# HEART OF **VENGEANCE**

**BOOK ONE**
OF THE VIGILANTE DUOLOGY

A BRAD MADRID STORY

# HEART OF **VENGEANCE**

**BOOK ONE**
OF THE VIGILANTE DUOLOGY

A BRAD MADRID STORY

## GLYNN STEWART

## TERRY MIXON

FAOLAN'S PEN
PUBLISHING
faolanspen.com

This edition published in 2018 by:

Faolan's Pen Publishing Inc.

22 King St. S, Suite 300

Waterloo, Ontario

N2J 1N8 Canada

ISBN-13: 978-1-988035-56-7 (print)

A record of this book is available from Library and Archives Canada.

Printed in the United States of America

1 2 3 4 5 6 7 8 9 10

First edition

First printing: August 2017

Illustration © 2017 Jeff Brown Graphics

Faolan's Pen Publishing logo is a trademark of Faolan's Pen Publishing Inc.

Read more books from Glynn Stewart at faolanspen.com

# CHAPTER ONE

BRAD MANTRUSO WAS BARELY HALF-WAY down the hundred-meter length of his uncle's ship, on his way to a date with the ship's junior navigator Shari, when all hell broke loose, a screaming alarm tearing through the air.

*Mandrake's Heart* wasn't a large or fancy spaceship, but it was all that his uncle Boris was able to afford, a hundred-meter-long, twenty-thousand-ton interplanetary bulk freighter that hauled cargo between Mars and the asteroid belt for whoever was willing to hire a tramp.

The young security officer had barely finished turning in his tracks when his uncle, Captain Boris Mantruso, spoke over the intercom, his voice warring with the loud alert.

"Emergency stations, people. We have Dark-damned IR signatures closing in from behind. Three little buggers and something in the fifty k-ton range. They don't read like Fleet and they're too fast to be transports.

"We have no choice but to assume they're pirates. I want everyone at their stations in five minutes. Bring your weapons and vac-suits. Move!"

Piracy was a sadly inevitable threat while sailing the spaceways, and it was even worse when your ship carried a load of monofilament.

His uncle had tried to keep the news about their cargo quiet, but that obviously hadn't worked.

Brad arrived on the bridge with less than forty seconds left in his allotted time. He'd swapped his fancy dinner clothes for a utilitarian gray vac-suit, strapping his weapon belt with his pistol and his monomolecular blade over the armor.

The bridge was an austere room, with a handful of stations for officers and their assistants. The only piece of decoration in the room was a series of intricately patterned crawling wires that covered the back wall—Brad's own careful handiwork in a nano-manufacturing vat.

At the front of the bridge were the two consoles for the pilot and his assistant, where Shari was already sitting when he dropped into the engineering console barely two feet away.

"It looks like dinner is off," the dark-haired youth told her as he slid into his chair, activating its artificial gravity field in case the main system went down.

"You get a raincheck, mister," she replied without looking up, her voice strained. They'd been doing the careful dance of teenagers who'd known each other half a decade and not *quite* admitted that they'd fallen in love along the way for six months.

The Everdark certainly had it in for him that this mess had hit today.

"Good," he said as lightly as he could, bringing up his displays. Since *Heart* only rarely needed a security team, his primary job was as second engineer—a job he had no formal training for but could muddle through, at least on *this* ship. "You don't get an easy out like a pirate attack."

He turned to his uncle. "Engineering is green, Cap'n."

Boris nodded. "Thank you." The burly spacer's eyes never moved from the main screen, which showed the approaching pirates.

Karen, the woman at the coms panel, twitched. "Incoming transmission, Cap'n."

"On screen."

The screen changed from basic movement vectors to the image of a man dressed in a black vac-suit—one almost identical to the one Brad and the others wore—with his helmet off.

The man held an aura of perfectly controlled power. Short-cropped black hair topped a scarred face with a pair of eyes that were as cold and blue as ice. The tattoo of a small red skull-and-crossbones highlighted his right cheek.

"*Mandrake's Heart*, this is the Cadre vessel *Lioness* and I am the Terror. Cut your engines and prepare for boarding. Evasion or resistance will be met with lethal force."

With that, his image died and silence reigned on *Mandrake*'s bridge.

Brad felt himself inhale involuntarily as his entire body tensed in fear. The Cadre was the most brutal pirate group in the Outer System —and the Terror was their leader. He wasn't noted for his mercy. If he captured them, they'd end up as slaves in the Fringe, doing the jobs too dangerous to risk an owner-citizen on.

"Like hell I'm letting them make slaves of us without a fight," Boris said, his thoughts obviously paralleling Brad's. "Better a clean death than a life toiling for monsters."

He glanced at Shari. "Or worse."

Boris turned to Michael, the lead pilot. "Give me as good an evasive pattern as you can. See if you can generate a vector they can't intercept us on."

"I can tell you right now that I can't, Cap'n," the pilot said.

"Try anyway," Boris ordered flatly, and then turned to Karen. "Can you send out a distress signal?"

The blonde shook her head jerkily. "They're jamming us. If I had a target, I might be able to punch a laser through, but no general transmissions."

Boris swore and turned to the rest of the bridge crew. "Split into groups of two. Brad, take Shari. Jordan, take Karen. Ryan, take Ferris. Cover the locks with guns and blades. Stop them if you can; bleed them if you can't. Michael and I will hold the bridge as long as we can."

Jordan, Ryan, and Brad were the ship's three "security officers." Each had other functions as well, but they were the best-trained fighters in the crew. They'd lead the resistance.

Brad stood slowly and turned to Shari as calmly as he could. "Let's go."

Boris looked at the two teenagers with haunted fear in his eyes. "Take the upper lock. May the Everlit guide your paths."

Brad bobbed his head at his uncle, struggling to keep a level voice and a calm mind as his heart tried to pound out of his chest. "And may they keep the Dark from yours."

He wondered if he'd ever see the last of his family again.

———

Brad and Shari stopped outside their assigned airlock, looking at it cautiously. Brad glanced over at her and drew his mono-blade. A small panel on the unadorned cylinder slid aside at the touch of his thumb, revealing a switch.

He flicked it and a meter of monomolecular filament uncoiled with a snap as electric current surged through it, extending the small ball at the end that was both necessary to keep the filament straight and an unavoidable impediment to using the impossibly narrow blade as a thrusting weapon.

The charged filament emitted an azure glow that lit the compartment. A moment later, a slightly paler blue joined his as Shari charged her own blade with its slightly different filament tuning.

The hum of the blade was calming, reassuring. Brad had never been in a real fight before, but he had hundreds of hours of practice with the weapon. Its weight in his hand brought back programmed muscle memory—memory that didn't include a fear-accelerated heartbeat.

He smiled at Shari as he drew his pistol with his left hand. Mostly ambidextrous, he'd trained to shoot with his off hand to allow this exact dual stance. He might not be the best shot—but in the tight confines of a starship, he didn't need to be.

Shari took up a two-handed stance with her blade. Unlike Brad, who had trained with both gun and mono-blade, she'd only learned to use the traditional weapon of a spacer.

Most spacers never bothered to learn to shoot. Pirates in particular seemed to shun the weapons in favor of blades. Maybe because the idea of having limbs lopped off—or heads—was terrifying to most of their victims—and even carefully designed guns tended to put holes in the spaceships they were trying to capture.

"I love you," Shari said, her voice carrying over the quiet hum of their blades. "I haven't said so before, but I might never get the chance if I don't say it right now. I love you and I have for a while. I'm so sorry we'll never find out where that takes us."

He'd known. He'd known for a while, but it was still a shock of warmth to his body to hear her say it.

"I love you, too," Brad told her softly. "Stay beside me and I'll protect you. We'll make it."

The timing was awful and the odds were bad. They'd most likely be dead in a few minutes, and he'd never know what admitting their love for each other would lead to.

"Activate your grav-boots," Boris said over the vac-suit's comlink. "I'm about to shut down internal gravity. They'll board in a couple of minutes. Be ready."

Brad checked his readouts, making sure his boots were active, and then glanced over at Shari. She nodded in reply to his unspoken question. Another piece of mundane, of ritual and process, that allowed him to calm his taut nerves and racing heart.

A sudden surge in the ambient temperature warned him that the pirates were close enough that their deceleration was washing the hull in energy. Moments later, the first thump of docking shook the ship. A second and third followed, the last on the hull right beside them.

As they watched, the intense red flare of an industrial plasma cutter burned through the airlock hatch and then began to melt its way up. They'd be through in seconds.

Somewhere along the way, Brad had fully regained his calm. His fear was gone; all that remained was a grim determination to protect his family and his ship.

"Get ready."

The cutter slowly moved across the top of the hatch and then down, leaving an intense afterimage in his vision. When it completed the last burn on the bottom, the remains of the hatch crashed to the deck, its edges white-hot.

Even before the metal stopped moving, Brad lunged for the opening. Muscle memory carried his blade through the armored vac-suit of the lead pirate before he'd made it into the ship. Gore splashed across the corridor as the bisected man crumpled to the deck, the first Brad had ever killed.

If Shari was to survive, it couldn't be the last.

Brad dodged aside, adrenaline warring with nausea and renewed fear as a shotgun inside the airlock barked. He fired a return shot in the general direction of the shooter without exposing himself. A muffled scream indicated he'd hit someone.

A live pirate exited the airlock and Shari attacked him. The slight man barely managed to interpose his own blade to block her two-handed slash as the young woman aggressively pushed him back.

Their blades bounced away from each other, but Shari brought hers snapping back to neatly remove the pirate's head. She stopped, staring in horror at the headless corpse.

Two more pirates charged out just as Shari finished her man. Both came after Brad, recognizing the threat of his pistol—a threat Brad managed to deliver on. It took four rapid shots, but he dropped the leader with his pistol and engaged the other in a duel of flashing blades. The man was decent.

The pirate deflected Brad's first slash and managed to lock blades with him, resisting the tendency of the blades to bounce away from each other. He pushed Brad back one step. Then another.

Three more pirates dashed into the space the man had created for them. Shari roared and charged, her blade swinging.

Fear for her flashed into him, and Brad twisted to fire a single shot into his opponent's stomach. The pirate fell back, clutching himself. Not willing to trust the man to die quietly, Brad shot him in the head, his adrenaline spiking before he could hesitate.

He spun to find Shari facing off against two pirates with the third floating gutted nearby, his legs attached to the floor but not his body. Before he could intervene, another pirate lunged at him from the airlock. This was getting old.

The air, filled with floating gore, betrayed the bastard. A glob of blood splashed across the man's faceplate, blinding him.

Training spoke again and Brad opened him up lengthwise. He

turned back to help Shari again—just in time to see yet another pirate step from the airlock and engage her.

Three against one would be terrible odds for him. She never stood a chance.

The new man slashed his sweetheart open, sending her crumpling away from his blade with blood spattering the corridor wall.

"No!" Brad brought his pistol up and shot the man in the head, far too late to do any good.

His entire body lit up with adrenaline as the remaining pirates turned and charged him. He shot the lead man in the sternum as he brought his blade up to parry the other pirate's attack.

Rage drove him and he launched a vicious flurry of strikes and the pirate desperately defended himself. He pushed the man back. When his opponent stumbled on one of his compatriot's bodies, Brad sliced through the man's upper body.

As the pirate crumpled, Brad released his pistol and grabbed a grenade from the pirate's belt, running on instinct and his uncle's "dirty tricks" training. He yanked out the pin and threw it into the pirate ship. The crystalline shrapnel in weapons like this was designed to kill people without knocking holes in the ship, so it should be relatively safe.

The sharp explosion stopped the fresh movement he'd been hearing. He grabbed his pistol before it drifted off, and risked a glance inside the airlock. No one else was coming out of there alive.

He deactivated his blade, holstered it, squatted beside Shari, and took her hand in his. She was still alive, but that wouldn't last long.

She coughed blood across the inside of her faceplate, trying to say something. Swearing, he pulled her helmet off and then removed his own.

"You're going to be fine," he lied softly, his throat tight.

Shari started to laugh, then coughed, spitting up more blood. "Like Dark...I am. Love you..."

Whatever else she might have said was lost as she went into another coughing fit and then went limp.

Brad lifted her hand to his lips. "I love you, too. I'll see you as soon as I take care of a few more things."

He didn't want to leave her there like that, but he had people to save and pirates to kill. Nausea and adrenaline rippled through him at the thought, but his *family* was on this ship—by blood or by crew, everyone on this ship was *his*.

No one had come out of the pirate ship, so he felt fairly certain that there was no one left inside. It was a risk, but he didn't have time to search it and still save the living.

Moving slowly he headed back down the corridor, he listened at each turn for pirates. Mentally crossing his fingers, he put his helmet back on and tried calling the bridge. There was no response.

He continued toward the rear of the ship, swapping his partially spent magazine for a fresh one with auto-pilot-driven fingers. When he reached the engineering hatch, he paused to catch his breath, struggling against the turmoil in his mind.

As he did, the gravity came back on. He didn't have much time.

Three voices carried through the open hatch, discussing how to get the engines running. A mirthless smile crossed his face. It appeared the little surprise the chief engineer had set up in the drives had worked after all. Now he just needed to get to the console and set off his own gift to the bastards.

Brad deactivated his grav-boots and drew his mono-blade, leaving it off for the moment. Activating it would alert the men he wanted to kill. As ready as he was going to be, he took a deep breath, steeled his nerve with the memory of Shari, and stepped into engineering.

One of the pirates was more observant than his companions and raised a shotgun.

Brad threw himself to the side as the weapon boomed. The flechettes tore through the open hatch and missed him. Barely.

He shot repeatedly at the man as he rolled back to his feet. The pirate fell heavily, hit at least once.

One of the remaining men charged him, his blade coming to life with a sharp *snap*, while the other scrambled for the fallen shotgun.

Brad activated his blade in time to parry the first man's attack before kicking him in the groin. Their suits were armored, but a man's testicles were far too sensitive for the protection to prevent pain and an automatic reaction.

As the attacker stumbled back, Brad emptied his pistol magazine into the pirate fumbling with the shotgun, then snapped his blade around as his enemy charged again.

He was only trying to parry, but a mistimed slash by the pirate bounced his blade into the man's neck, sending blood squirting across the compartment. The pirate's blade slipped from his suddenly nerveless fingers as he began trying to staunch the arterial spray.

That effort ended when Brad completed the kata and removed his foe's head.

Brad crossed to the main console, brought up the interface, and started accessing the fusion reactor's control systems. He'd only just begun when a slight hum behind him sent him diving to the side. A blue filament flashed through where he'd been standing.

He came to his feet with his activated blade in his hand, but had no time to do more before his new attacker was upon him.

Their blades clashed in rapid succession as each probed for weakness. The man was good. Better than good. Better than him.

Brad ducked a horizontal slash and tried to take the man's legs off, but the bastard nimbly jumped over his swing, grinning through his transparent faceplate.

That's when he saw the red skull and crossbones on the man's cheek. It was the Terror! Rage and fear alike filled him as he straightened.

"I'm going to kill you for Shari," he ground out between clenched teeth, using his anger to hold down his fear.

"Much as I'd love to dance, I have better things to do," the man said with a grin. "Have a nice trip. Kill the grav and open it!"

Brad had been so focused on his opponent that he hadn't seen the other pirates slip into the engineering compartment. One of them stood beside the massive equipment lock.

He tapped the controls and the hatch slid open right as the gravity cut out. He must've overridden the safety interlocks, too, because the air rushed out in an instant.

Brad was just a moment too late activating his grav-boots. The hurricane sucked him off his feet and hurled him out of *Mandrake's Heart* in a flash.

Spinning wildly, he caught glimpses of the ship as he tumbled away. That was it, then. It was over. Nausea from the fight and the spinning hammered into him and he vomited into his helmet, releasing his blade.

Safety systems in the helmet sucked away the vomit, and safety systems in the weapon deactivated the blade. It hung by its strap, spinning with him.

His weapons were useless now. Nothing could change his fate or save his ship. He was as dead as Shari. As dead as the rest of his family. His body just hadn't realized it yet.

His vac-suit had minimal emergency thrusters, but even as he watched, *Mandrake's Heart*'s engines flared to life. The freighter and the escorting pirate ships dove away into the deep dark, leaving him behind.

The Terror had turned him into a Dutchman. His frozen corpse would orbit in the unrelieved darkness of space for eternity.

For a moment, he considered ending it. It wouldn't be easy, not with his pistol empty and both weapons drifting by their safety straps, but he could manage it.

The stars were peaceful, though. He didn't want his last moments to be violence and death and hatred. He had a few hours of air, and he could find a better use for them than suicide.

He could spend his remaining hours remembering his family. His ship. The woman he'd never truly had a chance to love. His memories were the one thing the Terror couldn't take from him.

Death could have him when he finished.

# CHAPTER TWO

HE OPENED HIS EYES, then had to close them again immediately.

The light hurt. After a moment, he twitched his eyelids open a bit, keeping his eyelashes low to shield himself from the stark white brightness surrounding him.

He tried to remember how he'd ended up there, and started to panic. He didn't remember anything from before he woke up. He couldn't even think of his own name.

Even as he tried to jerk upright, his body failed him. Fear lashed through him as his limbs moved weakly, barely half-responsive to his commands.

"You're awake. Are you okay?" a masculine voice asked from beside him.

Even though he understood the words, he couldn't figure out how to answer. He moved his head slightly and licked his lips. That part of him seemed to respond, a minor sop against his growing panic.

The man who'd spoken sighed. He sounded relieved. "Thank the Everlit. You're in the infirmary aboard the Commonwealth cruiser *Freedom*. You gave us quite a scare. You've been out for nearly a full day. Lay back and relax while we get the doctor."

It was somehow exactly what he needed. "Doctor" was a promising word, one that meant help—and while he couldn't quite remember what the Commonwealth *was*, he knew it meant safety.

The man went away for a few minutes and someone else returned. The sound of the footsteps was different, so he knew this was someone else. He could only make out a vague shape through his mostly closed eyelids.

"Can you open your eyes?" a woman asked.

He shook his head, a spike of renewed fear hitting him at the thought.

"Let me turn down the lights and see if that helps."

The lights dimmed and he slowly opened his eyes. Between his blurry vision and the dim light, he could only barely make out the woman standing beside his bed.

"I'm Dr. Sarah Merrine. Can you tell me who you are?"

He tried to speak, to tell her he didn't know, but something clogged his throat. He began to panic again, but Merrine put her hand on his shoulder, a warm connection that helped him regain some calm.

She poured a glass of a clear liquid from a container, put a straw into the glass, and held it for him. "Drink some water. Just a sip or two."

He did so and found the cool liquid helped. He tried to speak again, but it came out as a frustratingly unintelligible garble.

"You spent nearly a day and a half on minimum oxygen," she said kindly. "There are a number of potential side effects from that. Don't worry. We'll get a handle on them now that you're over the worst part."

She reached out of his sight and picked something up. His slow mind supplied the thing's name. It was an injector.

"There appears to be some nerve or muscular damage to your face," she said in a matter of fact voice. "We'll need to take care of that as soon as possible. I'm going to put you under again so I can fix it."

The thought of sleeping again was terrifying. What if he didn't wake up this time? He somehow managed to raise his hand to stop her.

"It's all right," she said soothingly. "You're safe now. Rest and we'll have you feeling better very soon."

It seemed he didn't have a choice in the matter. He slowly lowered his hand and she pressed the injector to his arm. He heard a slight hiss and felt a tiny prick of pain. The doctor faded from view.

———

When he woke again, things were a little clearer. At least he could open his eyes without severe pain. His hands moved when he lifted them, letting him look at them. He still felt weak, but he could move, and that helped with his earlier fears.

The lighting in the room—an infirmary, his brain supplied—was significantly dimmer than it had been the first time. Dim enough that he could only barely make out someone sitting at a desk a few steps away, just on the other side of a translucent curtain.

The curtain only obscured part of his view, so he looked around at what he could see of the infirmary. Nothing seemed familiar. He was aboard a ship, but it wasn't his ship.

His ship? Why did he think he had a ship?

He struggled again to remember what had happened and had more success this time. He remembered gunfire and flashing lines of light. And fear. And hate.

He cringed away from the memories as his head began to ache. Well, maybe *ache* was too mild a word for what felt like nails stabbing into his temples. He groaned in pain.

The nearby figure looked up at the sound, stood, and stepped around the curtain. It was the woman who'd knocked him out. The doctor. Her eyes were concerned, but her presence was reassuring. She was familiar now. That helped keep the panic at bay.

She smiled. "How do you feel?"

He managed to get a single word out. "Bad."

"That's not surprising," she said sympathetically. "A number of nerve connections in your face decayed from oxygen starvation, as did some cerebral neurons. I had to regenerate them."

"How long?"

His voice sounded strange in his ears. Weak and rusty. Was this how he sounded all the time or was it just fear and injury talking?

"You were out another day with surgery and regen. You've been aboard *Freedom* four days now, if that's what you're wondering."

He frowned. Four days. What had happened to him before that? Why couldn't he remember anything other than the shooting and bright lines of light and the fear and pain?

"I can't remember," he admitted, his voice even weaker as the fear shivered through him.

The doctor watched him a long moment and shrugged slightly. "Frankly, I'm not surprised. You've mostly recovered from your Dutchman, but you're still suffering from the side effects from when you died."

He bit his lip, pushing down a spike of pure terror. He couldn't have heard her correctly. "I died?"

Somehow, he already knew what a Dutchman was. It meant he'd been loose in space, in just a suit. A horrible fate that most people didn't survive.

"You went into shock when we cut you out of your vac-suit," she told him gently. "Your heart shut down. I revived you, but throwing that on top of long-term hypoxia and low pressure, your body took quite a hit.

"Now that you can communicate, I need you to tell me if you're having any problems."

"I can't remember my name." His throat seemed clearer each time he spoke.

"That isn't unheard-of. The amnesia is almost certainly short-term. Things will start coming back over the next week or so. They'll come in flashes. Maybe a week after that, you'll recover everything. Probably all at once or close to it.

"Things might come when someone directly prods you about something. Like asking you a direct question. What's your name?"

He concentrated, pushing aside the pain for a moment. Out of the fog of fear and *nothingness*, something came to him. "Brad? I think I'm Brad."

He knew there should be more. A last name. But it wouldn't come.

"I can't remember anything more. I'm sorry." And afraid.

"Don't worry about it." She laid her hand on his arm, clearly understanding what he hadn't said. "This is excellent progress, even if it frustrates you. You'll get it all back in time."

She glanced at something above his head. "You should sleep again. You'll tire easily for a few days, so you need to rest."

He wanted to argue, but he knew she was right. Even this short conversation had been enough for just not panicking to have drained his reserves. He lay back and let the exhaustion take him.

———

Brad pulled himself into a sitting position as the captain—he somehow recognized the rank insignia—entered the infirmary. The officer pulled up a seat next to Brad's bed.

"I'm glad to see you with us, Brad. We were all very worried for you. My name is Mark Fields and I'm *Freedom*'s captain."

"Thank you for rescuing me," he said softly. He would have died if the cruiser hadn't lucked along. There was no question in his mind about that.

The man smiled. "That's what Fleet is here for. Sarah tells me you're suffering from temporary amnesia. I understand you might not remember what happened, but I'm going to ask you some questions anyway. 'I don't know' is a completely acceptable answer. No pressure. Clear?"

"I've tried remembering what happened," Brad said with a nod, "but I only get impressions of gunfire and blue lines of light."

"That makes sense." Fields gestured to someone near the door of the infirmary. The second man—this one in the uniform of a lieutenant —hurried over with a bundle, which he handed to the captain.

After a moment, Fields laid it on the small table beside Brad's bed. "We found these when we rescued you. Do they look familiar?"

Brad looked at the bundle. It was a belt with two holsters and two plain boxes in snap pouches attached to it. One holster held a slim black cylinder and the other an oddly shaped device.

Then his memory clicked. It was a weapons belt. The cylinder was a mono-blade, the device was a pistol. The black boxes were magazines holding bullets for the pistol. Somehow, he knew the weapons were his. And he *wanted* them.

He nodded slowly, controlling his desire to grab the weapons, and returned his gaze to the captain. "I know what they are and I know that they're mine. I even feel as if I could use them. Nothing beyond that."

Fields sighed. "I was hoping they'd jolt your memory a little more. That you could tell us what happened to your ship. Hell, I was hoping you could tell us what ship you came from."

Something flashed into Brad's mind. A fragment of a memory. In it, he turned just in time to see a man attack a young woman and slash her side open, sending her crumpling away from his blade.

He felt himself flinch and then shudder. The memory had been so vivid. The fear and pain—and *rage*—flooded his body and he exhaled sharply, breathing steadily to try and control his emotions again.

"Combat flashback?" Fields asked, his tone subdued and sympathetic.

Brad nodded, uncertain how the man had known. The term wasn't familiar to him, but it fit.

"I've seen the signs before and we knew you'd been in a fight. Your pistol was empty and your mono-blade filament had deformation consistent with a blade fight. Did you remember something specific?"

"A woman...no...a girl being killed. With a blade." Even just saying it hurt. Who had she been that it hurt this much?

"It's all right," Fields said gently, his eyes sympathetic. "Or, at least, it's over. We've searched the area we think you came from, but whatever ship you were on is long gone."

He glanced around the infirmary. "Dr. Merrine tells me you've recovered physically, so we're going to move you out of here today. She still wants to see you every day and you can call her anytime you need to, but we both think getting out among people will help you recover more quickly."

The captain stood, pulled his jacket tight, and picked up the weapons belt. "I'll send a petty officer to help you move. Try to relax. It will all come back to you eventually."

He tried to remember more, without success. Even the slightest thought of the girl in the memory brought flashes of powerful emotion. Pain. Fear. Rage…Warmth?

Who had she been? He'd clearly known her, but how well? Someone had killed her in front of him. He felt as if he should at least remember why.

A young petty officer with a bag over his shoulder interrupted his dark musings. He walked straight to where Brad sat and extended his hand. "I'm Petty Officer Second Class Mike Richmond. Just call me Mike."

Brad took the man's hand. "I'm Brad. I can't think of anything else for you to call me."

"Don't worry about it," Richmond replied with a cheerful grin. "I brought you some clothes."

He set the kit bag on the bed, opened it, and revealed several sets of ship fatigues with the insignia removed.

"Thanks," Brad told him, surprised to find tears in his eyes from the minor show of support.

"Not a problem. Throw one of those on and we'll get you straight to your new quarters." He stepped back and closed the curtain.

Brad dressed quickly, his body significantly more stable now than his emotions or mind. Once he finished, he opened the curtain, and the other man gestured toward the infirmary door.

They went through a number of tight corridors and passed men and women in uniform. It felt to Brad as if they were all staring at him, and he wondered if they could see how much mental pain he was in. Minutes later, they arrived at his new quarters.

"It isn't much," the PO said as he gestured through the hatch.

Brad looked around the tiny compartment. There was barely room for the built-in desk, bunk, and locker. "It's fine, Mike. It really is."

"Is there anything else I can get you?" the petty officer asked.

Brad turned to look at the blank wall opposite the door. "Yes," he said hesitantly. "Do you know what the Everlit an anvil-vat is?"

"Of course I do," Richmond said briskly, his eyes narrowing in question. "A vat of nanites used by nano-smiths."

"Good to know. I knew I wanted one, but I didn't know what it was."

"Wait a minute," the PO said. "You're a nano-smith?"

"Maybe?"

"There's only one way to be sure," Richmond said as he hurried out. "Be right back."

Brad sat there after the man had left, staring at the small room and wondering what other surprises lurked in the depths of his mind. He was afraid many of them would be horrible, like the girl's death.

What he remembered already terrified him and left him filled with anger. He almost wished the rest would never come back.

———

A short while later, he stared down at the anvil and the handful of pistol cartridges lying next to it. The captain had kept the weapons, but he'd agreed to give him some ammunition to work with.

Brad felt as if he'd done this many times before. The process hadn't come easily, but he'd eventually figured it out and now had a shiny pile of new rounds on the desk in front of him.

Mike looked over Brad's shoulder and smiled. "It appears you are indeed a nano-smith, my young friend."

"Yeah," Brad said dazedly, not entirely free of the tightly focused concentration necessary to bend the nanites to his will. He slowly removed the electrodes from his forehead and returned them to their receptacles on the anvil.

He suspected he wasn't a very *good* one. His brain was quite certain that duplicating an item he could drop in the vat as a sample was as easy a task as there was, and it had taken him over an hour to make a dozen bullets.

Mike's chrono beeped and he glanced down at it. "Shit. I forgot the time. I go on duty in twenty. Look, the anvil is ship's property, but Commander Douglas—the chief engineer—said you could borrow it while you're aboard."

Brad nodded, his eyes still resting on the anvil—a plain gray box about thirty centimeters on a side. "Thanks Mike."

The PO looked at Brad for a moment more before heading for the door. "Have fun, spacer."

He considered the anvil and wondered what else he should make. Somehow, he felt as if he should create something for the bulkhead. A vision of twisting wires arranged in an artistic flow appeared unbidden in his mind. It was simple in construction, at least, something he was pretty sure he could do, even if more complex items would be beyond him.

Had he done that? If so, he probably wouldn't be on board long enough to recreate it.

———

The next morning, a soft chime sounded at Brad's door. He looked up from where he was working with the anvil. "Come in."

The door slid open and Captain Fields entered. "Morning. How are you feeling?"

"Other than not being able to remember anything and being exhausted, I feel fine," Brad told him with a shrug. "Of course, the whole amnesia thing is rather annoying."

He didn't mention the nightmares. The spikes of fear when he was awake. The moments of unexplained fight-or-flight—or the anger bubbling along, just below the surface, without any kind of target.

Somehow, he knew that Fields was aware of all of that.

"Understandable. We'll be touching base at Ceres tomorrow," Fields warned him. "I'll have to turn you over to the local authorities. I'm not legally allowed to keep a civilian aboard past the nearest safe harbor except as a prisoner."

"I see," Brad said quietly. "I can't say I'm thrilled at the change, but it's the way things go, isn't it?"

"I'd prefer to keep you with us, if I can," the captain told him. "I could always use another nano-smith. Which leads me to your second option.

"If you want to stay, I can sponsor you for a midshipman's warrant. While you're under review, you're provisionally considered military personnel, so you could stay aboard."

His face took on a serious cast. "You'd almost certainly be accepted.

Spaceborn with any sort of sponsorship tend to be shoo-ins—as do any with *any* nano-smith skills—and you're both.

"Douglas scanned the reports on that vat." Fields gestured at the gray box. "He says you've clearly had some training but are mostly getting by on talent. With Fleet training, he says that alone would make you a damn fine engineering officer."

Brad considered the offer for a moment before shaking his head. It was a good offer, but there was too much anger in him now for any easy way forward.

"I appreciate the thought, Captain," he told Fields. "I think I'd have accepted it before all this happened. Now, though, I need to find some answers. Do something about what happened to me."

Fields returned his gaze levelly. "What sort of 'something'?"

"I've remembered more of what happened," Brad admitted. "A face. It's scarred, with black hair, blue eyes, and a tattoo on the cheek."

A face that filled him with hate when it crossed his mind. More hate than he would have thought one human could hold.

"A red skull and crossbones?" the captain asked sharply.

"Yes," Brad confirmed with a surprised blink. "Does it mean something?"

"It means you met the Terror," Fields said coldly. "He's a pirate. In a sense, he's *the* pirate. One of the most sadistic pieces of garbage you could ever meet. It couldn't be anyone else. No one would dare get anything like that on his face because of what the Terror would do to them."

"I see," Brad said softly. "I see indeed."

He turned toward his bed, letting his hate and his anger flow through him, warming him against the cold of a loss he didn't fully remember. In a sudden flash, he recalled hanging his weapons belt on the headboard of a different bed. "As I said, Captain, I can't take your offer."

"Son, don't go vigilante on me. The Terror is dangerous. He's one of the best bladesmen alive, with ships and men that only Fleet can handle."

"I'm sorry to say that Fleet isn't filling me with confidence," Brad said softly, studying the wall. "As for his skill with a blade, I'll just have to become better."

Fields sighed. "I can't stop you and I suppose Ceres isn't a bad place to start with something like that. It's the last real Commonwealth outpost before you reach the Outer System."

"Thank you for your kindness, Captain," Brad said sincerely. "It means a lot to me."

The officer smiled wryly, but his words were heavy with intended meaning. "Kindness and compassion are what separate warriors from killers. Remember that and you'll be fine."

Fields took a step toward the door. "I'll send your weapons with you when you leave. If you have vengeance on your mind, you'll need them. The law says you have a right to be armed, so don't let them bully you. They'll try."

"Then why can't I have them now?"

"Because Fleet has a few prerogatives," the captain told him with a small smile. "Get a good night's sleep. You'll need your wits about you tomorrow."

———

Barely twenty-four hours later, Brad quietly followed Mike into *Freedom*'s hangar with a duffel slung over his shoulder. The PO had Brad's weapons belt over his.

The bag contained the sum total of his worldly possessions: three plain jumpsuits donated by *Freedom*'s crew, a few additional magazines for his pistol, and a wrist-comp he couldn't access because he didn't remember the code.

It also held basic hygiene supplies and a number of comfort items, all gifts from the crew, like the bag itself. The vac-suit he'd come aboard with sat folded at the bottom. One of the cruiser's nano-smiths had repaired it, using one of the ship's larger anvils.

Brad looked down at the bag as they stopped beside the transport waiting for him. For a few seconds, gratitude managed to overcome the solid ball of anger and pain his emotions were becoming.

"I never got a chance to thank all the people who've helped me. Tell them I appreciate it."

The PO clapped a hand on his shoulder. "Don't worry about it, kid. Even though Fleet will probably compensate them, they'd have done it anyway. *Freedom* has a good crew."

The man grinned suddenly. "Now, you have a shuttle to catch. Pilot Mackenzie gets bitchy if people delay her departure times."

Brad forced himself to return the man's grin, took the proffered weapons belt, and headed for the shuttle. He had no idea what the future held for him, but he couldn't wait to get to it. He had some payback to deliver.

# CHAPTER THREE

BRAD WATCHED over Pilot Mackenzie's shoulder as *Freedom*'s shuttle slipped through the inner door of the main airlock of Cere City Spaceport's shuttle landing dome. It closed behind them as they headed for their assigned landing pad, sealing the massive dome once more.

They'd already flown over the main spaceport, where dozens of starships, relatively small but still too big to dock in the main port, were berthed. Those had temporary bubbles set up over their airlocks linked to the port entrances with a spider web of pressurized tunnels.

Inside the main port, however, there were oxygen and some gravity to hold the small craft from larger ships in place. As their craft reached its assigned spot, Mackenzie deftly fired the shuttle's thrusters to bring them into place. The landing gear touched the pad, and automatic tethers locked them in place.

The pilot killed the thrusters and turned to face him with her hand out.

"There's supposed to be someone waiting for you," she told him. "Good luck...and good hunting."

He wondered how she'd known what he intended to do. The captain didn't seem the type to gossip, so Brad must not be as clever as he thought he was.

Brad shook her hand, unstrapped himself, and stood. "Thank you, Lieutenant."

"My pleasure," she told him with a smile. "Now git."

He exited the shuttle onto the flat, black concrete, carefully watching for the border of the artificial gravity aboard the shuttle—maintained at a statutory point seven five gee, according to Mackenzie—and the point three gravities Ceres City kept their artificial gravity at.

Standing at the edge of the pad, next to the door into the terminal, was a woman clad in conservative business clothing. She waved him over.

"Are you Brad?" she asked as he stepped over.

"I am."

She didn't offer her hand. "I'm Jane Roland with the Ceres City Social Department. I'll be assisting you."

Her eyes rested on his face for a moment before drifting down to the weapons on his hips. Her lips hardened and her gaze rose to meet his again. "I need you to give me your weapons."

Brad met her gaze steadily, not speaking for a long moment as he carefully controlled his initial spike of anger. "I must decline."

Her lips compressed into a very thin white line. "I'm afraid I must insist. You're a ward of the state until your memory returns. As such, we must consider both the public good and your own safety. Do you understand?"

He allowed himself a smile. It was just as thin as hers and, he suspected, conveyed more of his hidden anger than he really liked.

"A friend of mine on *Freedom* thought you might take that line," Brad said softly. "He took the liberty of providing me with the appropriate sections of the Ceres legal code. Those sections hold a different view.

"Unless someone declares me medically incompetent—which Dr. Merrine on *Freedom* already ruled out—I have the right to keep and wear my weapons. Of course, I could voluntarily surrender them, but I'm not willing to do that."

"I think that's the wrong way to look at this, but I can't stop you," she admitted with a scowl and a reluctant nod. "Keep in mind that

Ceres Security takes an extremely dim view of people who brandish lethal weapons or act in a threatening manner.

"If you're done making certain I understand your rights," she said acerbically, "we need to go. Follow me."

———

The walk didn't take very long and he allowed himself to stare at the structures and people as they passed. He literally couldn't remember seeing anything like them before, though much of it seemed familiar.

The low building Roland brought him to was cut out of the native stone. The upper floor served as the lobby and held elevators going down into underground sections.

He had no idea how he knew the building practices on asteroid colonies, though. Another frustrating gap in his knowledge.

Roland paused outside an elevator, turning to face him. "The dorm for transients and wards such as yourself is on the third floor, counting downwards. For the immediate future, we'd prefer you only leave with one of the staff accompanying you. It's for your safety. Understood?"

That sounded prudent, so he nodded. "Understood."

He caught her quiet sigh of relief as she turned back toward the elevator. She must have expected him to fight her on that, too. He smiled bitterly. He was angry, not *stupid*.

They endured an awkward silence until they reached the third floor. The doors opened and she led him into a white-paneled corridor. Non-automatic doors painted the same shade as the walls were spaced along the wall every two meters.

The social worker pulled a data pad from her belt and checked it. "You've been assigned to room twenty-one. It's right over here."

A short walk down the corridor, silent except for occasional conversations coming from open doorways, brought them to a door with the numerals 21 on a small plaque at the top of the frame.

Roland turned the handle and opened the door, showing him into a small room that shared the same plain white shade as the rest of the facility. He was sensing a theme.

A small bed and a desk with a built-in computer were the only furniture in the room. They were plain, simple, and—unsurprisingly —white.

"The comp has limited access to the Ceres DataNet but no access to the Commonwealth SysNet," Roland said. "If you need assistance at any time, there's a call button by the door."

Brad nodded his thanks. "That's fine."

She looked him over carefully. "All right, then. Meal call is in about an hour. The cafeteria is further down the hall. You can't miss it. We'll talk again tomorrow, so I suggest you get some rest."

He shook his head after she'd left. It felt as though resting was all he'd ever done.

With a sigh, he set his bag onto the bed and unpacked. That took all of two minutes.

He joined the other dorm inhabitants for the meal but sat alone in a corner and didn't speak to any of them. He didn't know any of them. He wasn't even quite sure he knew *himself*.

He ate quickly and returned to his room.

Once there, he closed the door, locked it, and started the comp. It lacked a password prompt and he had access relatively quickly. Without thinking, he brought up a command window with a few keystrokes. Then he paused and looked at his hands.

He hadn't remembered how to do that a moment before. He hadn't even known what a command window was. Now he knew exactly how to verify what Roland had told him about the access he had on the system.

Even restricted to the Ceres DataNet—and, he was quite sure, having his searches monitored—the comp gave him access to a wealth of data. He couldn't make sense of a lot of it, but as he poked through it things fell into place.

He had ended up on the border between the Inner System—basically from the Sun itself out to the asteroid belt—where the Commonwealth of Nations held unquestioned control, and the Outer System where that control became…spottier.

Brad might not have known who he was yet, but he was starting to find holes in his knowledge that weren't due to the amnesia. He knew nothing about Earth, for example, except that it existed. History of spaceflight? Not a clue. How the Commonwealth had ended up in charge? A giant blank.

Shipping patterns along the border between Inner and Outer systems? *Those* he knew. How to use and maintain the two weapons on his belt? Almost instinct. But a lot of basic knowledge that the DataNet seemed to assume eluded him.

He looked around his room. Once he knew who he was, he wouldn't be staying there. The anger that ran underneath the surface of everything he thought and did wouldn't permit it. He needed to start making plans for his eventual exit.

Images of the man with the red skull and crossbones tattoo still haunted his dreams. He'd done as much research on the Terror and the Cadre as he could aboard *Freedom*. The man was a monster and his organization a blight on the Commonwealth.

Brad still had no idea how he'd beat them by himself, but he'd find a way. He had to.

———

He was eating breakfast the next morning when Roland found him.

Like everything else in the facility, the cafeteria was white. The tables were white plastic, the chairs were white plastic, the walls were native stone painted white. Even the floor and ceiling tiles were white. He'd half expected the food to be dyed white.

"Good morning," she said, sitting down at his table without asking.

He raised an eyebrow. "Good morning. Care for some synthetic egg?" He gestured at the yellowish-white substance on his plate that tasted vaguely like eggs.

"No, thank you. I've already eaten." He thought he detected a well-repressed shudder before she continued. "You go on, though."

Brad pushed the plate away. He didn't like the idea of eating while she watched him. "I was finished, anyway. What are the plans for today?"

"I have some tests I'd like you to do."

"My schedule appears to be open. Shall we begin?"

———

She took him into a small office away from the main patient area, where they started with a series of simple knowledge tests. First with a multiple choice test and then with him having to come up with the answers for himself.

The first set of questions was easy. He could select which were the correct answers almost every time, though some of the gaps in his knowledge became clearer as well. Recent history was…okay. Anything more than ten years old, anything outside the realm of merchant shipping, those he was vague on.

The second set frustrated and annoyed him. If the event or object in question had been referred to in the previous set of questions, he could often recall the correct answer. For those unconnected to earlier questions, it seemed almost random whether he could determine the answer or not.

The exceptions were the subjects he'd been vague on in the first questions, where he had no idea on the more open question, and anything related to ships and weapons—which he answered without even having to think.

Finally, Roland took him through a battery of more esoteric tests. Reaction times, strength, short-term memory. He was sure she'd have tested his long-term memory, too, if he'd had one.

When the clock twitched its way into the evening, Brad finally seemed to have finished enough tests to give Roland satisfaction.

"Well?" he asked. "What's your conclusion?"

She raised two fingers. "First, your amnesia seems to be fading. Once a subject is brought to your attention and you think about it, the information comes back, if you knew it in the first place. Second, you're spaceborn, have almost no formal education, and you've spent most of your life on a spaceship, learning how to fight and keep the ship flying.

"Tomorrow, I think we'll go to the spaceport. I suspect the ships there will bring back more than anything more we can do here. Maybe everything." She shrugged. "For now, I suggest you eat and get some more rest. We drove you pretty hard today."

———

When Roland entered the cafeteria the next morning, Brad was waiting. Suspecting she'd arrive at the same time as the previous day, he'd risen early and finished eating before she'd arrived. He'd also taken the precaution of securing his gear in his bag. It rested beside his chair.

His desire to take risks with his weapons was nonexistent at this point. Everything else just fit in the same bag.

"Ms. Roland," he greeted her, rising as she approached.

"Are you ready to go?"

"Certainly." He grabbed his bag and slung it over his shoulder.

She frowned. "You don't need that."

"I don't have a key to my room," he pointed out, "so it seems prudent to take what little I have with me on this excursion. It's not much, but it's all I have."

"We don't have a problem with theft here. You can leave that in your room and it will still be there when we get back."

When he merely raised an eyebrow and gestured toward the door, she sighed and led the way out.

He again studied the rapidly shifting crowds as they walked. The vast majority of people around them had the lankiness his hindbrain identified as the sign of the spaceborn. All of them moved quickly in the long, gliding strides allowed by the low gravity.

Roland made no attempt to ask him anything. She simply directed him where to go and otherwise said nothing.

It took them ten minutes to reach the tunnel access leading out to the net of domes that made up the spaceport. It sat just outside the main city dome. He'd seen that when he'd flown in.

Armed guards in the black fatigues of Commonwealth Marines guarded the spaceport entrance, blades and pistols at their waists and slug rifles held at the ready. The sight of the weapons sent a shiver of fear down his spine even as the Commonwealth uniforms reassured him.

The only one of them not armed with a rifle stepped up as they approached. "ID check."

"Jane Roland, Social Department." She flashed her wrist-comp across the man's scanner. "He's with me."

The marine waved her through and turned to Brad, who pulled out the temporary ident card Roland had given him.

The marine scanned it and then glanced at Roland. "All right. Pass through."

"Is that normal?" Brad asked as he followed her into the spaceport. "The marines, I mean."

She shrugged. "Not really. There was an attempted hijacking last night, so security is going to be tight for a while. Normally, they're less intrusive."

And less secure as well, he presumed, though the intrusiveness itself was mostly theater. How he knew *that*, of course, was beyond him.

That thought faded as they walked into the main observation dome of the Ceres City Spaceport. It was positioned on a stubby hill looking over the spider web of tunnels and hangar domes that stretched across forty square kilometers of asteroid rock.

His eyes roamed over the hundreds of ships scattered in front of them, each nestled up against a dome with a temporary pressurized tunnel leading to the ship. Some of the smallest ones—and all of the shuttles—were tucked into large multi-craft transparent hangar domes with massive airlock doors like the one he'd landed in.

"Impressive," he said softly.

"Indeed," she agreed. "It's the largest spaceport outside the planetary systems. Can you identify any of those ships?"

He looked at the closer ones and his eyes locked onto a sleek, black-painted, lethal-looking vessel near them.

"That one," he said, pointing. "It's a Centaur-class corvette. Three-thousand-ton base hull plus armament and cargo. Civilian construction, not Fleet."

"How can you possibly tell who built it?" she asked curiously. "Wouldn't the design be the same in all cases?"

He shook his head. "Fleet would have the name on the nose. Also, her fins are serrated. It looks pretty, but Fleet prefers stability over style. Both her engines are Skylark IV ion/fusion sets with three thousand kilonewtons each."

Roland seemed impressed, but Brad barely noticed as he spun and gestured at another ship. "That one is Fleet, though. A *Corsair*-class destroyer."

The ship he now gestured toward occupied one of the largest landing areas in the port. It was ninety meters long, painted white, and had notable protrusions where it mounted weapons. Her name—*CWS Buzzard*—was emblazoned on her nose.

"Twelve thousand tons with torpedo primary armament," he said. "She carries four parasite shuttles and a marine company. I see six Falcon V ion/fusion drives with six thousand kilonewtons each."

It was easy to identify the engines. Everything from the shape of their nacelles to the angle they attached to the hull differed from brand to brand and model to model.

Brad's mind picked up the various identifiers and gave him a name, manufacturer, and an encyclopedia entry's worth of information about them at a glance. She'd been right. The spaceport was a treasure trove of stimuli for his memory.

He knew a *lot* about ships. Data and knowledge reappeared in his mind in massive chunks. He couldn't tell you how either part of a hybrid ion/fusion drive unit *worked*, but he was pretty sure he could fix one. He could rebuild one from parts and make *some* of the parts himself if he had an anvil-vat.

The joy of knowledge, of restored memory, swept aside his anger for a moment—until his questing gaze settled on a ship near them, a medium-sized cylindrical bulk freighter. He gestured toward it.

"That's a Telstar III-Class bulk freighter," he told Roland, his voice soft for some reason. "Twenty thousand tons. About the largest ship anyone is going to bother landing on the surface. That one has eight Falcon IV ion/fusion engines with five thousand kilonewtons each."

Brad's eyes stayed on the Telstar for a long moment, and he blinked as a memory washed over him.

———

He was young. He knew that, though he didn't know how old he was. The man beside him towered over him. Not in a threatening manner, but because he was an adult.

Brad looked up at the man. "Uncle?" His voice was high-pitched. That had probably annoyed him at that age.

The burly man shook himself. "Sorry, Brad. Woolgathering."

He gestured out the tunnel window toward the ship. "That's her, nephew. *Mandrake's Heart.* I know she's not much compared to your father's ship, but I hope she'll come to feel like home in time."

The man's voice was scratchy, as if he'd been crying.

"Come on," he continued, clearly forcing himself. "If we don't get aboard soon, your aunt will leave without us."

————

Brad reeled physically from the sudden flashback, grabbing at a nearby bench.

"Are you all right?" Roland asked, her voice concerned.

Before he could reply, another memory came crashing in. It featured the same man but in a different place.

————

"Like hell I'm letting them make slaves of us without a fight," Boris said, his thoughts obviously paralleling Brad's. "Better a clean death than a life toiling for monsters."

He glanced at the blonde young woman at the assistant pilot console. "Or worse."

Boris turned to the lead pilot. "Give me as good an evasive pattern as you can. See if you can generate a vector they can't intercept us on."

"I can tell you right now that I can't, Cap'n," the pilot said.

"Try anyway," Boris ordered flatly, and then turned to another woman. "Can you send out a distress signal?"

She shook her head jerkily. "They're jamming us. If I had a target, I might be able to punch a laser through, but no general transmissions."

Boris swore and turned to the rest of the bridge crew. "Split into groups of two. Brad, take Shari. Jordan, take Karen. Ryan, take Ferris. Cover the locks with guns and blades. Stop them if you can; bleed them if you can't. Michael and I will hold the bridge as long as we can."

———

Brad waved Roland's hand away as she reached to help him, slumping down onto a bench. He gasped as another memory slammed into his mind with brutal force.

———

The gore betrayed the charging pirate. A glob of blood splashed across the man's faceplate, blinding him.

Brad opened him up lengthwise and turned back to help Shari just in time to see yet another pirate step from the airlock and engage her.

Before he could move to help, the new man slashed the young woman open, sending her crumpling away from his blade with blood spattering the corridor wall.

"No!" Brad brought his pistol up and shot the man in the head, far too late to do any good.

———

He gasped for breath as the flashbacks faded. He remembered everything now: *Mandrake's Heart*, the pirates, and the battle. And Shari.

His recollection of how he'd ended up in space was still a little fuzzy, but he remembered dueling the Terror in the engineering compartment. The man who'd destroyed his family, his life, and his sweetheart. The man who had quite literally taken everything from him.

Now he was glad he'd turned down Captain Fields's offer. There was no way he'd let anyone else avenge his family. No way the law would deal with the Terror like the bastard deserved.

He'd felt hate for the man before but hadn't known why. Now he did. No. The law would never support what he had to do.

His next step, therefore, had to be getting away from the law. He needed to get into the Outer System and start building a new life. One dedicated to wreaking his vengeance on the Terror and the Cadre.

Roland stared at him, concerned as he slowly stood. "Are you all right? What's happening?"

Brad Mantruso nodded calmly. The anger was still there, but remembering *why* he was angry gave it new focus. The fire no longer burned without answers. Now it was a forge, an anvil on which he would forge himself into a weapon.

"I'm fine, thank you," he told her. "I've remembered a few things—painful things—and need some space to process everything. I'd like to have some time alone to do that."

She looked as though she thought this was a bad idea, but eventually nodded. "Do you remember how to get back to the Social Department building? Come back when you finish. We'll talk then."

He watched her walk out of the port. It might take a few hours, but she'd eventually realize he wasn't coming back. He needed to be gone before she sounded the alarm.

True, he'd broken no laws, but the authorities would be concerned that a man lacking his memories might harm himself. Or others.

He couldn't allow anyone to know Brad Mantruso was still alive. Word might somehow get back to the Terror. He didn't want the man to know he was coming for him.

That thought made him laugh. As if the bastard didn't have thousands of people wanting to slit his throat already. Tens of thousands, probably. Possibly more. He was just the latest one in line. Possibly not even the angriest, though he'd never imagined in his life he could be this angry. Hate this much.

Well, he could ponder how to move up the queue after he devised a plan to get out of there. First things first. He needed to get lost in the crowd. If Roland came back to check on him, he needed to be elsewhere.

An hour later, he sat on a different bench, watching the people flow back and forth as he skimmed through the memory in his now-accessible wrist-comp. Financial accounts, a diary, birth certificate, certifications, credit status, and more sat in the tiny computer.

No one knew the owner of his account except him. Accounts were numbered so as to provide a measure of privacy and security in a post–physical currency age. That meant he still had his money.

Due to his stubbornness, he still had his weapons and gear. He'd need a few more items for the trip out, but that was a problem he could easily solve.

The shops in the port quickly provided all the supplies a traveler would need. The authorities would trace his movements eventually, but that couldn't be helped. Once they realized he'd left Ceres, their interest would cease.

Hefting his bag over his shoulder, he made his way to a ticket kiosk.

"Morning."

"Good morning," the woman behind the counter replied cheerily. "What can I do for you?"

"When does the next ship leave for the Outer System?"

"Which destination?"

"Anywhere."

When she gave him an odd look, he leaned forward and sadly shook his head. "I broke up with my fiancée, and her brothers want to have a long, painful discussion with me. I really don't care where I go, so long as it isn't here. Too many bad memories and the risk of them showing me the outside of an airlock without a suit, if you know what I mean."

Understanding blossomed in her eyes. "I'm so sorry to hear that. Let me see what I can find for you."

Her hands moved out of sight, accessing a computer. "The *Louisiana Rain* departs in fifty minutes for Ganymede. They'll still be boarding for another twenty-five. Does that work for you?"

"Perfect."

"That'll be one thousand credits for a dorm bed."

Brad hesitated, then shrugged. His uncle hadn't paid him well, but he'd had almost nothing to spend it on. His resources paled against the task he'd set himself, but he didn't need to share a dorm with potential threats.

"How much for the least expensive private cabin?"

She accessed her computer again. "Second class is the lowest ticket with a private cabin, sir. Four thousand, five hundred credits."

He lifted his wrist with the comp. "Do you take direct transfer?"

"Of course." She lifted a reader from behind the counter and held it out.

Brad moved his wrist-comp into its field and okayed the transaction. A soft beep from the reader confirmed the successful transfer.

The woman pushed several keys on her computer. "The *Rain* is in berth two-five-one. You have cabin A-twenty-five. My comp just transferred your boarding pass to you. Present it to the steward when you board. Have a good trip and good luck. I hope you find what you're looking for."

"Me, too," he said as he resettled his bag and headed away from the counter. Signs directed him toward the berth. He set out at a jog. He wouldn't want to be late to his own escape.

# CHAPTER FOUR

*Louisiana Rain*, a pretty standard passenger transport, squatted on its landing pad like an old and battered albatross. A white paint job, streaked in places with the black of heat-charred paint, added to the impression of age.

Brad recognized her as a Tempest IX liner. Fifteen thousand tons' mass with six Falcon IV engines. She probably didn't boost all that fast, but she'd get there all the same.

A pair of uniformed security guards stood at the entrance to the pressurized boarding tube leading into the transport's airlock. They were checking tickets against their list.

He stepped up to them confidently and offered his wrist-comp.

One of them scanned it. "Name, please?"

He hesitated for a moment. "Brad Madrid."

The guard didn't seem to notice his hesitancy. A moment later, the man's scanner beeped, confirming his boarding pass. Like many electronic documents, it was linked to his comp, not his name—the easiest way to provide a small amount of privacy in an era where *everything* was in the computers.

"You're good, Mr. Madrid. The lift is just inside the airlock. It'll take you up to A deck. Watch your step. Shipboard gravity is at point five."

Brad nodded his thanks. At almost double what Ceres Municipal Authority maintained, that was the sort of difference that could trip even an experienced spacer who wasn't expecting it.

He stepped between the guards as they turned to another passenger huffing toward the ship, struggling with his ungainly luggage.

The tiny cubicle he'd paid such a large amount for was about what he'd expected: a crowded little box two meters on a side, a dresser built into one of the walls, a coffin-like closet, and a tiny desk. A single bed occupied more than half the room. He'd have to find out where the lavatory was after they took off.

He sighed. *Rain's* travel time was nearly fifteen days. For some odd reason, he wouldn't be surprised if he got bored.

It took him almost an hour to find the gym after they took off. The crew had it tucked away in a half-hidden corner of the ship, well outside the areas normally frequented by the passengers.

He spent almost the entirety of his first sleep period in it, practicing, trying to burn off some of the adrenaline-fueled energy his anger gave him. He'd rather avoid the passengers during the day, anyway.

The blade katas he favored seemed different now. Before, he'd only gone through them as practice, as a test. They'd mostly been training but still at least something of a game. He'd never had to use them until the Terror had boarded *Mandrake's Heart*.

His cold-burning anger and the thought of everything he'd lost made him redouble his efforts. He brought the book he'd studied for most of his training—*The Path of the Blade*—up on his wrist-comp. He'd already mastered the basics, but there were advanced techniques it hinted at he could try to figure out.

That wasn't the same as finding a teacher with the knowledge, but it beat sitting in his room and brooding.

———

He spent the next two days using the gym throughout the entire sleep period before he saw anyone else in the room at all. When the stranger walked in, Brad was going through the motions of a half-remembered kata his teacher had shown him once. One he hadn't mastered.

The sound of the door sliding open startled him, and the practice blade slammed into his shin as he lost control of it. The capacitor attached to the thin metal blade discharged and his leg went into spasms. He hobbled to the bench and sat heavily.

It took him a moment to regain his breath, so he used it to study the man. He was shorter than Brad, barely topping a hundred and sixty centimeters, yet still had the lanky build of the spaceborn. He'd tied his blond hair back into a ponytail, leaving piercing blue eyes and sharply angled features visible.

"That rates a seven on the oops scale," the stranger said calmly.

"Thanks," Brad said shortly. "If you don't mind my asking, what brings you here at this hour?"

The stranger shrugged. "From the look of things, exactly the same thing that brought you. I only managed to find this place today, and I figured I'd come by while everyone else was asleep. The real katas, after all, tend to hurt unsuspecting bystanders," he added with a grin.

"True." Brad hesitated for a moment. "There should be room for both of us, if we're careful."

"Since there are two of us, why don't we see if we can show each other anything?"

Brad thought about it and shrugged. Carefully tucking the deactivated practice sword under his arm, he offered his hand. "Brad Madrid."

The blond man took it. "John Marshal."

Brad extracted another practice blade from the cabinet and tossed it to the other man. He caught it in a smooth motion.

"I think it would be best if we worked out where each other stands before we start learning from each other," Marshal said.

"What do you have in mind?"

The shorter man grinned. "I was thinking a little sparring match." With that, the blond raised the practice blade in salute, flicking the switch that armed the shock circuit.

Brad nodded wordlessly and raised his own blade in response. He armed the shock circuit and immediately lunged at the other man.

Marshal's grin faded as Brad's attack surged in. The man managed to parry, but Brad brought the practice blade flashing back in before he could launch an attack of his own. Four times the man managed to parry Brad's strikes, each time moving the blade just enough to deflect the attack.

He deflected Brad's fifth attack slightly harder, sending Brad's blade to one side, and flicked his into Brad's exposed shoulder.

Brad grunted as the circuit flashed its shock into him, and stepped back. He raised his blade in salute, acknowledging his defeat.

Marshal raised his own blade in response. "You're very fast and quite good, Mr. Madrid. What rank are you?"

"I don't hold an official rank," Brad lied with a shrug. "I'm not entirely self-taught, but it's been completely private."

Which wasn't exactly true, but it was Brad Mantruso that had earned the rank of First Blademaster. Brad Madrid had no such rank.

Marshal nodded. "I hold the rank of Third Blademaster." That was roughly equivalent to a third-degree black belt in the older martial arts.

The other man returned his blade to the salute. "Again."

This time, Brad held his blade at guard. For a moment, neither of them moved, and then Marshal lunged in. Brad knocked the other man's blade out to the side and thrust.

Marshal twisted out of the path of his attack and brought his own blade slashing back in. Brad allowed his left knee to collapse under him, dropping beneath the path of the blade as he brought his own blade snapping back toward the other man, twisting it across to slash into Marshal's side.

The practice blade sparked as it flashed its charge into the older man. Marshal grunted and lowered his blade in defeat.

"Well done. Very well done, in fact," Marshal said. "You have a great deal of natural talent, but—no offense intended—you could use more finesse."

Brad shrugged. "I've never needed it before."

Marshal looked at him oddly. "And you think you need it now?"

Brad hesitated for a moment, wondering whether this stranger could be trusted with even a fraction of the truth...and then nodded. "Yeah. I think I may."

"I can teach you," the older man offered.

"Why?" Brad asked, willing but suspicious.

"Because I've got nothing better to do for the next two weeks," the older man replied with a shrug. "Coincidentally, that's about how long I think it'll take for me to teach you most of what I know that you don't. The basics of it, anyway. You'll still have a lot of practice ahead of you to make it natural. Interested?"

Brad smiled. "Very. Thanks."

Several hours later, breathing heavily, Marshal tossed the practice blade to the side. "I think that's enough for one night."

"It's been educational," Brad replied. The other man had worn him out enough that the constant murmur of his anger was quieter now.

Brad collected the other man's blade and put them both away. The older man had put him through a series of drills, some of which he'd known, some of which he hadn't.

He turned back to find the older man watching him.

"I don't know about you, but I need a drink. Care to join me?"

"There's a bar on the ship?" Brad asked, before mentally slapping himself. It was a transport primarily carrying workers to the Outer System. Of course there was a bar.

"Yup. You drink beer?"

"No. I drink vacuum and starlight," Brad replied dryly, the other man bringing out a humor he'd almost forgotten.

"Well, I don't know if the bartender knows how to make fancy-assed drinks like that," Marshal told him with a grin, "but they do have some decent beer on this tub."

Brad inclined his head. "Show me the way."

———

The place seemed rather crude, with no decoration on the bare metal bulkheads or padding on the seats. Still, even at the early hour—or late, depending on how you wanted to judge it—the bar had a healthy number of patrons.

"So, what do you do?" Brad asked Marshal as they settled down at a corner table a few minutes later.

"I'm a pilot," the older man told him with a small gesture at their surroundings, with a hint of embarrassment. "A little down on my luck, obviously. Until about a week ago, I was a courier pilot with StarCorp."

Brad whistled silently. StarCorp was the largest corporation there was off Earth. They were big enough that even pirates hesitated before messing with them. StarCorp had both the cash and the will to see pirates who touched their ships dead. Messily.

"Yeah. It was one heck of a sweet deal. Money, glamor, excitement —I've even run away from or fought pirates a time or two." He finished his beer and signaled the serving robot for another. "A very sweet deal."

The mention of pirates soured Brad's mood, but he was getting used to controlling his anger now and covered his reaction. "So, what landmine did you step on?"

Brad silently noted the speed with which the pilot had finished his drink. He was less than halfway through his own beer.

Marshal shrugged. "To make a long story very short, I went clubbing, got drunk, and woke up in bed with the local boss's daughter. I was still drunk enough to tell the old man to go fuck himself when he came in."

Brad watched as the man's second beer arrived and he drained it. The *got drunk* part of the story was certainly believable.

"That still doesn't explain why you're on this tub. Last I'd heard, there's a shortage of pilots pretty much systemwide."

"Yeah, but nobody in the Inner System is going to touch someone that StarCorp has blacklisted," Marshal said quietly. A third beer arrived and the man treated it the same as the first two.

Brad nodded carefully. "So, you're going to the Outer System, looking for work?"

"Right. Out there, no one cares if you're blackballed or not." Marshal looked at Brad with a piercing gaze that belied his oncoming drunken state. "Your turn. What's a trained security man doing heading into the Outer System under a false name, 'Mr. Madrid?'"

Brad's anger spiked and he began to lean forward threateningly before he managed to stop himself.

"You seem to be making a few assumptions," he told Marshal with carefully forced calm. "Why would you think I'm using a false name and what makes me a security man?"

"You sure as hell didn't learn to fight in bars, kid. The way you move, the way you've learned to fight, those're marks of a professional fighter. You're not callous enough to be a pirate and you're too green to be a merc."

The other man grinned. "On top of that, it always takes you a moment or two to reply to 'Madrid.'"

Brad glanced down at the four empty beer bottles by Marshal's elbow. The two men had only been there twenty minutes. "I think you may be too observant for your own good, Mr. Marshal." He made sure his voice was cold.

The grin vanished off the other man's face. "I'm not going to tell anyone, kid. I don't have an agenda. I just want to help you out. I won't mention your past again. It's your business. Brad."

Brad hesitated for a moment before speaking. "I'll take you at your word, then. John."

Marshal nodded firmly and stood. "Excellent. I'll bid you farewell and good night, then. I'll meet you in the gym at the same time tomorrow."

"Sounds good." Brad twisted in his chair to let Marshal past. He turned back to the table and was about to order another drink when he heard a thudding sound behind him.

He turned to find that Marshal had somehow collided with another man and they'd both ended up on the floor. Both were standing back up, and the burly, shaven-headed guy had an ugly expression on his face.

"Think you can shove Doug Chenk around, pansy boy? You're going to wish you'd never been born."

"Hey, it was just an accident, man," Marshal said, backing away and raising his hands in a placating gesture.

"Then you won't mind when I 'accidentally' carve your face off, you little puffball," Chenk snapped, his hand darting inside his open leather vest.

Brad surged to his feet, drawing and activating his blade as he moved. It stopped Chenk's blade a foot from Marshal's face.

"This is none of your concern, tall boy," Chenk spat as he stepped back.

The other patrons were scurrying clear around them. No one wanted a wildly swung blade to cut them in half. The bartender was shouting something, but Brad couldn't spare the man any attention.

"Back off," Brad said curtly. He was perfectly willing to let the other man volunteer as a target for him to vent some of his rage, but this wasn't the place or time.

He watched the man carefully as he moved between the threat and Marshal. Chenk was a head shorter than he was but probably weighed half again as much. All of it muscle.

"Like fuck I will," the man snarled. "Get out of my way or join him in a gizzard sandwich."

The man matched actions to words by lunging at Brad. Brad deflected the thrust with a flick of his blade, unbalancing the other man in the process. He took advantage of that by shoving him away.

"One last chance," Brad said coolly. "Walk away and we can all forget this happened."

He saw Chenk's eyes flick left and right, taking in the dozen or so passengers in the bar, and swore mentally. The man wasn't going to back down in front of an audience.

"Fuck you, prick," Chenk hissed as he began to warily circle Brad.

Brad heard another blade activate behind him and knew that Marshal was preparing to enter the fight. With all the alcohol the man had consumed, he'd rather not risk it.

"I have this," Brad said as he brought his blade into the guard position and made a small *come on* gesture toward Chenk with his free hand. He got the expected reaction as the bald man lunged forward, his blade slashing at Brad's neck.

He parried the blade, caught the man's wrist in his left hand, and twisted it back. Tendons popped as the other man swore in pain. His blade dropped from suddenly nerveless fingers.

Safety cutoffs deactivated the charge to the filament as the blade fell, and Brad drove the heel of his foot into Chenk's kneecap with a loud *pop*.

The man hit the deck with a resounding thump and howl of agony just as a trio of *Rain*'s security men came charging in, stun-sticks at the ready.

He deactivated his blade and holstered it before turning to face them with his hands empty.

# CHAPTER FIVE

A PAIR of security men escorted him to the captain's office. Neither looked very friendly, so he leaned against the wall and waited in silence once they got there. Perhaps ten minutes went by before the door opened and a regular crewman came out.

"The old man wants to see you now," he told Brad. He glanced at the guards. "Just him, though. You can head back to your posts. I'll take his weapons for now."

"*Ja*, sir," one of them replied as he handed Brad's weapon's belt to the man. With that, the guards left.

The speaker gestured towards the door. "In with you."

Brad shrugged and stepped through the open hatch.

As he entered, he glanced around the room. It was relatively spartan, with only a single bookshelf—mostly filled with bric-a-brac rather than books—providing the sole break in the plain metal bulkheads. The desk was equally basic, a simple metal surface suspended on two filing cabinets with a computer console.

All in all, the room provided no excuse for him not to look at *Louisiana Rain*'s captain, so he did. The man's head was shaved, with slight blond fuzz apparently starting to grow back in. It was impossible to guess his height with him sitting down.

The man said nothing as his crewman laid Brad's weapons belt on the desk in front of him and departed without another word, closing the door behind him.

"My name is Hans Jaeger," he said with a noticeable German accent as he gestured toward the weapons on his desk. "I am the captain of *Louisiana Rain*. You may have these back. Please, have a seat."

Brad strapped the belt back around his waist and sat in the indicated chair, feeling more comfortable now he was armed. "I expected you to confiscate them."

"For fighting?" Jaeger asked with a chuckle. "*Hölle*, Mr. Madrid, I should probably be rewarding you. From what my bartender told me, and what the cameras showed, you ended that incident with the minimum amount of damage to all involved.

"Certainly, if you hadn't become involved, Mr. Marshal would most likely be dead and I'd have a messy situation on my hands."

He shrugged. "You did me a favor and I'm not one to let such things go unrewarded. Tell me, Mr. Madrid, what are you looking for in the Outer System?"

Brad blinked, a bit surprised at the unexpected question. "Work, mostly. There isn't much left for me anywhere else, and it seems like a good place to start over."

"That's a fairly common story." He held Brad's eyes for a moment before he continued. "According to your ticket, you're heading for Ganymede, correct?"

"Yes," he replied, still rather uncertain where this was leading.

The captain leaned back in his chair. "I know a woman on Ganymede—an agent for the Mercenary Guild—who might be able to help you find work. Interested?"

Brad hesitated for a moment. The Mercenary Guild was well known, even in the Inner System, where many of its members were considered criminals.

The Guild functioned as an intermediary between those seeking to hire mercenaries and bounty hunters and the mercs themselves. It also did things like recruiting crewmen and troopers for mercenary commanders.

It wasn't the sort of work Brad had originally been thinking of, but it had potential he hadn't previously considered. It would give him a better chance to find and kill the Terror than wandering around. Not to mention an outlet for the anger-fueled violence that ran just under the surface these days.

"Very," he replied firmly.

Jaeger plucked a business card from his tunic pocket and slid it across to Brad. It had basic information about the Guild and an individual on the card itself, and would have more detailed information on the chip inside it.

It simply read:

SARA KERNSKY

RECRUITING AGENT

MERCENARY GUILD

"Thank you, Captain," Brad said, tucking the card away.

"As I said, I return favors that are given to me. This concludes our business, but I have one more thing to say." The Captain raised a warning hand. "I'd appreciate it if you didn't draw your weapons again for any less pressing reason than you did tonight. Clear?"

"Clear, Captain," Brad said as he rose to his feet.

———

Brad found Marshal waiting for him when he arrived at the gym that night. The older man was sitting on one of the benches, a pair of practice blades leaning against the wall beside him. He looked up as Brad entered, and inclined his head.

"It seems you regard any debt worth paying as worth exceeding. I owe you my life."

"People die every day to disease, old age, or accident," Brad said with a shake of his head. "I see no reason to allow that number to increase when it's within my ability to change it."

He'd lost enough that, so much as it was in his power, the only people who were going to die around him were pirates. Though he was planning on killing a *lot* of pirates.

"Nonetheless, I owe you my life and I won't forget it."

"I don't demand repayment for what any man should do as a matter of course," Brad told him levelly.

Marshal nodded, rose to his feet, and picked up the blades. "I'm not offering repayment yet. I'm merely acknowledging that a debt exists and that you may call it due at your will."

Brad caught the practice blade Marshal tossed him and raised it in salute. "Maybe you can save my life one day."

"Maybe so," Marshal grinned as he returned the salute. "*En garde,* Mr. Madrid."

Brad raised his sword to the high guard position as the two began circling. "My name is Brad. Hell, Mr. Madrid isn't even my father."

———

Brad leaned back in his chair at the bar, quietly sipping his beer. Out of the corner of his eye, he watched Marshal making a pass at one of the unattached women on the ship. He liked the man, but he drank a lot and seemed incapable of resisting the temptation of a pretty lady.

The training had progressed very well over the last week. Brad thought he'd nailed the basics of what Marshal wanted to show him down, faster than the pilot had expected. The next week would cement them in his mind and make them natural. He still had a lot of practice to do, but it was a very good start to upping his game.

He finished his beer just as he noticed one of the security officers who'd picked him up after the earlier fight coming into the bar.

The man glanced at his wrist-comp, and the blood slowly drained out of his face. He turned and walked straight out of the bar.

Brad hesitated for a moment and then stood. Something was up. He smoothly followed the man deeper into the ship's corridors. He hung back, watching as the man met with three of his fellow security officers.

"Should we tell the passengers?" one of them asked.

"No," another—apparently the leader—replied. "The captain wants us to keep this under wraps unless we have to evacuate."

"Wonderful," one of the others said dryly. "He's the boss. Let's do it."

The quartet headed off.

Brad gave them a little time to move ahead and then followed. When he rounded the corner, he saw that he'd made a mistake. The men had passed out of sight in the complex of passages.

He swore softly and picked a corridor at random. A minute later, he decided he'd gone down the wrong one.

As he turned to head back, however, he heard a loud crash just around the corner ahead of him. One that he'd heard before: The heavy metal-on-metal sound of a cut airlock door falling to the deck.

Before he could do more than turn, a man wearing a plain black vac-suit stepped around the corner, carrying an automatic shotgun.

Brad jumped desperately to the side, his hand automatically going for his pistol. The man's shotgun cracked and flechettes snapped through the air where Brad had stood a moment before.

Relieved that he'd survived, he shot the man three times: twice in the chest and once in the head. The pirate grunted and fell backward to the deck.

Running footsteps sounded around the corridor as Brad realized the man—he had to be a pirate—had been the point man for a boarding team.

He rapidly holstered his pistol and grabbed the shotgun. He swung the weapon to his shoulder, exhaled, and held the trigger down as the pirates came around the corner, spraying the corridor with sharp metal.

What the flechettes did to the three men was indescribable.

Unfortunately, the rest of the boarding team—six more pirates— came surging around the corner behind them and opened fire at him. One of them had a Fleet auto-rifle—undoubtedly stolen—its high-speed rounds adding their own distinctive *crack* to the sound of the weapon firing.

Brad had already thrown himself down and was now rolling under the wave of fire as he tried to reload the shotgun. He hit the wall and drew his pistol with his left hand, emptying the magazine down the hallway at the man with the auto-rifle. He wasn't sure how many times he hit the man, but the pirate went down.

He dropped his pistol to finish reloading the shotgun, then shoved himself away from the wall. Almost too late. A flechette from a shotgun blast sliced across his leg but didn't do any major damage. He hoped.

A three-round burst from his reloaded shotgun blew away the man who'd tried to kill him in a blast of gore.

The next few moments were a bloody blur of crashing shotgun blasts. Brad took a hit in his left arm but managed to continue firing until his weapon locked open.

Miraculously, there was only one pirate left. He was fumbling with a new magazine for his pistol.

Brad surged to his feet, hurled the empty shotgun at the man, and drew his mono-blade. It activated with a hiss as he charged.

The man almost managed to get his pistol reloaded in time. Almost.

He took the man's head off and stood there panting in the midst of the dead. Adrenaline was pumping through him, and he let his anger rise with it.

Pirates.

He wasn't sure how he'd survived running into an entire squad of them, but there were pirates aboard the *Rain*, and the demon he'd kept leashed since waking up on *Freedom* didn't leave him much choice as to what happened now: they died.

Brad took a moment to make sure that none of his wounds was going to kill him, swallowing his gorge—and pride—enough to rip into one of the pirate's suit pockets for emergency autobandages.

Then he reclaimed his pistol and swapped the magazine for a full one.

These guys had been a lot more reliant on firearms than professional pirates. Those bastards had an almost-religious abhorrence for guns. This team must be new to the business.

Brad could work out what must have happened. The *Rain* was unarmed, so Captain Jaeger had allowed the pirates to close and board. He must've hoped to deal with them aboard the ship.

Not a winning strategy, but the man hadn't had a lot of choices. Still, he should've told the passengers what was happening and enlisted them to the defense.

Well, the pirates were short one boarding team now, but that didn't mean much. There'd be at least three ships—possibly more—attacking a vessel of this size. Each would send its own team. That many pirates would easily overrun Jaeger's security people.

Brad had seen one ship fall to pirates. He wasn't going to let it happen to another one, even if his left arm didn't quite want to work and his leg hurt. He could still walk and still shoot. It would have to be enough.

He stripped a bandolier of shotgun shells off a dead pirate and slung it over his shoulder. A pair of grenades on the bottom of the belt slapped against his hip.

He reloaded his new shotgun and hung it so he could access it quickly. He picked up the Fleet auto-rifle, which became his new best friend. The dead man had only a few additional magazines for it, but they might make the difference in a fight like this.

Brad retraced the path the pirates had used to get there. Less than ten meters down the winding corridor, he reached a sharp corner and paused, glancing around it.

A single pirate stood just outside the ship's breached airlock. As Brad watched, someone moved inside the ship behind him.

For a few seconds, he hesitated. He'd never opened a fight. Never intentionally shot a man who didn't know he was coming.

But *this* man was a pirate who'd come to kidnap *Rain*'s passengers. He brought the auto-rifle up and shot the pirate. The heavy recoil of the weapon punished his shoulder, but the slug brought the man down right away.

Shocked shouts from inside the ship marked at least two additional pirates. Brad pulled the pin from one of the grenades and lobbed it into the ship.

He threw himself against the bulkhead a few seconds before it exploded, sending sharp crystal fragments spewing into the pirate ship and back into the liner's corridor.

Thankfully, none of them hit him. He made a mental note to be a little more careful with grenades in the future.

Brad went in, rifle at the ready. It proved unnecessary. Neither of the pirates had been more than a meter from the grenade. It would take a forensic team to work out which bits were whose, and he drew on his anger to keep his stomach under control. He heard no other movement on the ship, but he had no idea how large it was.

He was about to find out when the sound from a blood-soaked commlink headset lying on the deck distracted him. It was a miracle the damned thing still worked.

Brad picked it up, ignoring the gore, and seated the earbud in mid-sentence.

"...guarding the ships," the voice spat from the earphone. "We've sealed the passenger decks to keep the prizes unhurt, and the crew seems to have dug in around the bridge. Get your lazy asses off those hunks of metal and get down here to help us!"

Brad caught two responses to the pirate leader's orders. So. There were only two other ships.

He activated the microphone. "Roger," he said quickly, mimicking the other responses and hoping they didn't notice that he wasn't one of the men left to guard this ship.

Only silence answered him, which he presumed to mean he'd succeeded. Wiping the controls off as best he could, he attached the com to his right wrist. Monitoring their communications might give him an inside track on their plans.

He slung the rifle over his shoulder and reseated the bandolier. His other hand rested on the handle of his mono-blade for a moment before he turned back towards the boarding lock.

————

A few minutes later, Brad saw just what the pirate leader had meant by *sealing the passenger decks*. Someone had cut open the access panel next to a door, manually closed it, and welded the hatch shut. Brad's planned route to the bridge went through there, so he needed a new plan.

He used his wrist-comp to bring up a deck plan of *Louisiana Rain*. A moment's study showed him an alternate route that didn't enter the passenger decks. He set out on it at a run. He didn't know how long the crew could hold out, and he was almost certainly running short on time.

Just as he was getting close to the bridge, he heard rapid footsteps ahead. Odds were good they belonged to another team of pirates.

He swore softly and listened. There were three or four of them, he thought. When they'd almost reached his position, he took a deep breath and leaned out, leading with the barrel of his rifle.

Three pirates, anonymous in their black vac-suits, froze at the sight of him. Two carried shotguns, the third carried an automatic grenade launcher—the heaviest weapon any sane person would risk aboard a spaceship. They really were new to this business—or they had seriously *meant* business.

His first burst of fire cut down the closest shotgun-carrier, and his next took out the second. Not before he managed to raise his weapon and fire, unfortunately.

Brad ducked back but took another hit in this leg, two inches above the first one. Worse, the auto-rifle took a flechette in the receiver. He could actually see it buried in the metal. He dropped the useless weapon and went for his mono-blade.

The grenadier had also opted for his blade. Smart. A grenade at this range was suicide.

Brad danced backward, parrying two rapid slashes with flicks of his own weapon. Then he saw the pirate reach for his comset controls.

Needing to end this before the man warned his comrades, he parried a third slash, allowing the momentum of the blades bouncing off one other to spin him around as he dropped to one knee. The pirate's weapon blocked high while Brad slashed him in two at the waist in an explosion of gore.

Brad breathed heavily, leaning against the bulkhead as he let his wounded leg and arm recover from the strains he'd just put on them. He scanned the bodies and his eye came to rest on the grenade launcher haphazardly dropped against the wall.

His anger had faded into a strange calm now, and a cold smile spread across his face at the sight of the launcher. The pirates had brought the weapon to break the crew's resistance, but that could work both ways. He picked it up and continued on his way.

———

Brad knew when he was nearing the bridge. The gunshots and whine of mono-blades colliding made that perfectly clear. The noises got louder as he approached the last corner, and he hefted the grenade launcher.

He'd never fired one before, but the controls were brutally simple. After his brief visit into the interior of the ship he'd grenaded, he had a sickeningly accurate idea of what its effects would be—but no part of him was going to argue that the pirates didn't deserve it!

He braced himself for a heavy kick and stepped around the corner.

The bridge's blast door was half closed, providing an impromptu barrier against the pirate attack. A small heap of vac-suited bodies—most showing the distinct damage of mono-blade strikes—showed the pirates had made at least one attempt to rush the door.

The fight had reduced itself to mostly pure gunfire now as the pirates took cover behind various uprooted tables and couches and did their best to soften up the defenses for another charge.

One of the pirates turned, possibly to see if their reinforcements were there, and saw Brad. As the woman opened her mouth to shout a warning, Brad lifted the launcher and fired.

He racked the slide, jacking in another grenade before the first one detonated, and kept firing. He was outside the grenades' lethal blast radius, but the clumps of horrified pirates definitely were not.

Brad emptied the launcher's five-round magazine in about as many seconds, walking the explosions down the corridor, toward the blast door. He probably wasn't accurate, but he was firing *grenades*.

Once the launcher clicked empty, he tossed it aside and hefted his shotgun.

A dark shadow appeared through the smoke, and Brad blew the pirate away. He waited for more to rush his position, but none came.

The ventilation and fire-prevention systems finally activated, rapidly clearing the smoke. Perhaps three pirates remained on their feet amidst the shattered debris of their makeshift blockade. All three turned toward Brad, raising their weapons.

Multiple shots rang out, so close together as to sound like one, and all three pirates dropped. No shots came near Brad, but he pointed the shotgun away from the defenders and spread his hands wide anyway.

Captain Jaeger stepped through the gap between the frozen halves of the blast door, pistols in both hands. He walked up to Brad, examined him closely, and then holstered his guns.

He offered his hand as members of his crew raced past them. Probably on their way to engineering and the pirate ships to corral any survivors before they escaped or caused any more mischief.

"Mr. Madrid," the man said softly. "Thank you."

Brad took Jaeger's hand. "My pleasure. I happen to dislike pirates a great deal."

A startled grin, probably brought on as much by combat fatigue as anything else, crossed the man's face. "Lucky for us."

He surveyed the corridor, now splattered with gore. "Very lucky for us, indeed."

The captain turned his attention back to Brad, just in time to catch the young man as blood loss caught up with him and he wavered on his feet.

"And luckily for you," he murmured, "we have a fantastic doctor."

# CHAPTER SIX

THE SEVERAL HOURS it took to clear the ship of the corpses, weapons, and other debris left behind by the pirates, Brad spent in the infirmary, getting several holes in his skin sewn shut and slathered with regeneration gel.

That was fine by him. While he had no objections to killing pirates, he didn't feel quite up to stripping and spacing the corpses.

Once the ship was cleared, the crew turned their attention to opening up the passenger sections. They rejected Brad's more-than-half-drugged suggestion to use one of the pirates' plasma cutters and chose to remove the welds in a slower, less destructive manner. That took an additional three hours.

By the time that was done, he'd rejoined the crew's security detail to make certain the access went smoothly. Being sewn up wasn't exactly relaxing and he was absolutely shattered.

Not as much as the rest of the passengers, he suspected. The pirates had cut all the com lines, so the crew couldn't even tell them the fighting was over.

When they opened the first door, they found a dozen passengers waiting for them, holding a motley collection of mono-blades, pistols, and long-bladed knives. To Brad's amused approval, Doug Chenk appeared to be in charge of defending this entrance.

The passengers relaxed at the sight of the crew uniforms. A female security officer stepped forward to address them. "All right, people, I know you want to know what happened, but we're still busy dealing with it. Return to your quarters and wait for the captain's announcement. He should be coming on as soon as we have the coms working again."

The crowd began dispersing and the security officer turned to Brad. "Thank you, Mr. Madrid," she said quietly. "You've done more than anyone had any right to expect."

She turned, gesturing the rest of her team away. "We can handle the repairs, and it looks like the pirates are done for. You can head back to your own quarters. The captain will most likely want to talk to you in the morning, but we're done for now."

"I was more than happy to help, but some sleep does sound good right about now." With that, he nodded and headed into the passenger deck.

Once he reached his cabin, he sealed the door behind him and dropped onto his bed with a sigh of relief. The ship's junior doctor had bandaged his various wounds, but he'd been too busy dealing with major casualties to do more.

Brad willed himself to undo his boots, but fell asleep before his tired body could obey.

————

For a moment after he woke, Brad couldn't figure out what had dragged him from his slumber. Then the door chime sounded again.

He groaned, stood while rubbing sleep from his eyes, and staggered to the door. "Yes?" he blearily asked the uniformed security guard standing in the corridor.

"Captain Jaeger wants to see you," the man said apologetically, his tone suggesting that more of Brad's anger at being awoken had leaked out than he meant.

Brad blinked away sleep, forcing himself to calm once more. "What time is it?"

"Seventeen hundred hours."

He'd been asleep for nearly twelve hours. Despite the events of the previous day, it had been dreamless sleep with none of the nightmares he'd expected.

"All right. I'll be a minute."

The guard nodded and Brad headed back into his cabin. He stripped out of his blood-soaked clothing and threw himself into the shower. A few minutes later, dressed in a fresh set of clothes, he felt much more human. He strapped his weapons belt on and opened the door once again.

The security man was leaning against the wall on the opposite of the corridor. When Brad exited, he straightened and gestured for Brad to precede him. "This way, please."

He followed the man through the ship. Here and there, techs had access panels open, repairing circuits damaged by everything from stray bullets to power surges. Most of them waved when they recognized him now.

When they reached the captain's office, the guard stopped. "He's waiting for you, Mr. Madrid"

"Thank you." He took a deep breath and then pressed the admittance chime.

The door slid open and Brad stepped inside to find Jaeger rising from his desk. "Come in, come in. Have a seat."

Brad sat. The top of Jaeger's desk had acquired several neat piles of data chips and readers, as well as one not-so-neat pile of hardcopy.

Jaeger gestured at the hardcopy. "I'm busy going over the salvage paperwork we're going to file on those pirate ships. It doesn't help that, as far as we can tell, they never officially registered them so there are no records of them *anywhere*."

"Sounds complicated," Brad commiserated.

"I imagine so, but it will prove lucrative for the company." The man settled back into his chair and considered him. "And for anyone that personally seized them, if they file the paperwork contesting any competing claims."

Brad frowned. "I'm not sure I follow you."

Jaeger smiled a little. "That's complicated, too. The Commonwealth's deep-space salvage laws, while derived from similar laws for oceans on Earth, have a few unique quirks regarding pirates and slavers.

"If one finds a ship drifting abandoned in space, there's a complicated process to locate the owner or heirs and determine the salvage fee due to the people that saved the ship. The salvager doesn't get ownership of the ship directly.

"Slavers and pirates are different. A ship seized in the commission of those crimes becomes the property of the company or individual that captured it. In this case, my crew fought off the pirates and seized their ships. The company that owns *Louisiana Rain* automatically becomes the not-so-proud owner of a few run-down pirate ships, as soon as we can detach them from our hull."

Brad settled a little deeper into his chair. "That seems pretty straightforward."

Jaeger smiled. "Appearances can be deceiving. The company is quite pleased that we've survived and that we brought them a lucrative and unforeseen windfall. That pleasure might be somewhat muted when they learn of the competing claim."

"Competing claim?"

"Indeed." Jaeger picked up the pile of hardcopy, removed a set of papers, and pushed them across the table to Brad.

He picked them up. "What are these?"

"Salvage papers for the largest of the pirate ships. It's based on Fleet's *Fidelis*-class heavy corvette. It masses about five thousand tons, but I'm not sure about what drives and weapons it carries.

"It also happens to be the ship you boarded. You killed the crew in that action, so under the letter of the law, you have a claim to that vessel. You quite literally seized it during an act of piracy."

"That seems like a technicality," Brad said with a shake of his head. The possibilities a *ship* opened up for him were huge, but it was just too much. "It was attached to your hull. While I took out their boarding party and crew, it probably wasn't the only boarding party from that ship. Your people fought and bled, too."

"I'm told that technicalities are the very soul of the law. When the arbiter questions me, I will have no choice but to confirm that you personally and single-handedly boarded that enemy ship and killed every pirate aboard it. As much as my company will scream, that makes it yours. Or it will once the proceedings are complete."

Brad frowned. "Your employers are going to be pissed. Why are you doing this?"

"We owe you," Jaeger said simply. "If you hadn't done what you did, my crew and I would be dead right now. My company will just have to make do with the other two ships."

Brad did some quick calculations in his head. "Captain, you're talking something like sixty million credits of armed spaceship. That feels a little excessive as a thank you gift."

"How highly would you value your life and the lives of those under your care?" Jaeger asked gently. "I think it sounds about right to me, though I suspect the actual value is somewhat less than that, once you look at the repairs and upgrades it probably requires.

"And, as I said, I'm certain the company will contest your claim, but I feel confident you'll triumph in the end."

Brad looked at the papers, stunned. "What am I supposed to do with a five-thousand-ton warship?"

Even as he asked, ideas began to flow into his head. Working as a merc was one thing, but it would take a power base and independent transportation to hunt down the Terror. This ship could give him both.

"Remember the contact I gave you for the Mercenary Guild?" Jaeger asked. "She can help you find a crew as easily as finding you a place in a mercenary company. Also, if I send along a glowing-enough commendation—which I will—the Guild will probably help you get started."

He paused. "Also, my people loaded about half of the weapons and equipment we salvaged into that ship's cargo hold. The ships were a good place to put all the salvaged materials, after all. Finally, since pirates are not fans of banking institutions, it wouldn't surprise me if there were stashes of money aboard the ships. All of those things will help you get started."

Brad still hesitated, so Jaeger leaned forward. "Mr. Madrid, my crew and I owe you our lives. One ship and a bunch of guns and armor we could never use are the least we can do. Sign the claim and I'll dutifully send it to Ganymede."

He nodded slowly and signed the papers. "Done."

"And done," Jaeger said smoothly, taking them. "I'll send these with a competing claim on the company's behalf. We'll see you at the arbiter's office. May the best man win...Captain Madrid." He added a slow wink to the last.

"I suggest you complete an inventory of your own. You'll want to be certain the details in the claim are correct. If you find something off, I can assist you in amending the paperwork."

Brad climbed to his feet. "I'm not sure what to say. Thank you, Captain Jaeger."

The other man smiled. "It seems as if you knew exactly what to say after all. Good luck and good hunting, Captain."

———

Brad sat in the command chair aboard the corvette. The bridge was small, only three duty stations: helm, fire control, and communications. The command chair sat between the other three consoles, nicely positioned to see everyone's screens.

Behind him, a highly overdone plaque above the bridge entrance announced that the ship had been named *Bloodthirster*. That was definitely going to go. He made a mental note to look up how one went about rechristening a ship.

He looked down at the arms of the command chair. From his studies, the same place on a Navy ship like *Freedom* held a set of repeater screens that could call up data from any console on the bridge. The repeaters could even allow the captain to fly and fight the ship alone if he was truly desperate.

Brad added *command chair repeaters* to the open file on his wristcomp. It became just one more entry in a long list of modifications he wanted to make. The pirate ship was a rather crude hack-job on a solid base design, effective but far from efficient.

He stood with a sigh, crossed to the helm console, and surveyed the controls. They were complex but no more so than any other ship. Thanks to Shari, he could probably fly it in an emergency, but he'd need a real pilot.

The memory of her death came flooding back over him. Rage and grief briefly swamped him before he pushed them back. He would have his vengeance, but he needed his wits about him now.

Fortunately, he knew where to find a pilot. One who owed him.

First, though, he needed to finish his initial examination of the ship. Engineering was next and he dreaded what no doubt awaited him there.

———

Two hours later, Brad was in *Rain*'s bar, going over his list. Foremost on it were the ship's drives. The corvette had mounts for three drive units but had only two, and they were of completely different types.

One was a Skylark III, putting out two thousand kilonewtons of thrust. The other was more than twice as powerful, a Falcon IV providing five thousand kilonewtons.

Not only did the engines look different, which messed up the symmetry of the ship, but the unbalanced thrust would cause significant problems controlling it under power.

The second concern was the corvette's weapons and targeting scanners. Both, in Brad's opinion, were useless.

The scanners could probably hit something *Louisiana Rain*'s size, but anything smaller would almost certainly evade them. Not that it mattered. The guns were the mass-driver equivalents of giant blunderbusses. Pinpoint accuracy, no matter how good the scanners were, was impossible.

Marshal set his beer down next to Brad's elbow. "So, the conquering hero has decided to join us, has he?"

"Well, I can't spend all my time being fawned over by busty women, can I?" Brad asked reasonably.

Marshal snorted and sat down. "Touché. The beer's on me, this time at least. My own little repayment for saving our asses."

Brad shrugged and then downed half his beer. "I should take advantage of this while it lasts, huh?"

"Definitely."

Silence descended for a moment as both men sipped their beer. "Have you worked out what you're going to be doing once you reach Ganymede?" he asked.

The pilot shrugged. "Look for work, obviously. There aren't all that many fully qualified pilots this far out. That makes it an employee's market."

Brad regarded the man over his beer. He figured Marshal was being overly optimistic. The look in the man's eyes suggested that he probably thought so too. In the Outer System, people were perfectly willing to let less-qualified pilots fly them.

"You want to cut to the chase and get a job now?"

Marshal sat up straight, his quick move belying the number of drinks he'd probably had. "What do you mean?"

Brad grinned. "I seem to have seized a pirate ship. Or I will have, once the arbiter makes the final call on Ganymede. The law seems pretty clear, and Captain Jaeger has already annoyed his bosses by sending a statement that backs me up. So, it seems I need a pilot."

"You *own* a ship?" Marshal demanded, openmouthed.

"It's a corvette and she needs a lot of work, but it seems I do." Brad stared at Marshal steadily. "So, what do you say, Mr. Marshal? Are you willing to work for me?"

The pilot was silent for a moment. "I think one of us going to end up regretting this, but you've got yourself a pilot."

———

The next six days went by in a blur. He and Marshal threw themselves into examining the corvette. Most of the physical gear they left in place, not even hunting for the money stashes that they'd lose if the claim process didn't go their way.

Brad spent more than half of his waking time on the computers, breaking past the various encryptions and codes on the ship's systems. They were a mess.

He found a few tidbits of interesting information along the way, ranging from the names of the crewmembers—a file he shot over to Captain Jaeger, as it should help in collecting any standing bounties on the dead men—to the program the corvette's pilot had used to counteract the thrust imbalance of the ship's drives.

As an afterthought, he added *new operating system* to his list of desired upgrades.

The ship had an obsolete—but perfectly serviceable—Fleet anvil, so he could take care of some of the repairs and upgrades on his own once they had more time.

Marshal turned up while he was considering the possibilities of that, and dropped off a list of upgrades he'd come up with in his own, slightly more time-consuming survey of the ship.

It was more substantial and undoubtedly costlier to satisfy, he was sure.

The two of them were still discussing it when Captain Jaeger signaled from the airlock. Brad walked down and met him.

"I thought you'd like to know we're almost inside Ganymede's traffic control perimeter," the other man said. "It's time for us to part company. Can you make it in under your own power?"

"I think so," he said. "Come on up to the bridge and let me verify that with Marshal."

The liner captain looked around at the former pirate ship as they walked. "You're going to have a lot of work to do to bring this up to spec. I know someone on Ganymede that might be able to assist you with that, for a price."

"That would be good. We can do some, but we're going to require a major refit in the not-so-distant future."

Once they stepped onto the bridge, Brad passed the news on to Marshal.

"Can we actually fly ourselves in?" he asked.

The pilot considered the controls for a moment before nodding. "Yes. The program to mesh the engines is a mess, but a low-velocity docking with station computer backup is a pretty low bar to meet. I suppose we should get our gear."

The liner captain shook his head. "With your permission, I'll have the purser pack for you. I wouldn't want to disrupt your departure preparations."

The purser had already shown his appreciation, and that of his people, by giving the corvette's living quarters a thorough cleaning. Brad suspected that he'd also replaced some of the consumables, because he doubted the pirates went in for high-thread-count sheets.

Brad looked at Marshal and nodded when the pilot did. "That sounds great. Please pass our thanks on to all your people."

He offered Jaeger his hand. "And thank you, Captain. For everything."

Jaeger shook his hand. "We still owe you, Captain Madrid."

He handed Brad a business card. "This is for the yardmaster at the Io Shipyards I mentioned earlier. I took the liberty of contacting him already and he says he can clear a berth for you once the arbitration is complete.

"Good luck, gentlemen. I'm certain you'll succeed in whatever you choose to do."

———

Two hours later, Brad lounged in the command chair, watching over Marshal's shoulder as the man slowly detached the corvette from the liner. The pilot handled the delicate adjustments of the imbalanced thrusters like a maestro, gently clearing the larger vessel.

"Our assigned docking bay is oh-six-nine, Marshal," Brad told him. "The beacon is on frequency one-zero-six-zero-six."

Marshal nodded, and typed the number series into his console. A flashing red crosshair, with the numbers 069 floating next to it appeared on the main screen. The view slid sideways as Marshal triggered the maneuvering thrusters again, turning the corvette to face the beacon.

"We're clear of *Louisiana Rain*." Marshal said.

"Take her in."

# CHAPTER SEVEN

THEY'D BARELY FINISHED DOCKING the ship when someone announced themselves at the airlock.

Marshal raised an eyebrow. "That was quick. Are we expecting anyone?"

Brad shook his head. "It's probably the arbiter. Get the board shut down while I go see what we need to do next."

He made his way to the airlock and examined the image on the small screen beside it. Three men stood outside the airlock. Two of them looked bored, but the short, balding man in front was angry. Red-faced angry.

Not the arbiter. Probably someone from the company that owned *Louisiana Rain*. That likely meant there was about to be a fight about their presence on the ship.

Well, best to get that out of the way as soon as possible.

He opened the airlock and stepped out. Before any of the men could react, he closed the lock and secured it. No one would be getting in without Marshal opening the door or him allowing them in.

The man in front stepped into Brad's personal space and stuck his chin out aggressively. "You have no business on that ship, Madrid. I insist you vacate it at once."

Brad stood his ground, letting his anger leak into his gaze and his stance. "You obviously know who I am. Who are you?"

"Fabian Breen, with Astro Transport. The owners of the vessel you have illegally seized. You will turn this vessel over to my security officers at once or I shall have charges pressed against you."

"I believe the ownership of this vessel is going to be determined by an arbiter," Brad said levelly. "I'm willing to turn the vessel over to his or her care, of course. You're more than welcome to wait here for that to take place, but I'm not letting you onto this vessel."

No matter what the law said, Brad knew that possession counted for a lot. He wasn't about to turn this ship over to Breen, or he might never see it again. What was that old saying? It's easier to beg forgiveness than to ask permission.

He could easily see the company moving the ship elsewhere and then getting into a legal fight about the size of the fine they'd have to pay. That wasn't happening.

The man's face reddened further and he took another half-step forward. His face was now mere inches from Brad's.

"You do not want to cross me, Madrid. Do yourself a favor and get the hell out of my way."

Brad gave in to his demon a little. He placed a hand on the other man's chest and shoved him back with all the force he could muster. That sent Breen staggering into the guards behind him.

"You don't frighten me," Brad growled. "I've killed pirates face to face with a blade in my hand. You're just a minor annoyance."

He allowed his hand to drop near his holstered blade. "If you really want to make this into a fight, you're going to have to do much better than blustering."

Based upon the redness of the man's face, he was in danger of suffering some kind of blood pressure–related incident. "You're an idiot. Take him, men."

The two guards glanced at one another but made no move to advance.

Breen whirled on them. "Did I stutter?"

"Um…sir?" one of the guards asked hesitantly. "Perhaps we should call Ganymede Security."

"That won't be necessary, I hope," a voice said from farther down the corridor.

Brad look past the men in front of him and saw a slender woman approaching. She had a couple of men behind her as well. Unlike Breen's men, *these* wore matte-black clamshell body armor and carried stubby-barreled riot guns.

She stopped just short of Breen and his men. "Gentlemen, my name is Kenna Blaze and I represent the Arbiter Guild. Might I inquire what the nature of this public disagreement is about?"

Rather than try to talk over Breen, Brad decided to allow him to have his say.

Blaze held up a hand and cut the man off after only a few sentences of his rant. "I believe the Guild was quite clear in their communication with Astro Transport, Limited. Until we have reviewed the evidence and can make a ruling on the competing claims, the Guild will maintain possession of this vessel in trust for the eventual owner."

Breen looked as though he might explode. "This is outrageous! I will have your head."

He stormed off down the corridor and his guards followed him with apologetic shrugs.

Once they were gone, Blaze looked at Brad. "Are you Brad Madrid?"

At his nod, she continued. "My men will take possession of this ship until such time as I am prepared to make a ruling, so you'll need to find alternate quarters. The ship will remain at this dock until I issue my final ruling. Do you have any questions?"

He shook his head with a smile. "Not really. My pilot and I will get our personal belongings and leave the ship under your care."

"This may sound intrusive, but I'll need to see the inside of your cases before you leave the ship," she said apologetically. "Anything that is not part of your personal belongings must remain here until I issue a ruling."

"No objection from me. We're already packed, so it should only take a few minutes for you to examine everything. If I might ask, how long does it normally take the Guild to make a ruling in cases like this?"

She allowed him a small smile. "I've already begun reviewing the evidence, and there are many previous cases to provide precedent. I anticipate making a ruling within the next few days."

While nothing she said provided any clue as to how she might rule, her smile told him that he was on fairly safe ground. He only hoped he wasn't reading this entirely wrong.

———

The next day, Brad checked the fit of his new suit in the mirror. The quarters he'd rented while the Arbiter Guild settled the ownership of the corvette were small, but hardly cramped by his spaceborn standards.

In less than forty minutes, he was meeting the local representative of the Mercenary Guild, and even armed with Captain Jaeger's glowing recommendation, he wanted to make the best first impression possible.

Done going over his own clothes, he met Marshal in the hotel's lobby. The pilot wore a light gray suit similar to Brad's dark blue one. He bore his mono-blade on one hip and his pistol on the other, also just like Brad.

At the sight of the weapons on Brad's belt, Marshal grinned. "We seemed to have mastered at least one mercenary habit. Never go anywhere without your weapons."

Brad returned the grin with a subdued smile. "Indeed. I'm worried that I look a trifle…young for what they're expecting. I'm only in my twenties."

"Skipper, the instant they look at your eyes, they're going to raise whatever their estimate is by ten years," Marshal said, his voice suddenly serious. "You've seen the elephant and it shows. Trust me."

"I hope you're right. Let's go."

———

Thirty minutes later, they stood in front of a set of offices that looked identical to every other set they'd passed. A small sign next to the door declared this one, however, to be the Ganymede Office of the Mercenaries Guild.

A burly man in a black ship suit waited just outside. He extended his hand. "Mr. Madrid? I'm Guildsman Mike Randall. I'm here to escort you in."

Brad nodded. "Lead the way, Guildsman."

Upon entering the offices, Brad found the front room similar to other offices he'd seen over the years. There was the large desk with the multiple comsets manned by several young men and women, there were couches, and there was a door to the rest of the building.

From there, it diverged quite heavily. Where another office would have potted plants, either grown in the hydroponics section of the domes or—in the more powerful firms—imported from Earth or Mars, this office had weapons and armor set up neatly on display racks.

They ranged from swords and plate mail from Earth to modern combat armor and mono-blades. Each display had a small placard stating whose weapons they were, where they'd been made, and why they were on display.

The holos and paintings that would have been inspirational posters or garden scenes in another office were battle scenes here, starships and the like.

Brad was distracted from his survey of the rooms fascinating decor by Randall looking up from his quiet discussion with one of the receptionists. "The Factor is waiting for you, gentlemen. This way."

The security door at the other end of the reception room slid open before they reached it and Randall led them down a wood-paneled hallway. The Guildsman stopped next to a laminated metal door and touched an intercom key. "Ms. Kernsky, Mr. Madrid is here to see you."

"Send him in," a melodious voice ordered from the speaker.

Randall stepped back as the door slid open, and gestured Brad and Marshal in.

Brad took a deep breath and entered the office of the woman who held his future in her hands.

The impression of luxury given by the outer corridors increased when he entered the Factor's office. Waist-high wood paneling surrounded the room, surmounted by a light brown laminate on the plaster walls, perfectly matching the wood. A plush maroon carpet covered the floor, supporting a large wood and stained-ceramic desk.

Holding a place of pride above the desk was a large picture of a warship spewing flame from hull breaches, about to crash into an asteroid or moon. From the graininess of the image, Brad realized it was an actual still, recorded from a ship's visual records.

With an effort, Brad tore his eyes away from the picture to focus on the room's mistress.

As he did, the redheaded woman stood and extended her hand across the desk. "I'm Sara Kernsky, the senior Factor for the Mercenary Guild on Ganymede."

He crossed to the desk and took her hand, and then gestured to Marshal. "Brad Madrid. May I present my pilot, John Marshal?"

Marshal took Kernsky's hand and calmly bowed over it. "*Enchanté,* Miss Kernsky."

A small smile crossed the woman's face as she gestured them to chairs set in front of her desk. "Have a seat, gentlemen."

Brad sat, crossing his hands on the table in front of him, waiting for her to speak.

"I've looked at your application to the Mercenary Guild," she said as she sat back down. "I also took the opportunity to speak with Captain Jaeger.

"While he's sent a few good men my way, I confess that he's never recommended anyone as highly as he has you. As far as I can see, you might actually be as good as he indicated.

"However, you are an enigma, Mr. Madrid. As far as I can tell, you have no past."

Brad met her gaze calmly. "I hesitate to divulge my past unless it's absolutely necessary."

The woman raised a hand, palm up. "It's not. The Guild doesn't insist on knowing everything about you, and I prefer to base my judgment on the firsthand accounts of men I trust rather than older data."

"And what does your judgment come to this time?"

She snorted. "With the exception of a handful of men who'd

already been in the Guild a long time, you're one of the most qualified people who's ever walked into this office to apply for assistance.

"Don't get overjoyed too quickly, however," she warned. "There's more to being a bonded member of the Guild and the leader of a company than ability." She gestured to the picture above her desk. "Do you know what that is a picture of?"

Brad blinked at the seeming tangent. "Not really."

"It's the Cadre cruiser *Black Skull*. She was the Terror's flagship at the time, the other of the bastard's pair of stolen Fleet cruisers. She tore a swathe ten light-seconds wide through shipping. Wiped out a dozen merc companies.

"In the end, the Guild activated its 'overriding contract' clause and set twelve of the larger companies after it, nearly forty warships."

The Factor turned to gaze at the still. "We caught up with him off Uranus, quite a bit off the beaten track. They'd just finished slaughtering the crew of a science vessel doing a mineral survey. We hit her with everything we had."

She shrugged eloquently. "The heaviest ship we had was a destroyer. She was a cruiser, but there were forty of us. We lost twenty-six ships outright and eight more would never fly again, but we crippled her engines and watched her ram into Miranda at six kilometers a second. The still is from the visual records of the frigate *Midsummer*—one of the ones that never flew again."

"We?" Brad asked.

Kernsky turned back to face him. "I was *Midsummer*'s commanding officer, the most junior captain of four in the Red Wing Mercenary Company. When the battle was over, I was the senior officer and sole captain the Red Wings had left.

"The payment for the overriding contract was far more than we would have earned from any other agreement, but it wasn't enough to rebuild an entire squadron from scratch. We split the money between the survivors and went our separate ways.

"The Red Wings weren't the only company to die that day, but if the Guild calls us to do it again, every mercenary company will. Do you understand why, Mr. Madrid?"

"Because it needed to be done and someone had to do it," Brad said instantly. The demon of his anger might drive him but he would *not* let it control him. He was in this to stop the Cadre doing to others what they'd done to his family.

Kernsky smiled at him. "Precisely. I'm provisionally accepting your application for Guild membership as a bonded company, pending the favorable ruling of the Arbiter Guild on your ownership of the corvette."

He raised an eyebrow. "And if they don't find in my favor?"

"I happen to have friends in the Arbiter Guild," she replied, her smile widening. "The word I'm getting is the review is little more than a formality. You have the weight of precedent on your side.

"If they somehow find against you, I'm certain I could place you in a reputable company without any problem, so I feel comfortable welcoming you to the Mercenary Guild, Mr. Madrid. I'm looking forward to seeing what you do next."

# CHAPTER EIGHT

BRAD WOKE REFRESHED, even though his evening had run a bit late, as Marshal had wanted to hit the night spots. He probably should've refused, but things had been so hectic since the attack on the *Rain* that he wanted to decompress himself.

What he'd seen had given him more cause to worry about his pilot. The man's drinking showed no sign of abating now that he had gainful employment. Brad had hoped part of the man's intake was fueled by the uncertainty of his work situation.

Apparently not.

If Marshal didn't cut back on his own, Brad was going to have to become less subtle in his hints. He'd rather not do that—he wasn't even entirely sure how to—but he wasn't going to have Marshal's behavior put anyone in danger. On a ship, the pilot was always on call if trouble came calling, on duty or not.

He pondered potential methods of getting that point across while he showered and dressed for the day. No easy solutions presented themselves, so he'd just have to work it out when the time came, as painful as that might end up being.

A check of his wrist-comp indicated it was far too early to expect Marshal to be awake, even if the man hadn't hooked up with the tall brunette he'd met just before Brad had excused himself the previous evening.

Considering how well they'd been getting along, a night of solitude seemed unlikely.

He ate breakfast at the hotel restaurant. It wasn't anything to scream about, but he wasn't going to complain. He made a mental note that someone in his new crew had to fill the role of cook in addition to other duties. Two people would be better.

His wrist-comp signaled just as he was putting his dishes in a handy bin. It was his room forwarding a call. He accepted it and saw Kenna Blaze, her expression thunderous.

"Good morning, Arbiter Blaze. What can I do for you?"

"Did you return to the ship last night?"

Brad frowned and shook his head. "No. Why do you ask?"

"Someone broke into it through an exterior maintenance airlock a few hours ago and assaulted my guards."

He straightened in alarm. "Are they all right? Is the ship all right?"

She considered him for a long moment before her expression softened slightly. "My people will recover, though one of them is in the hospital. The other had just enough warning to signal for help from Ganymede Security before the intruders overwhelmed him.

"As for the ship, I'm afraid there's damage to the control consoles on the bridge. Someone unsuccessfully attempted to bypass the lockout I installed on the ship. Security probably drove them off before they could manage it."

Brad's mind raced, but his suspect list was short and his anger flared. "It had to be Breen. I'm fairly confident the arbitration will work out in my favor. He's the one that pushed things yesterday."

"I've already spoken with him and he vehemently denies involvement. It doesn't matter what either of us suspect unless Ganymede Security turns up hard evidence."

He sighed, pushing his demon back down. Nothing was ever easy.

"How does this change things?" he asked.

"It moves things forward. The meeting to present your official claim is scheduled for two this afternoon in my office."

"Official claim? I thought I made that already."

A hint of a smile shadowed her lips. "The paperwork you filed is a preliminary claim. Astro Transport, Limited, have one filed with my office as well. Those becomes official when the two of you make your cases before me. Don't be late."

"Once we make our claims, how long will it take you to reach a decision?" Brad asked.

Her lips edged slightly higher. "Not very long at all, I'd imagine. I've been reviewing the data both parties provided as well as the records from the ship itself. Unless I hear something completely unexpected at the hearing, I anticipate rendering my decision at that time."

"I promise to be punctual, then."

"See that you are. If one of the parties isn't present at the hearing, I'll be forced to make a summary judgement for the party that is there, no matter if the evidence might normally indicate another outcome."

That put a fine point on it. "I'll be early. Thank you for explaining the process. Would it be possible for me to examine the damage to the ship?"

"Under escort, yes. I've placed additional people on the ship to deter any future acts. That means your access will be monitored and restricted. Still, the law allows for the claimants to see something like this, as it might materially affect their claim. If so, you can amend your paperwork at the hearing."

"Thank you. How do I make the inspection happen?" he asked politely.

"I'll notify the men at the dock to expect you. Present your ID and they'll escort you inside."

Once the call was done, he headed straight for the dock, controlling his anger as best as he could. His demon wanted to confront Breen about it, but that would hardly improve matters. He had no proof at all that pointed at the man.

In fact, a fight might complicate the arbitration. Brad had too much at stake to allow his anger to get the better of him. Better to make them pay by winning.

———

It only took stepping onto the dock to see that Arbiter Blaze was taking this situation seriously. Four men in unfamiliar uniforms stood outside the ship's lock. None of them was smaller than a gorilla and all were heavily armed.

Okay, the gorilla comparison was stretching things a bit, but they were some of the largest examples of humanity Brad had seen recently. Or ever.

The men wore dark uniforms with a number of patches on their sleeves and chests. The largest was a coiled python on the top of the left sleeve.

Mercenaries, Brad assumed. He wondered which company they belonged to. He made a mental note to add uniform design to his always-growing list of things to do.

Their guards' attention settled on him as he walked forward. One stepped up to meet him. "Can I help you?"

"I'm Brad Madrid," he said calmly. "You should be expecting me."

"Identification, please."

Brad presented his wrist-comp. The only ID it showed publicly was his Mercenary Guild license, but that should be more than enough.

The man scanned it with a portable reader and closely examined his screen. He then looked Brad up and down once more.

"You can go in," the man said with apparent reluctance. "Two of my people will be with you at all times and you can't take anything."

"That's fine. I just need to verify the damage."

The man jerked his head and one of the others opened the airlock. That man and one of his fellows followed Brad inside.

It only took a minute to get to the bridge. It looked as if someone had taken a sledge to the helm. No one would be flying this ship anywhere without rerouting or rebuilding the controls.

Well, this was going to add to the refit bill for sure. Nothing he could do about it, though. It seemed more like vandalism than an attempt to steal the ship.

That thought made him pause and control his anger again. He turned to the merc at his shoulder. "I'm going to go through the pieces."

The man raised an eyebrow. "I'm pretty sure that console isn't salvageable."

"Probably not, but the damage seems a little excessive. I want to check something else before I go."

"Knock yourself out." He leaned against the communications console and watched with a bored expression.

Brad started identifying the parts of the console one by one, the process of laying it all out almost meditative for him. It was occasionally harder seeing inside the larger pieces, but he managed to figure it all out. In less than ten minutes, he'd decided the break-in hadn't been to steal the ship after all.

Someone had wanted the helm's control unit. It was missing.

What the hell had they hoped to gain by taking it? It was bizarre to expect Breen to break into a ship and steal something like that.

Maybe it really hadn't been the arrogant executive. Maybe the control unit had held some bit of information someone wanted to make certain never saw the light of day.

That pointed a shaky finger at the dead pirates. Had someone associated with them wanted to make certain no one traced where they'd been?

If so, taking the helm controller was overkill. It probably hadn't kept anything detailed enough to trace the pirates' movement. That kind of information was kept in the computer core. Flight data was one of the things he hadn't managed to crack the encryption on.

Brad stepped over to the communications console. "Do you mind?"

"That depends on what you want to do," the mercenary said without moving. His partner at the hatch grinned at the exchange.

"I want to check the computer to make sure it wasn't tampered with."

The man seemed to consider that for a moment before he shrugged. "Keep it simple. I want to be able to track what you're doing."

Brad nodded and brought the computer interface up. Rather, he tried to. The console remained stubbornly blank.

"I'm no expert, but isn't that supposed to do something?" the man asked.

"Yeah. It's not connecting to the core. I need to open the room and take a look."

The mercenary gestured for him to proceed.

Brad headed out of the bridge with them at his heels. The computer room was adjacent to the engineering compartment. He saw a problem as soon as he got into the appropriate corridor. The hatch was slightly ajar and the access panel was smashed.

"That doesn't look promising," he muttered under his breath.

"Stand clear," the lead mercenary said, pulling his pistol and angling toward the hatch. His companion settled for putting a hand on his own weapon and watching Brad closely.

The man opened the hatch and went in. He returned a moment later, already holstering his weapon. "All clear, but it looks as if the bastards wanted to trash more than that one console."

That's what Brad had been afraid of. He stepped up to the hatch and peered inside.

The computer compartment was a wreck. Someone had smashed everything and stolen the core for good measure. The destruction was total.

———

It took him another two hours to go over every section of the ship. The intruders hadn't wrecked anything else, it seemed.

Which hardly trivialized what they'd ruined. He really didn't want to know how much a new computer core was going to set him back.

Technicians from the Arbiter Guild had arrived in the middle of everything to document the damage, but they hadn't interfered with his examination. Brad was more than a bit surprised that Arbiter Blaze hadn't accompanied them.

A bedraggled Marshal finally showed up. Brad had left a message for him to come as soon as he'd reported the damage. It had taken another hour for his pilot to return the call.

Brad was in the captain's cabin when one of the mercenaries delivered the pilot. He fixed his man with a less-than-happy stare, letting almost all of his anger leak through for once.

"Glad you could make it," he said flatly.

"Sorry. Late night." At least Marshal had the decency to look sheepish.

"Uh-huh. I suppose it doesn't matter *this time*." He subtly emphasized the last two words and was pleased to see some recognition in the man's eyes.

"I'll do better, boss. Promise. What all did he trash and why?"

"The computer core and the helm console. I'm not sure it was Breen, though. I think it might've been the pirates."

Marshal frowned when he explained his line of reasoning. "That seems awfully convoluted. Did they go after the other ships? If it was just ours, I don't get it."

It took Brad a moment to get what Marshal meant. The two smaller ships the *Rain*'s crew had captured.

"I have no idea," he admitted. "Let's find out."

He made a call to the number Arbiter Blaze had given him. She answered a few moments later.

"Mr. Madrid. I hope you aren't calling to add to the already-impressive list of damages to the ship."

"Not this time," Brad told her. "I had a question about the other ships taken in the raid on the *Louisiana Rain*. Were any of them broken into?"

She shrugged slightly. "I'm not sure. Since there were no competing claims, Astro Transport has possession of them. I suppose you could call Mr. Breen and inquire."

That got a smile out of him. "I'll ask him at the hearing."

"That might be for the best. For what it's worth, I haven't heard anything from Ganymede Security about other break-ins. Might I ask why you want to know?"

"I was exploring the idea that Mr. Breen might not have been responsible for the damage. Maybe it was someone that wanted to make certain no one knew precisely where this ship had been. If so, the other pirate ships might have had something similar done to them."

She considered that for a long moment and nodded slowly. "It's an interesting idea. I'll ask in my official capacity during the hearing. Which is in less than two hours, I remind you."

"I'll be on time. We're done here, anyway. I'll grab something to eat and be at your office in an hour."

"Very good. I'll see you then." She cut the channel.

Marshal frowned. "Are you telling me that I rushed all the way over here for nothing?"

Brad bit back his immediate reaction to snap the man's head off. Barely. He took a deep breath and counted to five in his head.

"No," he said calmly once he had done so. "I called you over when I needed you. It's not my fault I finished before you arrived."

The pilot opened his mouth to say something but seemed to decide against it. That was probably for the best.

Brad shook his head and started for the exit.

Their mercenary babysitter followed the duo back to the airlock. He stopped when they were clear, and joined his companions.

Deciding to make a fresh start, Brad raised an eyebrow at Marshal. "Do you happen to know a place to get something for lunch? We have a little bit of time."

"I saw a café not too far from here. Look, I'm sorry. I was up late, but that's no excuse. I'll be better once we eat."

Brad certainly hoped so.

They went a few corridors in from the docks and Marshal gestured toward the place he'd remembered. *Café* might have been too formal a word for the place, but it had a bustling lunch crowd. Brad saw dock workers, mercenaries, and regular civilians bustling in and out.

He also just happened to catch a glimpse of someone looking in their direction from past the place. The only reason he was sure the man was looking at them was his reaction when he noted Brad staring at him.

The man raised his wrist-comp to his lips and said something as he started forward. He slid his hand under his jacket.

Oh, crap.

Brad planted his back to the nearest wall and looked for other hostiles.

He immediately spotted two men trailing them from the docks, and a third angling in from a side corridor. There might have been more in the mass of people swirling around Marshal and him, but Brad had seen more than enough to know they were in deep trouble.

# CHAPTER NINE

BRAD CHARGED the man coming from the corridor off to the side. The assailant was behind a large group of tourists. His view of Brad and Marshall couldn't be good.

If he could, Brad would stick to fists. He really didn't want to start a gunfight in a crowd. No way that would turn out well. Much less a blade fight. The very thought made him shudder.

Marshal backed his play, cutting in front of the tourists and making enough noise to draw every eye around them.

That turned out to be just enough of a distraction. The man Brad was looking for had turned partway toward the pilot and was heading for him, his hand in his coat, too.

That meant the thug only had a second's warning when Brad dodged between two women with armfuls of bags and smashed his fist into the man's face.

The guy was tough. He only staggered back, bringing his hands up to defend himself.

Instead of a gun or blade, the man held a truncheon of some kind. So, this was likely a beating rather than plain murder. That made things a bit simpler.

Even without a blade in his hand, Brad counted himself as a decent fighter. One more than capable of using terrain to his advantage.

He snatched the steaming coffee from a passerby's hand and tossed it into his attacker's face. The scalding liquid completely disrupted any coordinated action on the other man's part. He screamed and grabbed at his face with both hands.

Brad snatched the truncheon out of his nerveless fingers and gave him a good jab to the gut. That took any thought of fight out of the man.

From the sound behind him, the other attackers were closing in. That got the crowd upset, which only added to the chaos. He hoped that no one got trampled.

Marshal dodged between a couple of gawking dockworkers and slammed his elbow into the side of the attacker's head. The man went down hard.

"Let's go!" Brad shouted, taking off into the corridor ahead of them. It seemed clear of potential threats.

The pilot pounded after him. "There's a bazaar around the next corner, to the right. Head into it and we can get back onto the docks before they know which way we went."

The best fight was the one you didn't have to have. Brad hoped they could escape. Otherwise, things would likely escalate and cause him more grief.

Killing pirates was one thing. Ganymede Security had barely questioned Brad once the details of the attack on *Louisiana Rain* had been established. A fight here was a completely different thing. They'd grill him if anyone got hurt, much less killed.

The bazaar turned out to be more significant than Brad had imagined. It sat in an open compartment big enough to hold thousands of people. Vendors filled hundreds of booths and were selling every imaginable product.

It was astonishing how bright and colorful everything was. A booth at the very entrance was covered in scarves of every imaginable hue. Other people sold a vast array of products all seemingly designed to catch the eye.

The smells of the place were something outside his experience too.

Those clashed more than the visual element but less than the noise. Everyone was shouting over everyone else, trying to attract potential buyers and hawk their wares. They probably hadn't even heard the fight in there.

Marshal had obviously been there yesterday, because he led Brad down one of the wide spaces between booths. In moments, they were part of the crowd.

"Slow down," Brad said, grabbing the pilot's arm as he stuffed the truncheon into his belt.

"We have to get out of here before they catch up with us," Marshal said as he tried to cut between a group of shoppers discussing the benefits of some homeopathic remedies a spindly man in a white robe was pushing on them.

"That's just going to make us stand out. Slow down and let the crowd mask us. Be one of the shoppers."

Brad stopped at a booth selling hats and grabbed two at random. He barely heard the amount the woman wanted for them as he presented his wrist-comp. It wasn't much.

The purchase completed, he handed one to Marshal and put the other one on. It would change his appearance some, but he needed to do more.

A vendor half a dozen stalls down sold clothing, including jackets of various types. Brad was just going to grab two at random, but a rack of midnight blue ones with faint gold piping caught his eye. They were subdued but looked sharp. They might make for decent uniform jackets.

He knew his size and made an educated guess at Marshal's. Moments later, he was slipping the jacket over his tunic. It fit pretty well. A glance told him that he'd made the right call on the pilot's jacket, too.

Brad leaned forward. "Can I get this style in bulk? Maybe a dozen or two?"

He had no idea how many crewmen and mercenaries he might end up commanding when this was all settled, but they'd need uniforms. One more expense to his already-impressive list.

"Sure," the man said as a ruckus broke out at the entrance to the bazaar, drawing the vendor's eye for a moment. "Whatever you need. I have six dozen back at my shop in various sizes. I'm just rolling the style out, so no one is using them yet."

Marshal kept glancing back toward the noises in the crowd, so Brad tugged him closer. "Look closely at the detail work, Marshal. Focus on it. Tell me what you really think."

"That you have ice water in your veins," the pilot muttered. "It's a jacket. It looks fine."

Brad's "ice water" was fueled by anger at the situation. The irony wasn't lost on him.

The vendor had a mirror so potential buyers could try things on. Brad used it to watch for their pursuers while simultaneously admiring the cut of the cloth. He saw two of the men rush past the booth without a second glance. The change in appearance had thrown them off.

That ruse might work for a little while, but once they realized they'd lost their targets, they'd circle back around. He and Marshal needed to get a move on.

"I'd like to reserve what you have and hold the design. I'm forming a mercenary company."

The man grinned. "I can do that, but exclusivity costs a bit more."

Brad winced at the amount, but if he wanted to have a distinctive look like this, it wouldn't come cheaply. Sure, others could duplicate it, but he'd be first. They'd be the copycats.

He paid for the jackets and design exclusivity, snagged one of the vendor's cards, and smiled as he told his comp to also give the man his Guild ID. "Mark them down for Brad Madrid. I'll be in touch shortly. Thanks."

Rather than following the two men, Brad led Marshal back the way they'd come. The men would assume they were headed for the docks. Instead, the two of them would make their way deeper into the city.

Marshal obviously thought this was a rash choice, but he limited himself to glancing around nervously.

Brad half-expected one of their pursuers to spot them, but they slipped out of the area with hardly a peep. Once he was relatively certain they weren't going to be attacked again, he dropped the truncheon into a handy bin.

He glanced at his wrist-comp and did a double take. The hearing started in less than half an hour. So much for getting something to eat.

"We need to get to the Arbiter Guild," he told the pilot. "If I'm not there when the hearing starts, Breen can move to have my claim dismissed."

"I'll bet he sent those guys to delay you."

"Probably. Let's hope he doesn't have anyone else lurking around to ambush us."

———

The trip to Blaze's office took another ten minutes. It turned out there were more men lounging around the Arbiter Guild, but Brad had no idea if they were hostile or not. Rather than take chances, he selected a cluster of mercenaries walking past the building and attached himself and Marshal to them.

The dark jackets and hats weren't really close to what the other men were wearing, but they did the trick long enough to get close to the entrance.

Brad saw one of the watchers straighten abruptly and point at him with a shout. Thankfully, Brad was close enough to the door to get there just ahead of the rushing thugs. Marshal slammed the glass door in the men's faces.

A young man with bright red hair and a slender face sat behind the long counter. He smiled at the two of them. "Mr. Madrid?"

"That's me," Brad said as he waved cockily at the impotently raging men outside. "I'm here for the hearing." He glanced backwards. "And we're being chased."

"That won't be a problem," the young man said calmly. "If you and your associate would care to take a seat in the waiting room, Arbiter Blaze should be ready shortly. If you'd like coffee or tea, we have a service in there. Please help yourselves."

Brad knew there was nothing stopping the thugs from coming in after them, regardless of the receptionist's calm confidence. For a moment, he thought the leader of the men might do exactly that. Then the man snarled something to his companions and stalked off.

That had been close.

He had no doubt that Breen was behind this, even though he might be innocent of breaching the ship. Well, the man would put in an appearance shortly or Brad would be the only one at the hearing. He'd know soon enough.

The two of them had barely settled to their seats when the man himself came in. Brad listened with growing anticipation to the receptionist confirming his identity. This wasn't going to be boring, no matter how it played out.

Breen appeared at the door to the waiting room and glowered at Brad. "I'm surprised to see you here."

"I'll just bet you are," Brad agreed dryly, biting his tongue on a more *direct* response. "I met some friends of yours. Isn't that kind of thing a little beneath a company like Astro Transport?"

"I hear Ganymede Security is looking for a man matching your appearance that assaulted some dockworkers. I should call them."

"Please do. I'll be happy to explain what happened in excruciating detail."

Someone cleared their throat and Brad saw Arbiter Blaze standing behind the executive. "Since everyone is here, why don't we get things started. Please step into my office."

Brad climbed to his feet and looked at Marshal. "Why don't you stay out here and keep an eye on things while I make my statement?"

The pilot nodded. "I'll make sure and let you know if our new friends come looking for us."

"Excellent."

Breen was already gone, so Brad walked through the door Blaze was holding open for him behind the counter. She led the two men down a short corridor and through a wide door.

Her office was more sedate than Sara Kernsky's but might have cost as much to outfit. The paneling was some kind of pale wood that went from floor to ceiling. The carpet under their feet was plush and bright white. A wide screen—currently turned off—dominated one wall.

Several stands placed around the room held stone busts. He had no idea who the people were, but the work seemed quite lifelike.

The chairs set before her desk were heavily stuffed dark leather. His was quite comfortable he discovered when he took his seat.

She took them both in with a single glance. "Now, before we get started, this hearing will be recorded and you will both be under oath. Is that understood?"

Once they nodded, she made a show of turning on a desk recorder. "Arbiter Kenna Blaze, Ganymede. Hearing five two one two-A. Also present are Fabian Breen of Astro Transport, Limited, and Brad Madrid. Gentlemen, please state your names for the official record."

Brad allowed Breen to precede him and then spoke. "Brad Madrid."

"Do both of you swear to answer my questions fully and truthfully?"

"I do," Brad said.

Once Breen had done so, Arbiter Blaze continued. "This arbitration revolves around the ownership of the pirate vessel known as *Bloodthirster*. It is known to have attacked the Astro Transport, Limited, liner *Louisiana Rain*.

"Both of you have filed preliminary paperwork asserting ownership. Do you wish to make your filing official at this time?"

Both said they did.

"Then your claims are entered into the official record. Would either of you care to amend your filing at this time?"

"I would," Brad said. "I need to state for the record that the ship was vandalized last night."

Breen scowled at him. "What?"

"Someone broke into the ship last night, wrecked the helm console, smashed the computer room, and stole the computer core. I don't suppose you know anything about that?"

"The parties will limit themselves to addressing me," Arbiter Blaze said firmly. "Mr. Breen, the facts are substantially what Mr. Madrid has indicated. In addition, two employees of the Arbiter Guild were injured defending the ship. Were you in any manner responsible for these incidents?"

Breen gave her an affronted look. "Of course not! This is outrageous!"

"No," she said patiently. "It's a perfectly valid question."

She turned her attention to Brad. "Mr. Madrid, were you in any manner responsible for these incidents?"

"No, I was not."

"Let the record show that both parties assert their innocence. Ganymede Security is currently investigating the incident and will report to my office in due course.

"As the vessel was under Arbiter's seal at the time of the loss, we will pay for the replacement of the damaged or stolen equipment. We shall recover the funds from the guilty parties once they are located. Which I have confidence will occur in due time."

The guild paying for the damage surprised Brad a little, but it made sense now that he thought about it. It would help.

"Now let's get to the meat of the matter," Arbiter Blaze said. "I've reviewed both of your claims thoroughly and consulted the existing legal precedent. I also impounded the security recorders from the ship before the attack.

"Which, in hindsight, was a mistake. The recorders' files were destroyed with the computer cores. I regret that I didn't extract all of the data, only the immediately relevant information. I assure you both that guild procedures will be updated to avoid this type of lapse in the future."

She tapped her computer and the wall screen came to life. It was a still image of the ship's security feed. It covered engineering, the bridge, the airlock, and several major corridors.

The area near the airlock was filled with armed pirates. Based on the numbers, this was just before they boarded the liner, Brad suspected.

"The recording begins just prior to the attack," she confirmed a moment later. "I will play it quickly to a point that is key to the proceedings. Copies of this bonded recording will be provided to both parties as part of the final determination."

Arbiter Blaze started the playback and the video streamed forward. Brad saw the pirates working their cutter and then rushing out, presumably into the liner. The pirate ship seemed deserted other than three men in the airlock. Then the grenade Brad had tossed in exploded in their midst.

Well, that was brutal. It was a good thing he'd missed lunch, after all.

He'd been so involved in the fighting at the time that his memories had glossed over how bloody the airlock had been when he'd stepped inside it. Now, though, his mind was reminding him how the carnage had smelled of blood and guts.

Moments later, he watched the recording of him stepping into the airlock with his weapons ready. That's where the recording froze.

"Based on many hours of review, I've determined that the only pirates on board the ship *Bloodthirster* at this time were located in the airlock at the time Mr. Madrid killed them and boarded the ship."

"But he left," Breen argued. "Employees of Astro Transport, Limited, then secured the ship. Madrid was barely there. My people scoured it against all possible threats after they'd killed the other pirates on the liner, including others that very likely came from this ship."

Arbiter Blaze nodded. "I am not disputing those potential facts. They are irrelevant. According to existing law, killing or capturing all parties aboard a ship engaged in piracy and boarding the vessel are all that is required to assert a valid claim to the vessel.

"Finding no evidence that stands against Mr. Madrid's claim, the Arbiter Guild rules in his favor and awards him sole ownership of the ship *Bloodthirster*."

Breen shot to his feet. "I'm appealing this biased ruling!"

"As you should already know," Blaze snapped, "all judgments of an Arbiter such as myself are final. If you'll step outside, my associates will see that you receive all the official records relating to my decision, Mr. Breen."

The man fixed her with a glare that would've melted steel, and then stalked out of the office without another word.

"Let the record show that Fabian Breen has left the hearing," she said dryly as she focused her attention on Brad. "The judgements of the Arbiter Guild often lead to hard feelings, particularly when significant sums of money are involved. Do you have any objections for the record, Mr. Madrid?"

He smiled and shook his head. "No, ma'am."

"Very well. I hereby declare these proceedings closed."

She made a show of turning off the recorder and settled back in her seat. "Understand that this is simply speculation on my part, but you might want to arrange extra security for your ship once you officially take possession.

"The Pythons come highly recommended by the Mercenary Guild and are currently available. The Arbiter Guild has already paid them for three days, so you have until the evening of the day after tomorrow to find suitable replacements. I'd suggest the Pythons, as their rates are quite reasonable and they are now familiar with the ship and docking area."

Brad nodded. "I'll be sure to get that covered before their contract lapses. Thank you."

She rose to her feet. "My assistant will provide you with the final paperwork and I'll see the security system is put back to rights. Once you find someone to repair the damage to the ship, please have the bill for the computer room and helm console sent to me.

"Once again, the Arbiter Guild apologizes for what happened to your ship while it was under our supervision."

He extended his hand to her. "You did everything a reasonable person could do."

"Best of luck, Mr. Madrid."

Brad found a young man waiting for him outside her office with everything he needed. Fifteen minutes later, he stepped out into the lobby.

He found Marshal sipping some coffee in the waiting room. "We're done."

The man quickly downed his drink and threw the disposable cup away. "Judging from how fast Breen stormed out of here, you came out on top. Congratulations, Captain."

Brad took the offered hand. "We've got guards on the ship for two more days. We can spend the night in the hotel, since we're already paid up. Tomorrow, we'll take possession and move in for real."

"Do you think Breen will try anything else?"

"I kind of hope he does," Brad admitted. That would let him unleash his anger on *somebody*. "If so, we'll deal with it."

"What next?"

Brad grinned. "Now we go back to the Mercenary Guild. It's time for a career change."

# CHAPTER TEN

IT TURNED out Ms. Kernsky was too busy to fit him into her schedule until the next morning. This time, Brad was smart enough to leave the late-night shenanigans to Marshal. He hit the sack early, rose feeling good, and had a leisurely breakfast before his appointed meeting time.

He more than half-expected Marshal would oversleep, so he wasn't too upset when the man was a no-show. Honestly, this really wasn't the kind of meeting he needed the pilot for, anyway.

Brad was wary as he made his way to the Mercenary Guild. Even though he was relatively certain Breen was done with him, he couldn't rule revenge out of the equation. After all, the bastard had tried to have him beaten up so that he could steal his ship.

He'd need to come up with a new name for the vessel, too. *Bloodthirster* wasn't going to cut it.

The receptionist passed him through to see Ms. Kernsky without much of a delay, who smiled as she rose to her feet and extended her hand across her desk.

"I'm glad to hear the arbitration went well. Congratulations on getting the ownership of your ship settled in your favor, Captain Madrid."

"Thank you."

He took the seat she indicated. "What happens next?"

She sat and brought something up on her computer. "Now we see if I can help you form a company around your ship. My understanding is that it's in critical need of work.

"The Guild might be able to assist with that, but we'll need to work the details out first. And you'll need to be on our rolls as a mercenary company."

She slid a datapad across to him. "This is what you're looking at to incorporate as a mercenary company."

Brad picked the datapad up and started reading. One item immediately caught his eye. "The fee is somewhat higher than I expected." Almost twice what he'd been led to believe, in fact.

He and Captain Jaeger had discussed the rough costs of his becoming a mercenary after the pirate attack. The man had had his sources ask a few questions.

Kernsky smiled. "The fee you were probably thinking of is for a copper rating. We have five possible levels for mercenary companies: copper, bronze, silver, gold, and platinum. Those are graded based on ability and reliability.

"Because of Captain Jaeger's glowing recommendation and my assessment of your actions aboard the *Louisiana Rain*, I'm proposing a bronze rating."

"What difference does the rating make?"

"It allows you to access better Guild services. Among other things, we maintain a different database of recruits for each level. There is, of course, some overlap, but a bronze company will tend to get more capable personnel than a copper.

"Also, up to a third of a bronze company's refits and repairs are paid for by the Guild. We'll pay ten percent of the total outright and cover up to twenty percent with long-term loans. A bronze rating will also draw a higher class of mission with a correspondingly better payment scale."

That was a no-brainer. He signed the contract and handed the datapad back to Kernsky.

She skimmed it quickly and slid it into a reader slot. "There. Now we can discuss your next steps. From what Captain Jaeger told me, you're planning on an extensive refit. Will that happen on Ganymede?"

"Captain Jaeger arranged for a berth at the Io Yards. We're planning on going there next."

Kernsky nodded. "All right, I'll begin pulling together a dossier of possible recruits for you while that happens. What sort of people are you looking for?"

He considered the size of the ship and his resources. "Crew for the ship and an eight-trooper ground squad. I'll need both a senior and junior engineer, a coms expert, a tactical officer, and seven grunts."

"I take it you intend to command the boarding team yourself?"

"Most of my skills are in that area, so it makes the most sense."

She nodded again, making additional notes on her computer. "Many of those positions can be filled at your leisure, but you might want to have an engineer on your payroll to oversee the refit."

"I have some experience in that area myself."

"You could oversee the refit yourself, of course, but it would lock you down on your ship almost full-time. It might be best to fill your senior engineer position now. I have someone to recommend: Mike Randall. He's a very good engineer and is available."

Brad raised an eyebrow, considering the man he'd met outside. "If he's a good engineer, why is he working at the Guild hall instead of on a ship?"

"You haven't been around him long enough to see," Kernsky said with a sigh, "but he has a few personal faults that always seem to bring him back here. We pay him a small retainer when he ends up here, but I'm sure he'd much rather have an engineering position."

"What sort of faults are we talking about?"

"He has a tendency to tell his superiors exactly what he thinks," she told him dryly. "For example, he called his last ship a 'rat-infested sinkhole' for six months. Pretty much every day, even when told to stop. He's not shy about critiquing his superior officers, either."

"I can see why that might not endear him to people. How good of an engineer is he?"

"Before his mouth got him cashiered, he was the senior engineer aboard a Fleet battleship."

Brad widened his eyes in surprise. There were only three battle-ships in the Commonwealth Fleet and two of them never left Earth orbit. The other never left Mars orbit. They were considered the last line of defense for Sol's more heavily inhabited planets against pirates or potential Outer System aggression, so they got the best Fleet had.

"That might help balance out some character flaws," he observed. "I'm willing to take a chance if he is."

"Shall I talk to him?" Kernsky asked with a smile.

"If you don't mind, I think I will. Is there anything else?"

"No, that about covers it. I'll need the details on your company name and so forth when you make a final decision, but we're good for the moment."

"Thanks for your help and for your confidence in me."

Kernsky inclined her head. "Randall should be in the reception area. If he asks, tell him I approve. Now get going, Captain. I'm already looking forward to sending you on your first mission."

———

Randall was indeed lounging in the reception hall. He sat in an open-legged sprawl across a chair, reading a datapad. The man was graying with age, quite a feat in this era, but he was still both burly and muscular.

Brad could see him buried in a drive and covered with grease. He crossed the room and stopped beside him. "Mr. Randall."

The engineer blinked up at him. "Mr. Madrid, isn't it?"

"You have a good memory. Captain Madrid now. Which actually brings me to you."

"Oh?" The man's eyebrows quirked, but he didn't move a muscle otherwise.

"Ms. Kernsky told me you were a good engineer and currently between jobs. I'm taking my new ship into a major refit very shortly, and I'd like to have a senior engineer aboard to oversee the work. She recommended you for the job."

The man studied Brad. "I presume she told you I'm an ornery old bastard who doesn't believe in tact?"

"That might have come up."

Randall snorted. "Well, it's true. I'm interested, but technically, I'm still under contract with Heimdall's Raiders. They suspended me without pay for conduct unbecoming. I'd imagine it won't take much longer for them to decide to boot me."

"I can speak with them and speed the process along, I'll wager. If you want the job."

"What's the ship's name?"

He wasn't going to keep calling it *Bloodthirster*, so he needed something new and meaningful.

"*Heart of Vengeance*." A snap decision, but it felt right. "That's not in the official records yet, but it will be by oh dark thirty."

"I like it," Randall said firmly as he stood. "Once my release becomes final, you've got yourself a senior engineer."

"I'll talk to someone with Heimdall's Raiders today. If I can smooth things along for you, I'd like you to drop by tomorrow morning at bay zero-six-nine." He offered his hand. "Welcome aboard, Mr. Randall."

––––––––

It took only a simple inquiry to determine which room Heimdall's Raiders were using at the Guild. It seemed every mercenary company of a certain size kept offices there.

That made sense, Brad supposed. It would be hard for potential customers to contact you if you were always off on a ship somewhere.

The smaller outfits—like his currently unnamed company—would use Guild factors to match them with appropriate contracts, but the bigger, more established outfits had someone representing them in person. If he and his company grew large enough one day, they'd have to follow suit.

Brad stopped outside the office and examined the emblem Heimdall's Raiders had chosen. It was a mighty warrior with a huge sword and bright eyes slashing at a great serpent. The image was much more detailed than the coiled python favored by the men guarding his ship at the moment.

Of course, it also reflected the Raiders' higher status. The Pythons were a silver company and Heimdall's Raiders were gold. And his company was a lowly bronze, he reflected wryly.

The image was marketing. He'd have to consult with someone about getting something done once he had a company name to go with his ship.

He liked the godly connotations of Heimdall's Raiders. He'd have to look up some gods of vengeance when he had time. No one was going to mind if he stole the theme.

The man sitting behind the desk inside looked up as Brad walked thought the door. "Morning. How can the Raiders help you today?"

Though dressed in a uniform, the man didn't have the appearance Brad expected of a mercenary. He was reed-thin and young. Perhaps he was just the mercenary version of a receptionist.

"My name is Brad Madrid and I need to talk to someone about one of your people. Mike Randall."

The eyeroll was brief and the man stopped it almost at once, but not before Brad had seen it start.

"Let me see if Commander Branson has time to see you," the man said with a sigh he didn't bother to conceal.

He pressed a button on the com center on his desk, and a gruff voice asked what he wanted. "There's someone here to see you about Randall, Commander."

"Send him in." Branson didn't sound in the least surprised.

The young man rose, led Brad down a short corridor, and gestured toward an open door. Inside the indicated room, a large man with dark red hair cut in a tight buzz was coming around a beat-up desk made of gray metal.

"You must be Brad Madrid. Ms. Kernsky called to let me know you might be dropping by. I'm William Branson. Have a seat. Can I get you a drink?"

Brad stepped into the man's office and shook his head. "I'm good, thanks. Your man out front didn't seem surprised that random people would be stopping by to talk about Mr. Randall."

The mercenary commander smiled, showing a hint of teeth as he shook Brad's hand. "The old saying is that 'his reputation precedes him.' That's not always a good thing. It certainly isn't when it comes to Mike. Great engineer, terrible subordinate."

"So I've heard."

"Park it and we'll talk."

Brad sat and waited for the other man to get back behind his desk before continuing. "Ms. Kernsky probably told you that I've newly come into a ship and need an engineer. She's of the opinion Randall would be a good fit once his status with Heimdall's Raiders is resolved."

"I like how you phrased that. It makes a stinking mess sound so straightforward. Believe me, it's not. My bosses paid a pretty significant bonus to sign Mike on six months ago. I don't believe they're going to actually fire him once his suspension is over."

That wasn't what Brad had expected to hear. "I see."

"Personally," Branson continued, "I don't see him as a good fit with the Raiders, but they want to recoup the investment they made in him. Even if he drives everyone nuts."

The man considered Brad for a long moment. "Once Ms. Kernsky contacted me, I called my boss and discussed the matter with him in general terms. He's willing to release Randall, but it's going to cost you."

Another expense. Wonderful.

Brad leaned back in his seat a little. "There are plenty of engineers floating around the Outer System. I'm not sure it's in my best interest to pay extra for one you've already admitted has significant negatives."

Now that they'd both laid out their initial bargaining positions, the real negotiation could begin. The other man's eyes told Brad that he knew that too.

Branson's smile widened a trifle. "I've done a quick bit of research on you, Captain Madrid. You're just starting out, but Ms. Kernsky had good things to say about you. We're not talking about money here.

"The Raiders are willing to release Mike Randall to you in exchange for future subcontract work at a discount rate. Ms. Kernsky will negotiate an appropriate level of effort, so you won't be committing to something worth far more than one guy. Think of it as a favor between mercenary companies."

Brad pondered that for a moment and then nodded. "I can live with that, I think."

The other man grinned. "You say that now. Wait until you have to live with Mike for a few months."

# CHAPTER ELEVEN

BRAD WATCHED the Io shipyards grow slowly in *Heart*'s viewscreen. The third-largest moon of Jupiter seemed to float in the upper right quadrant of the screen, jeweled with the lights of domed cities.

The seven massive space stations that formed the nodes of the third-largest shipyard in Sol—smaller only than the complexes orbiting Earth and Mars—dominated the screen. Each of them was a cylinder roughly a kilometer and a half long and three hundred meters around.

Massive connecting tubes—dozens of kilometers long and often hundreds of meters in diameter—connected the huge nodal stations to the hundreds of lesser facilities, which ranged from large-scale nanosmith workshops to zero-*g* manufacturing facilities.

All in all, the massive network filled a sphere of space nearly thirty kilometers across with over three hundred manmade objects, and provided homes and workplaces to a quarter of a million human beings.

Somewhere in the tangle was a collection of about thirty construction berths—probably on one of the nodal stations—under the auspices of Kawa Repair and Construction. The firm was owned and operated by one Hiroshi Kawa, the man whom Jaeger had convinced to hold a berth open for *Heart*.

Brad regarded the yards for a moment and then crossed to the communications console. Marshal was running the ship from the tactical console. Without the computer program to balance the drives, he was significantly less chatty than his usual self. Mike Randall was keeping a similar eye on the drives.

Once Brad had the coms system online, he signaled the shipyards and routed a call to Kawa. A moment later, the screen lit up with the image of an attractive young Asian woman.

"Kawa Repair and Construction, Reiko Kawa speaking," she said in a melodious voice. "Can I help you?"

"I'm Captain Brad Madrid on *Heart of Vengeance*," Brad said. "I'd like to speak with Hiroshi Kawa, please. Captain Jaeger of *Louisiana Rain* referred me."

The young woman nodded immediately. "Certainly, Captain Madrid. He's been expecting your call. One moment, please."

A standby message flashed onto the screen for a moment, then was replaced by the image of a wizened Asian man. It was hard to tell his height since he was sitting, but he gave Brad the impression of being short.

Jet-black eyes pierced Brad as Hiroshi Kawa spoke softly. "Captain Madrid. It's good to finally speak with you. Jaeger told me you wanted a refit. What exactly do you need done?"

"Do you have an hour? This was a pirate ship until a week ago, and I don't like the design, Mr. Kawa. That doesn't even consider the additional damage it suffered a few days ago."

"Please, call me Hiroshi. Whatever you need, I guarantee my people can handle it."

"I'm sure they can. My chief engineer and I will need to go over what's necessary—and what I can afford—with you and your people once we dock. Can we arrange an appointment now?"

"Certainly. How far out are you?"

"About an hour."

"Then I shall see you when you arrive," the yardmaster instructed crisply.

---

Randall met him at the main airlock once they'd docked and he'd shut the drives down. The *Heart*'s new chief engineer hadn't bothered changing jumpsuits. Spots of oil covered one sleeve and he still had his tool belt on.

Brad regarded the man for a long moment and then shrugged. He doubted Randall would listen if he ordered him to go clean up, and they really didn't have the time, anyway.

When they left the ship, they found Hiroshi waiting for them just aboard the station. Standing up straight, the wizened old man came to maybe five feet. Maybe. Nonetheless, he exuded energy as he bounced forward to shake their hands.

"Welcome to my facility." He gestured for them to proceed him down the corridor. "Come this way."

The yardmaster led them down a corridor to a door with a nano-shaped metal sign proclaiming Kawa Repair and Construction above it.

At the old man's approach, the door slid smoothly open to reveal a small reception area. Inside, the flooring shifted from plain metal to plush carpeting. The walls were a soft, relaxing beige.

Hiroshi bustled them both in and waved at the young woman at the desk. "I believe you spoke to my granddaughter, Reiko."

Brad inclined his head to her. "Yes, I did. Good afternoon, ma'am."

Reiko Kawa smiled at him. "Good afternoon, Captain." She looked to her grandfather. "The green conference room is ready for your meeting."

The old man nodded. "Excellent. Thank you, Reiko." He turned back to Brad and Randall. "This way, gentlemen."

A winding, ramped corridor took the trio down a level to a standard door. Hiroshi stepped up to the panel and waved his wrist-comp at it. The door slid open and he gestured them both inside.

The room was decorated in a dark green with one entire wall showing the view into a small atrium filled with a small forest of tiny pine trees. Brad didn't know much about Earth flora, but he suspected they were genetically modified. The real thing *had* to be bigger.

Hiroshi strode to the end of the table and gestured them to sit. He tapped a control, and a small opening appeared in the table, allowing a platter with drinks and sandwiches to rise out.

"Help yourself to refreshments," he said as he leaned back. "Now, tell me what exactly you want done."

"We put together a list of the modifications we'd like," Brad said. "The computer replacement and helm console will be covered by the Arbiter Guild. Mike?"

Randall pulled a data chip from his pocket and slid it to Hiroshi wordlessly.

The yardmaster tapped another control and a computer screen projected itself in front of him. He slid the chip into a reader and studied the file in front of him.

———

An hour later, Hiroshi had finished going over the list with them in detail. "I can see why you dislike the original design, Captain. Based on what I'm seeing here, the modifications you propose make sense and will greatly enhance the performance of your vessel. They will, however, cost around eight million credits, by my estimation."

Brad froze for a moment. Even with the Guild loans, that was significantly more than he could afford. "I fear we will have to make some modifications to my list."

"Before you start crossing things off, there is something you should know," Hiroshi said. "I have been retained by both the Mercenary and Shipper Guilds to handle the sale of the other ships involved in the attack on *Louisiana Rain*. I've only sold one so far, but that does provide you with a somewhat larger credit balance."

Brad blinked. "What does selling those ships have to do with me? Doesn't the money go to Astro Transport?"

"Didn't Hans tell you? Four percent of the sale value is marked as going to you for your services in capturing them. That's solely at the discretion of the ship's captain, and a separate matter from the ship you now own. Well outside the control of Astro," the old man noted with a knowing smile.

"As I said, I've only sold one ship, but that puts just over a million additional credits in your pocket. The other is larger and should bring you roughly double that amount, and I'm willing to credit that estimated amount toward the total, as I will sell her well before the refit is complete."

With the ten percent the Mercenary Guild was covering outright and the additional twenty percent in guaranteed loans they provided, that still left about two and a half million credits on the tab, by Brad's estimation.

With the sale of the pirates' weapons and the money found on the ship after he'd seized it, he could just about cover the remainder, but it would leave nothing to operate the ship with or hire people.

"That does make me feel better, but it's still somewhat out of my range. Mike and I will have to trim a few items from the list, I'm afraid."

The old man nodded. "Perhaps. Or I may be able to assist you in another manner. You see, it happens I find myself in a position where you might be able to render me assistance."

Brad raised an eyebrow. "You need a mercenary company?"

"In a manner of speaking, yes."

He pressed a button on the table and the door slid open. A black-clad, nondescript man with short-cropped black hair and mildly Asian features stepped into the conference room.

"Captain Madrid, this is Saburo Kawa, my youngest son. His employer ran afoul of Mercenary Guild regulations a few months ago. They dissolved his company and left my son at loose ends.

"Unfortunately, Saburo is the black sheep of the family. He's been kicked out of more mercenary companies than I once believed existed. He hasn't found any takers this time around."

Brad considered the young man. His company already had one potential loose cannon living inside the captain's head. He wasn't sure he needed another one.

"That's quite an accomplishment," he observed. "How did you manage it?"

"Is it my fault that two thirds of merc officers think a shiny gold bar makes them worth ten times as much as a noncom who actually knows what he's doing?" the man asked somewhat crossly.

Brad snorted softly and glanced at Mike Randall. The two of them might get along famously. Or fight like blood enemies.

"Ms. Kernsky indicated you would be hiring a squad of ground troops," Hiroshi said. "My son has a good record of accomplishment on the battlefield, if not the home office. As much as it pains me, I will support him one last time.

"In exchange for hiring him, subject to his record meeting the requirements of the job, I will personally arrange for a small lending syndicate to cover your remaining repair and refit costs. My son understands this is the last chance for him, and he will make *every* effort to be an asset to you."

Admittedly, Brad would still need to repay the money, and Hiroshi would make his expected profit from the work, but this was a big opportunity for Brad.

Seeing how he was pondering the offer, Saburo added a few chips to the pot. "I can bring a veteran squad with all their basic equipment with me. One that used to fight for a gold-level company."

Brad frowned. "How?"

"The Golden Warriors fell apart when their commanding officer was arrested, and they didn't do it gracefully," Saburo said sourly. "My squad stands with me. If you hire me, they'll come if I ask."

"I see." He stood slowly and stepped over to the man and gazed down into the man's eyes. Saburo was more heavily built than he was, but he had a good twelve centimeters on the yardmaster's son.

"I honestly don't care if you bring an entire battalion with you," he said grimly, letting a flicker of his anger into his gaze. "If you can't follow my orders or fight, I won't make the deal."

Saburo puffed up. "I can fight. Probably better than you can."

"Don't wager on that until you've seen the security tapes from *Louisiana Rain*," the old man advised his son with a chuckle.

A corner of Brad's mouth quirked. It hadn't occurred to him that the security tapes might be making the rounds. He turned his attention back to Saburo with an effort.

"And the other?" he asked softly. "Can you follow orders?"

"I can," the man replied more quietly. "I've been a noncommissioned officer in the Guild for fifteen years. I've served in eight different companies with distinction." He shrugged a little. "As my father pointed out so politely, I've been kicked *out* of six—there's some overlap, but I've done time in ten units. I'll tell you if you're making an ass of yourself or stop you if you're asking the impossible, but I'll follow orders."

Brad stepped back and looked over at Hiroshi. "And you think he and I can work together? You know him better than anyone else ever will."

Hiroshi nodded. "You'll spend half of your time irritated with him, a quarter of your time wanting to kill him, and the rest of your time thanking the Everlit you have him at your back. You've been lucky so far. With him and his men, you may actually survive when your luck runs out."

"I see." Brad said softly. For a long moment, he was silent as his memory angrily replayed the many reasons his demon didn't think he was all that lucky.

Finally, he met Saburo's gaze again. "If you're prepared to follow, I'm prepared to lead."

Saburo snorted. "I'm willing to give this my best shot. That's a more realistic promise."

"Good enough. We'll be sitting in dock for a refit, though. Think your people can handle that?"

The smaller man shrugged and grinned. "We'll manage. It'll give me time to review those tapes and see what I can teach you."

This was going to be interesting. Brad extended his hand. "Welcome aboard."

# CHAPTER TWELVE

TWO WEEKS LATER, Brad stood in his newly rebuilt computer room, admiring the upgraded systems. The replacement computer wasn't new, but it was significantly more powerful than what ships of this class usually sported. That was going to prove to be an unpleasant surprise for someone in the near future.

Hiroshi had given him the option of a brand-new system or a used but more capable one. That had been a no-brainer. More computing power would help them in many ways.

For one thing, it would make their new weapons more effective by giving them better targeting solutions and faster response times. Once they actually had new weapons. Hiroshi was keeping the details of what he had in mind there close to his vest.

"You have a surprise visitor," Marshal said from the corridor.

Brad looked up from the direct access console and frowned. "I wasn't expecting anyone."

"Obviously. I did say *surprise*." The pilot grinned. "And she's very cute."

"That's the most important takeaway you have for me about an unexpected visitor?" he asked as he rose to his feet. "Details, man."

"She's Fleet," he said, his face settling back into his normal expression. "Fleet Security, to be precise."

"Then I'd best go see what she wants. Did you put her in the galley?"

"Sure did. Gave her some tea, too."

Brad smiled. "What a considerate host you are. Are you planning to hit on her once we're done?"

The man looked mildly offended. "Who do you take me for? I already did that. She's seeing someone."

"One of these days, that's going to get you into a world of hurt."

"Thank goodness I know a bunch of mercenaries that can pull me back out."

Brad threw up his hands in mock disgust and headed for the hatch. The man was incorrigible.

The ship's galley wasn't that big a space, but on a heavy corvette with just over a dozen people in the final headcount, it didn't have to be. In a pinch, twice that number could crowd in at the small tables.

The mess and attached galley had been the very first things Hiroshi had refurbished. Brad hadn't been certain the man had his priorities right until he realized that everyone was using it: crew, workers, and visitors. It truly was *Heart*'s heart.

He walked into the compartment and found a young, very attractive woman in a Fleet uniform sitting at one of the tables.

She rose as he stepped over to her. "Captain Madrid? I'm Lieutenant Jean Greer, Fleet Security. Thank you for seeing me on such short notice."

"I always have time for Fleet," he told her with a smile. "Your people saved my life. Let me grab some tea and you can tell me what you need."

Brad stepped into the gleaming kitchen and poured himself a mug. The equipment around him didn't look like it belonged on a ship at all. It certainly wouldn't have fit on *Mandrake's Heart* when he was growing up. This place looked like a brand-new restaurant kitchen.

That only made sense. Hiroshi had picked up a complete set of gear from a café on one of the Io space stations that had gone under before they'd even opened..

The yardmaster had claimed there was very little he had to modify to make a station restaurant kitchen work on a ship and the equipment was both more capable and less costly than the variety normally marketed to ships.

Brad trusted the man to know what he was talking about. He certainly had no complaints about the quality of the food a skilled cook could make with it. When one was lucky enough to have a skilled cook, that was.

That thought brought a wry smile to his face. Saburo's claim that his people could do basic kitchen work was accurate enough. Unfortunately, what could keep one alive wasn't the same as what tasted good. They'd do in a pinch, but he'd be interviewing a cook—also, thankfully, a medic—shortly.

The extra man was worth the money. Brad would let the mercenaries with the "cooking skills" kill people in the more traditional way going forward.

Tea in hand, Brad made his way back to the lieutenant and sat across from her. "What can I do for Fleet today, Lieutenant Greer?"

"I've been working on the information that came out of the attack on *Louisiana Rain*. Captain Jaeger sent us images of the dead attackers and scans of what fingerprints he could.

"As one would expect, most of them were either unidentifiable or known criminals. One of them, however, was a surprise. A missing Fleet Marine." She tapped her wrist-comp and sent him several images.

He pulled them up on his own wrist-comp and studied the man. The first image was obviously from Fleet records. The man had close-cropped brown hair and seemed unremarkable.

The second image was a dead pirate. One that looked vaguely familiar.

"I think I killed him," Brad said slowly. "I'm not completely sure, but I found a Fleet weapon on a guy that looked like him. That's why I took him out so fast, actually."

"We're pretty sure that's correct," she confirmed. "He went missing with his weapon, and the serial numbers match."

Brad took a long sip of his tea. "I'm not sure what I can tell you about him other than that. Our interaction was very brief and nonverbal."

That made her smile a bit. "I understand. Honestly, I'm hoping you could share your impressions of the attack itself. Did it feel like a regular pirate attack, or were there some aspects that felt off?"

He nodded immediately. "They liked their weapons a lot more than most pirates I've ever heard about. Pirates prefer blades, pistols for backup. A few have shotguns, but that's about it. They rely on the general fear of monofilament blades and pirates to keep order among the crew and passengers.

"These guys had a grenade launcher and lots of guns. They sealed the passengers away from the fighting and then tried to wipe the crew out."

"That matches my impression pretty well," Greer confirmed. "Did you find anything interesting on the ship during your refit?"

"Not so far. The refit is still underway, so it's always possible something interesting will turn up. What are you thinking? Hidden compartments?"

"Those would be fascinating, no doubt, but I'm more interested in the larger areas of this ship. Were there any facilities for holding people?"

Brad frowned and thought back over what he'd seen in the original search of the ship. "Sort of. They had a bunch of cuffs in the main cargo hold."

"Would you mind if I took a look?"

"Not at all. The cuffs are gone, though."

"That's fine. I just want to get a feel for the room."

They drank their tea and he put the mugs into the washer. Someone would kick it off once it was full.

The main cargo hold wasn't empty now. The refit crew was using it to sort equipment as it was brought aboard. There was still quite a bit of open area, though.

"This is a bigger space than I imagined a warship of this class needed," Greer said, turning in place to look around once they were inside. "What do you use it all for?"

"We'll need quite a bit of space to store ammunition and other combat equipment once we're operational, but I agree with you. This is a lot bigger than the basic plan for the *Fidelis* calls for. The previous management obviously made some modifications. Maybe to haul their take away if the target ship can't move under its own power."

She nodded thoughtfully, walked over to the closest bulkhead, and started walking down it. After only a few steps, she paused and knelt to examine something more closely. It was a small hole in the metal of the wall, just big enough to run a strap through.

"Are these standard?" she asked, looking up at him.

He nodded. "Sure. It makes sense to secure cargo with straps. If we have to maneuver under heavy acceleration, things would get tossed around."

"Do you normally see this many, though?"

Brad looked past her and saw what she meant. There were attachment points roughly every foot. He hadn't noticed before as the cargo space had been at the absolute bottom of his priority list—a chunk of it was even due to be sectioned off for torpedo magazines in the next two days.

"Not normally, no."

Greer stood and brushed her hands off. "I don't think these people were pirates in the traditional sense. I think they were slavers."

———

They examined more of the ship as she explained what she was thinking, but nothing else provided any insight into her investigation. It did leave him a lot to consider as soon as she'd left, though.

Slavers. The word alone woke an entirely new level of rage inside him.

He'd known the Cadre and other pirates took people from their prizes. A few made it back to civilization every year with horrible tales of lawless enclaves out on the Fringe where the poor bastards toiled away for the pirates.

Brad had hoped to find out more one day, because there was a chance someone from *Mandrake's Heart* had survived the attack that left him a Dutchman.

Not Shari, of course. He'd seen the life drain out of his girlfriend, but maybe his uncle or some other member of the crew had been taken. If so, he might be able to find them. Eventually.

The idea that there were professional—to use the term loosely—slavers was a shock, though. In a way, that was even worse than the piracy itself. It gave a kind of legitimacy to the Cadre enclaves when others tried to fill roles in supplying their needs.

Greer had left a folder of information with him, asking that he review it discreetly. It had been surprisingly thick and contained what certainly appeared to be unredacted investigation files.

The direct evidence was sparse. Not many people got back home once they'd been taken. The pirates always took steps to make certain no one survived to tell any awkward tales when Fleet caught them in an infrequent raid.

Not that the raids themselves were infrequent. No, Fleet was always trying to find out where the Cadre was operating. It was the general lack of success on Fleet's part that had Brad worried.

The Cadre had Fleet penetrated. Perhaps not directly, but extremely thoroughly. Someone was feeding them information.

It was silly to think Fleet didn't know. They had to. So, why hadn't they caught the spies? What was keeping them from locating the Cadre?

The answer was simple and chilling. Someone powerful was protecting the pirates and, by extension, the slavers.

Lieutenant Greer had been very chatty about Fleet's investigation into the slavers as the two of them had searched *Heart* for any other oddities. That, in conjunction with the folder of investigative notes, made him certain she'd had a deeper agenda than sparking any thoughts he might have over the events on *Rain*.

No, the more he considered the idea, the more likely it sounded. She was hoping he'd look into the matter himself.

Perhaps partly as a way around the ears and eyes she'd probably known he'd suspect were watching her and the investigation closely. More directly, he suspected she hoped he shot some slavers up and did what Fleet seemed unable to do: find their bases and unravel their secrets.

If so, he'd happily play along. There was no way his demon would let him pass up the opportunity. The slavers were worthwhile in and of themselves, but they'd lead him to the Cadre, too.

If they were going to tangle with slavers, though, they'd need some additional equipment. Mercenaries were good at shooting people. Less so at shooting only some people while protecting others.

He went in search of Saburo and found the noncom in the bay he shared with his squad.

The man looked up from the pistol he was cleaning. "Captain."

"Do you have a few minutes to discuss some contingencies I was thinking about?"

"I've always got time to work out operational details. Have a seat."

Brad did so after unholstering his weapon. He removed the magazine and carefully ejected the round in the chamber. Once he was doubly sure it was empty, he started disassembling it for cleaning. If he was going to be sitting there with all the equipment, he might as well use it.

"I just spent a few hours talking with a Fleet investigator about this ship, among other things," he said as he ran a cleaning patch coated with oil down the barrel of his pistol.

The mercenary noncom nodded. "I heard Pilot Marshal discussing her."

Brad could only imagine what Marshal had said. "Moving beyond her purely physical attributes, she seemed to be a very smart cookie."

He explained what she'd said, what she hadn't, and the wealth of information she'd left in his care.

The other man listened intently, his eyes narrowing as the scope of the files became clear. He said nothing until Brad finished. In fact, he cleaned his pistol in silence for a good while after Brad finished, even switching to a new weapon before he spoke.

"I think you're on to something, Captain," Saburo said after a long while. "She's a lot smarter than Marshal gave her credit for. All that and cute, too. She had our good pilot in range long before he knew she was scoping him out."

"We'll keep him in the dark on that," Brad said with a smile. "We wouldn't want to blunt his ego."

That earned him a snort and a grin.

"In any case, I get where you're going," Saburo said. "If we just happen to chance across some slavers, we'll want a means to disable them without killing their prisoners. In fact, we'll need to actively protect any prisoners from hostile countermeasures while we kill their captors."

"Exactly. I know elite police organizations have some things that might work, but no one has been going after these kinds of people with capture in mind. No one will have worked out the tactics and gear we'll need.

"I want you to run this past your people and your father. He knows people. He might have a source we can tap to get specialized gear we don't even know exists."

Saburo nodded slowly, his eyes narrowed in thought. "He might even be able to come up with something no one has considered before. My father is an engineer by trade and an exceptionally clever man. He has many other clever men and women in his employ."

"We need to keep things quiet," Brad warned. "If these slavers—or the Cadre, for that matter—have as many eyes and ears scattered around as I expect, they'll get word of any unhealthy curiosity. I'd prefer to avoid that."

"Don't take me for an idiot," the man said bluntly. "I know how to maintain operational security, and my father didn't build a successful business by letting people see what he was up to."

This wasn't the first time Brad had evoked this kind of response from the mercenary. Unlike the man's former commanders, he didn't care if he got some talkback, so long as Saburo respected his ultimate authority and shared his goals.

That didn't make interaction easy, of course. And, as he'd partly expected, Saburo and Mike Randall got along like oil and water. Occasionally oil and water that were on fire.

To their credit, though, neither one of them did any more than argue like an old married couple. They worked together seamlessly on the things that mattered.

"There's a difference between keeping things quiet and going out of your way to make sure no one learns what we're up to," Brad said soothingly. "I want to be sure you and your father actively make sure that there are alternate, believable explanations for everything you're doing. That keeps us all safe from preemptive reprisals."

The other man's eyes narrowed even further, not in anger but in consideration. "You believe the slavers have us under surveillance."

"We have what they consider one of their ships. They'd like to get it back and make us pay, I'm sure. On top of that, we just had a friendly visit by Fleet Security. If we start doing something that smacks of hunting slavers, they'll focus even more attention on us."

The smaller man nodded sharply. "Good thinking. Let me consider our options. My father and I can come up with believable cover stories. Better yet, we might even be able to identify any potential watchers now that we have reason to suspect direct surveillance."

Brad finished cleaning his pistol and reassembled it. "What do you imagine we'd do to any watchers you manage to identify?"

The mercenary grinned coldly. "Nothing I'll admit to a senior officer, but accidents happen. People disappear."

"Make sure you have no doubts before you even think about that," Brad cautioned the man. "This isn't the kind of thing you want to make a mistake over."

He stood before the other man could respond, loaded his weapon, and holstered it. "Run your thoughts on equipment past Randall. We'll need to involve him in installing anything larger than hand weapons."

Saburo scowled. "Why did you have to ruin what was promising to be an enjoyable mental exercise like that?"

"It's how I roll. Keep me in the loop."

# CHAPTER THIRTEEN

BRAD LEANED back in his command chair, surveying *Heart of Vengeance*'s vastly changed bridge. The ship was in so much better condition now and he could hardly wait to take her out on the shakedown cruise for her new systems and engines in a few days.

The rest of the crew was ready to get off the shipyard too. Perhaps no one more so than Saburo. The mercenary noncom was annoyed that he hadn't identified anyone associated with the slavers or the Cadre.

The best he'd been able to manage was finding an industrial spy in the employ of his father's largest competitor. He'd had to settle for telling Hiroshi and letting him "discover" the mole rather than dealing with him personally, and that had made the short man grumpy.

Well, he'd get the chance to make someone hurt before too much longer.

A scuff at the hatch made him glance up just as Jason Finley, his new tactical officer, entered the bridge.

"Good morning, Captain," the man said cheerfully.

"And a good morning to you, too."

Finley and his lover, Shelly Weldon, had turned up to their interviews together. She'd made a good fit for the communication officer's position. Brad wasn't thrilled with having a couple aboard the ship at first, but they'd both impressed him with their skills, so he'd taken a chance.

It had paid off. The two of them worked together extremely well, even if they occasionally had spats like most couples. Better yet, Shelly had a way with their cantankerous engineer. She was the Randall Whisperer. That was worth a lot by itself.

Rather than heading for his console, Jason stopped beside Brad's chair. "There's a guy at the airlock looking for you. Should I let him in?"

Brad wasn't expecting anyone. They'd finished filling their crew complement a month earlier when Randall had finally found another engineer—a young native of Io named Jim Shoulter—that he could tolerate for more than twelve seconds.

"That depends on who he is and what he wants," Brad said slowly. "Did he give you a name?"

"Nope," the tactical officer said. "He was all mysterious and just handed me this." Jason handed him a blank-faced data card.

Brad brought up a secure reader on his wrist comp. The card listed his visitor as Jack Mader, a special assistant to the Governor of Io. Interesting if true. Anyone could have a card made up to say whatever they wanted.

"Show him in," Brad said. "I'll meet him in my office." The tiny room off the bridge was hardly worthy of the name, but he had to conduct his business somewhere.

"Be right back." Jason turned on his heel and headed back to the airlock to collect their visitor.

Jason showed the governor's man into Brad's office a few minutes later. And, of course, he had to add a florid bow.

Brad shot his new tactical officer a reproving glare, but the man just grinned. The man was irrepressible. The hatch slid shut behind the departing tactical officer, and Brad faced his visitor.

Mader was silently standing there, studying the mercenary company's logo on the wall behind Brad's desk. It showed a massively built Viking warrior with the hilts of two swords visible over his shoulders. The man's expression was cold, hard, and promised significant pain to the people who had displeased him.

Of course, the image had hidden meaning for Brad. To the rest of the system, it stood for the Vikings mercenary company. To him, the image represented Vidar, the silent god. The Norse god of vengeance.

They called him the silent god because he didn't speak of vengeance. He just went about making it happen.

That suited Brad perfectly.

Brad pushed the thought aside and focused on Mader. The man wore what seemed like a perfectly genuine smile, which somehow managed to put Brad's teeth on edge.

"Have a seat, Mr. Mader. What can the Vikings do for you?"

The man sat in the indicated chair somewhat primly, as if he were afraid of getting his trousers dirty. "The governor wishes to speak with you, Mr. Madrid. With you personally."

Brad repressed the urge to correct the man in his use of titles. It would only lengthen a meeting he could already tell was going to strain his patience.

"I'm at the governor's disposal, of course." Especially since the only reason Brad could see for a meeting probably led to employment for the Vikings. "When and where?"

"The governor is currently on Node Six of the Io Yards. When she finishes her conference there, she'll return to Io via shuttle. On the way, they'll discreetly detour here. I've already arranged for Mr. Kawa to provide a conference room."

"I see. How does that translate to times and places?"

The man's smile twitched at Brad's dry tone. "This evening at eighteen hundred standard in Mr. Kawa's red conference room. Come alone and unarmed."

That made Brad frown. "I'd prefer not to go anywhere unarmed. It's not that I distrust the governor. I don't trust anyone quite that much."

"Nonetheless, I must insist," Mader replied sternly.

Brad was insulted enough to consider rejecting the meeting for a moment, but allowed the prospect of gainful employment to sway him. He might end up regretting the weakness, but he'd play along. This time.

"Very well. If something makes me regret this, I'll take my displeasure out of your hide," he warned, letting his irritation turn his voice ice-cold.

"I believe that concludes our business, Mr. Madrid," Mader said flatly as he rose to his feet. "Good day."

"Captain Madrid," Brad corrected icily. "It's considered polite to use a ship commander's title rather than *Mister*."

"I see. Thank you for the information."

It amused Brad to note the man still couldn't bring himself to use the correct title, a spark of amusement that let him swallow his anger. He didn't need to work with Jack Mader. He could tolerate the man for a little while.

As soon as the hatch opened, Jason was there to escort him back off *Heart*.

Brad leaned back in his chair and pondered why the Governor of Io needed a discreet mercenary company. She had quite a bit of military force already under her command and could access any number of gold or platinum level mercenaries. This should be interesting.

―――――

Reiko greeted Brad as soon as he came into the office. "Good evening, Captain Madrid."

"Evening, Reiko," he replied with a smile for the young woman. "Am I early?"

"Right on time. The governor is waiting in the red conference room. Her aide is with her," she added, her face twisting very slightly.

Brad stopped and considered the young woman more closely. Her judgement had seemed sound to him so far. He wanted to know if her opinion matched his.

"What's wrong with Mader?"

She shrugged with a hint of embarrassment. "He smiles too much, even when he doesn't mean it."

"That matches my impression," he said with a chuckle. There was something inherently false about Mader, beyond just a politician's fake smile.

Reiko rewarded him with a small smile. "You can go right in."

It took him less than a minute to reach the red conference room, the one farthest from the entrance. He activated the door chime and Mader's voice spoke over the intercom. "Come in, Mr. Madrid."

Brad snorted but did as he was instructed. The red conference room was actually the smallest of Kawa's conference rooms, but it was amply spacious for the pair who occupied it. And, of course, red dominated the walls.

The tall blonde woman at the head of the table was Governor Johnson. He'd read up on her in preparation for the meeting. Mader stood at her right side.

Mader drew a sensor wand and crossed the room to scan him. A moment later, he nodded to the governor. "He's clear."

Brad shook his head and snorted. "Governor, you need a new sensor system."

He reached up to his throat and removed the monofilament garrote Saburo had lent him. It had an outer sheath to prevent him from accidentally cutting his own throat, but that would easily give way if he'd actually needed to use the weapon.

It had a small pendant hanging from it as well, completing its disguise as a necklace. He'd chosen a Norse rune for the occasion. The one that meant *vengeance*, of course.

"I'll want that back," he told the outraged aide as he handed it over.

Johnson smiled and shook her head. "And what other weapons are you carrying that you haven't told us about, Captain Madrid?"

"None, though I do have a transmitter. If there's trouble, my men are right outside the office and will come running."

"Perfectly acceptable. Have a seat, Captain Madrid. Wait outside please, Jack."

The man's already-stiff smile became even more so, but he bowed his way out of the room.

Johnson watched him leave and then turned back to Brad. "I'm told your refit should be finished in the next two days."

Brad nodded, taking a seat across from her. "That's what Mr. Kawa says, and I have no reason to doubt him."

The governor nodded.

"In three days, the passenger liner *Tempest* will be leaving Io bound for Mars," she told him. "I want your ship to shadow her."

That was an unusual request. "Why?"

"My son is heading to New Boston to study for a master's degree," Johnson explained. "I'm concerned with the increased pirate activity in our area and want to be certain no one takes him hostage to get a handle on me."

"You mean the Cadre," Brad said tonelessly. He couldn't appear *too* eager.

"Among others, but yes," she said. "However, my son refuses to travel aboard a Commonwealth or militia warship. And while I could arrange for one to accompany the liner, it would be abusive of my authority to do so. Which brings us to you and your ship."

"You want me to escort *Tempest*," he concluded.

"Yes. *Tempest*'s captain will know, but I'd rather you not reveal your presence unless there's an attack."

"How much fanfare does this trip have?"

"I put out a lot of disinformation about my son's itinerary," the governor said with a sigh, "so I'm hoping no one will expect him to be on this particular ship. Even he thinks he'll be leaving in two weeks. If I'm wrong and there is combat, I'll pay the Guild-mandated bonuses and expenses, of course, but I'd rather this be a quiet shakedown cruise for you."

Considering how deeply he suspected the Cadre was plugged into the areas they prowled, Brad suspected that was a distinct possibility.

"Why me?"

"I spoke with Ms. Kernsky a few days ago, and she thought you'd be the perfect fit for this mission. I trust her judgement."

"Unless someone throws a heavy warship at us, we can handle the mission," he said after a moment. "How much are you offering?"

The governor slid a data pad across the table.

He picked it up, glanced at the screen, and his eyebrows rose. The offer was nearly forty percent above the going rate for a ship from a silver company, much less a bronze.

Brad offered his hand across the table. "It's going to be a pleasure working for you, Governor."

———

He glanced around *Heart*'s cramped wardroom. Given the nature of the mercenary company, nearly half of its personnel qualified as officers of one stripe or another. Counting Brad, six of them were in this compartment.

At the opposite end of the table, Marshal lounged in the executive officer's traditional seat. While he was officially only the pilot, everyone knew he was the company's effective second-in-command.

To Brad's left, Saburo sat cross-legged, regarding the rest of them calmly and looking as enigmatic as ever. While the Japanese trooper only considered himself the senior noncom, Brad thought of him as the ground combat officer.

Beyond Saburo, Randall had apparently discovered the arms on the chairs swung down, allowing the bulky engineer to avoid having to cram himself into the chair. One less thing to complain about, though Brad knew he'd find something else quickly enough.

Jason and Shelly sat across from them. Both seemed mostly focused, but Brad was almost certain the two were holding hands under the table. Ah, young love.

The irony that the two officers were both older than him did not escape him.

He laid his hands on the table and cleared his throat. "As I'm sure you've already guessed, we have a job. Before I give you the details, I want to touch base with everyone on our current status. Randall, how's the refit going?"

The engineer shrugged. "It's effectively done. We'll seal the last of the holes in the armor by nine hundred hours tomorrow. We'll be spaceworthy by noon."

"Excellent! Jason, how's the armament?"

"With the refit complete, we have six twelve-barrel Gatling drivers and four torpedo tubes. We have something around half a million driver rounds, so I don't think we need to worry about running out of ammo anytime soon. With our new sensors, we could shoot a cockroach off somebody's hull at a thousand klicks."

"And the torpedoes?"

"I finished loading the magazines right before the meeting started. We have a hundred on tap."

"Also excellent. Shelly?"

She smiled widely. "Coms are up and running. Most of my systems are the original installations anyway, just new software. I'm good."

Saburo didn't wait for Brad to look at him. "The troops are ready to go. We've got guns, blades, ammo, and armor. Give us a target and we will slice and dice it."

Brad grinned. He appreciated that enthusiasm—and understood it far more than he'd once have expected.

"For this mission, we're staying in space. We may need your squad for boarding, so we won't be leaving you behind, but you should be able to ride this one out in comfort."

"Ha!" the noncom snorted. "You've jinxed us now, for sure."

"Marshal?"

"The new helm console is in and checks out," the pilot said laconically. "We won't be completely sure about the new drives until we take the ship out for a spin, but the tests all look good. I should be ready to rock and roll whenever the rest of the ship is done."

"Great news," Brad said with more than a hint of satisfaction. "We'll take *Heart* out for a good test run tomorrow afternoon. That'll set us up for our mission, actually.

"It's a basic escort job with a few twists. First, our package is the Governor of Io's son and is riding aboard a civilian liner, *Tempest*. We're going to shadow the liner in case someone wants to pay them an unfriendly visit."

He swept his eyes around the table, making sure they were all with him so far.

"The second twist is that the governor doesn't want anyone to know we're there unless we have to play defense. Only the liner's captain is going to know. If one of his sensor officers spots us, he'll bring them into the plan.

"Otherwise, he'll keep quiet. I'd like to make this a test of our capability for sneaking up on someone, so we play everything close."

"Are we expecting an attack, or is this just a precaution?" Shelly asked.

"The governor doesn't expect an attack, but I think the Cadre is plugged into events more deeply than she imagines. They'd love to have the governor's son in their possession."

Saburo had been nodding the entire time. He didn't say anything, but Brad knew the man shared his concerns.

"What kind of opposition might we expect if the Cadre shows up?" Jason asked.

"*Tempest* is armed but only has a single quartet of quad barrels. Most likely, we'll only be looking at a frigate or regular corvette. I'm perfectly confident of our ability to take them."

Jason snorted. "Even another heavy corvette wouldn't be a match for us now. We could go toe to toe with a pirate destroyer and I'd still put my money on us."

"That's my take as well," Brad agreed. "All right, folks, I think that covers the general situation. *Tempest* leaves day after tomorrow at ten hundred hours. We'll have two shifts to do a shakedown test.

"Focus on main systems and flag anything that needs immediate attention. We'll work up the secondary systems on the trip to Mars."

He grinned at them. "The Vikings are now open for business."

# CHAPTER FOURTEEN

BRAD WATCHED Saburo carefully as the noncom settled into a combat stance, his cat's claws spread. He was using practice gloves, of course. It wouldn't do to have the mono-filament blades extending from the fingers of a real one to lop off something Brad cared about.

The men regarded one another for several long seconds before Saburo charged. For a moment, the slashing claws seemed to be coming from every direction, and it was all Brad could do to interpose his practice blade against each strike.

Then Saburo got an inch too close and Brad hooked his ankle around the man's leg, sending him tumbling backward. He lunged in to finish the fight, but Saburo blocked the blade with crossed claws. That wasn't going to stop him for long.

The mercenary locked his claws around Brad's weapon and did something just a bit too quickly for Brad to see. The blade tore out of Brad's hand, went spinning across the room, and bounced off the locker mounted to the gym bulkhead.

Saburo took advantage of Brad's momentary shock to lunge at him.

Brad managed to twist clear of the first lunging claw, grabbed the noncom's wrist, and threw the other man over his shoulder.

The smaller man rolled and surged to his feet, but one of the cat's claws was gone, lost in the fall. He inclined his head in salute and charged again.

This time, Brad was ready. He snapped his foot out in a low kick, which ran into an iron-hard block from the man's non-clawed arm. Brad used the energy from the block to spin around and slam his fist into the smaller man's stomach.

Saburo hesitated, his lungs momentarily stunned into inaction. As Brad came around to finish the job, the mercenary came back to life, caught his arm, and threw him to the floor. Half a moment later, the cat's claws slashed down against Brad's throat.

The shock set him to twitching and Brad raised a hand in surrender. "All right, all right. I give up!"

"Give up, my ass. I just ripped your throat out."

Getting beat sent a ripple of sullen anger through him, but Brad suppressed it. Saburo was an experienced mercenary. That kind of thing mattered. Brad would just have to keep learning so eventually he came out on top.

Saburo stripped the remaining practice glove from his hand and helped Brad up. "Unconventional weapons, my captain, confuse the poor sucker who ends up fighting you."

"No shit."

"Ready for another round?" Saburo asked. "I have other tricks in my bag."

Brad snorted. "I'll just bet you do. I'd prefer to let some of the bruises heal before we go at it again."

"True," Saburo acknowledged, pressing one hand to where Brad had slammed a fist into his stomach. "To be honest, I didn't expect you to fight so well once I'd disarmed you."

"My first sensei believed the best foundation for learning to fight with a weapon was learning to fight without one. It obviously wasn't enough." The last slipped out in spite of his determination to keep a lid on his demon.

The intercom chimed, silencing the mercenary's response. "Captain, this is Shelly."

Brad crossed to the bulkhead and pressed the button that answered the call, glad for the reprieve. "Brad here."

"We've got a thermal, sir. Jason is still narrowing the size down and establishing the exact vector, but it's probably on an intercept course for *Tempest*."

*Heart* had been silently shadowing the liner for three days now. Brad was actually surprised they'd struck so quickly. He'd expected them to hit closer to Mars. Someone had been right there, waiting for the governor's son to leave Io.

"Good job, you two. I'll be up in five minutes."

"Gotcha. Bridge out."

He turned to Saburo. "I'll have to take a rain check on that rematch."

The noncom inclined his head and grinned. "Rest up, Captain. I'll be ready for your tricks next time."

Brad changed back into his uniform quickly. The midnight-blue jacket with the faint gold piping set the tone for the ship suit of the same shade he wore under it. It looked damned sharp.

The left shoulder held the Viking patch of his mercenary company, and the right had a patch of a fist holding a beating heart. The latter represented *Heart of Vengeance*. If he ever got a second ship, the people serving there would have a different emblem.

His lapels held the silver triangle of stars that marked a Guild ship's captain and his collar bore the short gold chain of a company commander. And, of course, he was armed with his usual weapons. They were part of everyone's standard uniform.

He'd insisted Saburo and Marshal start training everyone. They might be crewing a ship rather than being dedicated fighters, but he wasn't going to lose anyone else because they couldn't use a blade, guns, and their bodies as weapons in a pinch.

Once he was ready, he headed for the bridge at a jog.

Shelly looked up as he entered. "The bridge is yours, Captain."

"Thanks," he said as he sat in his chair and brought up the repeaters. "Jason, what have we got?"

The tactical officer pressed a key that flicked his display to the main screen. A small graph in the corner indicated it was showing a sphere of space three hundred thousand kilometers across. A green triangle floated at the center of the screen with only its vector marked. That was *Heart*.

About thirty thousand kilometers above the green triangle was a golden one. Its vector was oriented along the same course as *Heart's*, and the icon also indicated the vessel's mass and armament information. Big, full of rich people, and almost unarmed.

That was *Tempest*. Those two light codes had been on the screen in nearly identical positions since *Heart* had snuck up on the liner and started shadowing her.

New to the screen was the red circle in the lower left quadrant of the screen. Data flowed underneath it, changing as the sensors refined their data.

"She's about thirty thousand klicks away from us and about fifty thousand from *Tempest*," Jason said. "Her current velocity is about five klicks per second.

"She's pulling four meters per second squared, and her thermal signature is consistent with ion/fusion drives pushing a ship of about our weight. Emission signatures fit a quartet of Falcon IVs pulling maximum acceleration."

Brad nodded. *Heart*, with her trio of new*ish* Skylark VI drive units, could outdo that by only five percent. "What's his course?"

"If he's headed for a zero-range intercept, he'll cross *Tempest's* course in just under sixty-seven minutes. He'll be in weapons range quite a bit before that. If he goes for zero-zero to board, he'll reach them in one hundred and two minutes with turnover in forty-one."

Brad studied the screen for a moment. "Does *Tempest* know they're there?"

"I doubt it. Even if she does, *Tempest* can only pull two meters per second squared. All she could do is delay the inevitable for a few minutes."

Brad nodded, and then glanced at Shelly. "Do we have an intercept course?"

"Plugged in and auto-updating as we speak," she confirmed. "Marshal will confirm it as soon as he gets here. We caught him in the shower and he thought we'd appreciate not seeing him naked. I heartily concur."

Marshal came striding into the bridge just in time to hear that last. "Plenty of women are *very* happy to see me naked. Just not under these particular circumstances. Not so far, anyway."

He planted himself at the helm console and double checked the course. "It looks good, Captain. Ready to execute."

"Do it."

For a moment, acceleration pushed everyone back into their seats, and then the artificial gravity compensated, bringing them back to the standard point five *g*'s it was set to.

The main viewscreen continued to show a repeat of the tactical displays. Now a green arrow extended from *Heart* toward the red arrow projecting from the bogey on an intercept course. The pirate had to have detected them by now, but he hadn't reacted.

"Jason, what's our time to weapons range?"

The tactical officer shrugged. "I could hit them with the mass drivers at this range if I was lucky and they didn't maneuver."

Brad nodded. The theoretical range of a mass driver was infinite, but the hundred-gram steel slugs only moved at about a thousand kilometers per second. At long ranges, that meant all your opponent had to do was alter his acceleration by a minute amount and you'd miss.

"Time to torpedo range?"

"We'll reach our ten-thousand-kilometer powered envelope in twenty-seven minutes. That's about ten minutes before he'll turn over if he continues on a zero-zero course."

"Thank you. Hail him for me, Shelly."

"You're live in three, two, one," she said.

Brad let a cold expression cover his face. "Unidentified vessel, this is the Guild warship *Heart of Vengeance*. Identify yourself and heave to."

Seconds ticked past—far more than it would take the message to cross the gap between the two ships.

"Unidentified vessel," Brad repeated, "if you do not heave to, we will assume hostile intent and destroy your ship."

Again, there was no reply. Brad felt his mouth tighten with dark satisfaction, and killed the communications channel from his repeater.

"Can you put a driver round across their bow?" he asked Jason.

"Easily. Should I use an explosive round and detonate it in front of him to make sure we have his complete attention?"

"Do it."

Jason turned to his console and manipulated the controls. On Brad's repeater screen, a tiny green speck appeared on the display.

"Warning shot fired," Jason reported.

Brad watched the round cross the twenty thousand kilometers between the two ships and vanish.

"Warning shot detonated," his tactical officer said.

"Shelly, let's try one last time." That was more than his demon wanted to give the bastard, but he wanted the record to show he'd done everything right.

She hit a key and nodded.

Brad faced the camera one last time and he knew his expression was even colder than it had been before. He wanted them to see his rage. "Unidentified vessel, that was your final warning. Withdraw immediately or be destroyed."

Once again, there was no response, so Brad killed the channel with a satisfied smile.

"He's shifting course towards us," Jason said. "Time to effective mass driver range is now six minutes."

That at least made the enemy's intentions clear. Now no one could blame him for what he was about to do.

He studied the tactical display on his repeater. "Set Gatlings five and six for torpedo defense and engage with one through four at twenty thousand kilometers. We'll open fire with torpedoes as soon as we reach powered engagement range and I give the order."

"Copy that," Jason replied, keying commands into his console.

Brad watched the range indicator drop. Once the enemy hit the twenty-thousand-kilometer mark, the tactical officer opened fire.

Green specks flashed onto the screen as each of the Gatling mass drivers fired its first barrel. Two seconds later, a second set of specks appeared as the next barrel rotated into position and fired. He watched them fly with hot approval.

Since each barrel took twenty-four seconds to reload and cool, a round every two seconds was the maximum rate of fire they could maintain.

The first set of green specks was two thirds of the way to the target and the fourth set had just flashed onto the screen when a set of red specks appeared.

"He's returning fire," Jason reported coolly. "Sensors reading six projectiles."

"Evasive maneuvers," Brad ordered.

He felt the ship shift before the artificial gravity dampened the change in momentum. On the screen, the first set of green specks flashed by the red circle. The enemy had also dodged.

A second set of red specks had joined the first. "I can confirm that he has six mass drivers," Jason reported. "Four second lag between rounds. Odds are we're facing hexabarrel Gatlings."

Brad merely nodded, watching the specks on the screen that marked weapons trying to kill him and his crew. "Time to torpedo range?"

"One minute—we hit him!" Jason's surprised exclamation was marked by a flash on the screen and data codes marking atmosphere loss next to the symbol for the enemy ship.

More complex data codes for the vectors began to appear next to the symbol as the enemy began to maneuver more aggressively. Then *Heart* seemed to shudder as Marshal failed to dodge fast enough and half a salvo of driver rounds slammed into their hull.

Brad keyed the intercom to engineering. "Mike! Damage report!"

"Doesn't look like they made it through the reactive armor," Randall said. "Hull integrity still good."

Brad breathed a sigh of relief. "All right. Keep me in the loop if that changes."

"As if I wouldn't," the man said before he cut the connection.

The reactive armor strips had been one of the more expensive refits to *Heart*, but they could deflect driver slugs away from the hull in some cases.

"Torpedo range," Jason said.

"Fire at will," Brad said savagely.

"I have no idea what everyone has against that Will guy. First salvo away."

Even as the tactical officer spoke, *Heart* shuddered as the torpedoes blasted away from her. Four squares flashed into existence on the screen.

"The enemy is returning fire," the tactical officer reported a moment later. "Three torpedoes inbound. Gatlings five and six engaging."

Brad watched as the two sets of squares began the two-minute journey between the ships. It would probably be the exchange of heavy munitions like this that ended the fight. And end it they would, one way or the other.

The torpedoes weren't much more than hundred-kilo slugs of metal strapped to small drives. It was the general consensus of those who used them that adding anything short of a nuke to them made only a negligible difference.

He didn't doubt that many would like the extra boost a nuke would add, but the Commonwealth reserved those for Fleet units, with draconian penalties for anyone caught trafficking in them, much less using them.

"Enemy torpedoes destroyed," Jason said thirty seconds later.

"How are ours?" Brad asked.

"Still good. The idiot focused all his Gatlings on us. He hasn't managed to retarget to any of our torpedoes yet. Our tubes are reloaded. Do you want me to fire another salvo?"

"No. Let's see how he deals with the first."

A sudden shudder ran through the corvette. Then another. A display showed parts of the hull changing color from green to yellow as more of the reactive armor was expended stopping enemy slugs.

"Marshal," Brad snapped.

"They got lucky. I'm varying our thrust a little more to get out of the hotspot."

"Gotcha!" Jason shouted as their torpedoes overlapped with the red circle of the enemy. It flashed and turned into a flashing X.

"Three solid hits," the tactical officer reported briskly. "No indication of continued acceleration, and he's ceased firing. I'm still picking up his fusion reactor, so part of him is still intact."

"Kill him," Brad ordered, cold hatred seething through his veins.

Jason nodded wordlessly and pressed a button on his console.

All six Gatlings went to maximum rate of fire, emptying every barrel in four seconds to send seventy-two projectiles flashing toward the pirate ship at a thousand kilometers a second. Seven seconds later, the first of them impacted. A blue-white flash that was visible at that distance indicated the failure of the enemy's fusion bottle.

"Enemy destroyed," Jason said into the silence. "All screens clear."

Shelly turned from her console. "Captain, *Tempest* is hailing us. Captain Vasilev is on the line."

"Put him on."

The main screen shifted to the image of a dark-skinned man in a white-and-gold uniform.

"Captain Madrid," the other man said, inclining his head. "From the bottom of my heart, I thank you on behalf of my crew and passengers."

Brad smiled a little. "I'll pass your kind words on to my crew, Captain Vasilev."

"Thank you. I don't believe there's much point in pretending *Tempest* is unescorted anymore. That being the case, I suggest you place your ship in a standard escort position.

"Then I'd like to extend an invitation to you and your officers to dine with myself and my senior staff aboard *Tempest*."

"We'd enjoy that. Though I'll leave half of my people on duty here in case our friend wasn't completely alone. The rest of us can come over another time."

"Excellent. Until then, *Tempest* out."

# CHAPTER FIFTEEN

HEART'S SHUTTLE was designed for efficient movement of troops and supplies, not comfort. The cockpit at least, unlike the rear compartment set up for Saburo and his armored mercenaries, had padded acceleration couches.

Brad sat in the copilot's seat, watching *Tempest* grow larger as Marshal took the shuttle in. Behind them, Saburo occupied the third seat in the cockpit. Jason and Shelly were keeping an eye out for trouble back on *Heart*.

Under a normal interpretation of *senior officers*, Brad would've brought Randall along with them, but the engineer had made his view on that very clear. He was busy replacing the reactive armor strips that had been used and checking the mass drivers for wear and tear.

Marshal murmured into his mic and released the controls. "Their approach computers have us now. Sit back and relax."

A few bursts from the shuttle's drive aligned them with one of the liner's boat bays. For a moment, the hundred-ton craft—tiny next to *Tempest*'s hundred-thousand-ton bulk—seemed motionless as the bay doors opened. Then a short burn gently floated them into the bay.

As they entered, the craft slowed as it encountered the catcher field.

A few moments later, the shuttle came to a halt, waiting in front of the bay's inner door.

When the outer doors had closed behind them, the inner doors slid open. The catcher field reversed and pushed the shuttle forward into the main bay. Artificial gravity caught them and pulled them to the deck as soon as they were in place.

Once the shuttle had settled down, Brad glanced over at Marshal and nodded. The push of a button extended their ramp, and the three men stood. Glancing out the port, Brad saw a door in the side of the bay open, and a small group of people entered.

Brad smiled and gestured for Saburo to precede him—he quite literally couldn't get out of the cockpit until the other man did—and then followed him out. The presence of breathable air on the other side of the airlock deactivated the normal overrides and allowed Brad to open both doors simultaneously.

He led the way down onto the deck just in time to meet their welcoming committee. Captain Vasilev led the group.

Vasilev took Brad's hand in both of his, shaking it enthusiastically. "Welcome aboard *Tempest*, Captain Madrid."

"The pleasure is mine. This is my pilot, John Marshal, and Saburo Kawa, my combat team leader."

Vasilev shook their hands and then motioned for a young man in an exquisite dark blue suit to come forward. "This is Colin Johnson. He requested to be here."

The young man seemed to half-glare at Brad, threatening to rouse the anger than never seemed to fully sleep inside him. "It seems my esteemed mother won't hesitate to break her word when it suits her 'best judgment.'" The last two words came out in a tone that could only be described as a whiny sneer.

Before Brad could respond, the man jerked as if kicked. Considering the capable-looking man standing behind Colin—whose demeanor screamed *bodyguard*—that was quite possible.

"Nonetheless," Colin continued grudgingly, "in this case, she was correct. Thank you for your efforts." He offered his hand in an almost-dainty gesture.

Brad studied the man as he took a deep breath to calm the demon and accepted the offered hand. It would've been kind to call the grip effeminate.

"I would've preferred an uneventful trip myself, Mr. Johnson, but needs must when the devil drives."

Colin inclined his head and released Brad's hand. "I hope none of your people were injured?"

"No. *Heart* took some damage, but it's all repairable."

"You are fortunate to have such a capable ship, Captain," one of Vasilev's staffers commented.

"Fortune has nothing to do with it," Vasilev snorted. "I imagine it involved a great deal of hard work and money, da?"

Brad shrugged. "Our lives depend on that ship. It was worth every credit."

Vasilev nodded. "I think that's a sentiment most spacers would agree with. Now, gentlemen, the cooks have a wonderful dinner prepared. It would be a crime to let it get cold."

———

Brad watched *Tempest* slot into her docking bay on the massive Mars Orbital Station One, more commonly known as MOSO. The attack had provided the sole excitement of the multi-week journey from the Jovian system to Mars.

Now *Heart*'s contract was officially fulfilled, though *Tempest* had been perfectly safe since they'd entered the ten-light-second radius around Mars that the Commonwealth patrolled most heavily.

Bringing the liner to MOSO and under the guns of the Mars Defense Command forts and the Commonwealth battleship *Eternal* had simply made it formal.

"Shelly, do we have our docking clearance?" he asked.

"Yup. Docking bay one-seven-zero. The beacon code is niner-four-niner-five, and it's already in the computers."

"Thank you. John?"

"Underway," the pilot said, his hands busy on his controls. "Be nice to see some land for once."

Jason snorted. "Not all that much land on MOSO. Just metal."

The pilot made a rude noise. "At least there are bars. And women."

"Very true."

"Watch your step, Guns," Shelly said with a mock growl. "You wouldn't want to have to sleep on a nice, hard deck for the next few weeks, would you?"

Brad sat back and smiled as his bridge poked at one another. They were good people and he was damned lucky to have them.

————

Brad sighed as he attached the final appendix to his official report and leaned back in his chair. He hated paperwork, but it was the one unavoidable thing in this business. Everything had to be documented when you killed someone.

While the contract had authorized lethal force in defense of the governor's son and the liner, Guild regulations and Commonwealth law required him to explain the events in as much detail as possible.

In this case, he had the sensor records and his bridge security recordings to document how he'd given the pirates every opportunity to change their minds. Some bureaucrat might whine because he'd finished the pirate off at the end, but the law gave no cover to pirates caught in the act.

He wouldn't have risked his ship or crew trying to capture people with an automatic death sentence over their heads anyway. Desperate people did desperate things.

Brad flicked back to the main body of his report and began scanning it again. Just as he reached the section covering the fight, his intercom beeped.

He saved the report and responded. "Madrid."

"Captain, I've got a transmission from a Mr. Ambrose Weaver," Shelly said. "He wishes to speak with you."

"Put him through." Brad hadn't been expecting anyone to contact him.

"Patching him through now," she replied, then the intercom shut off with a quiet click.

Brad turned back to his console in time to see the image of a graying man dressed in a neat suit appear on the screen.

"Captain Madrid."

"Mr. Weaver. Might I ask the purpose of your call?"

"Of course," the man replied genially. "I'm Governor Johnson's agent on Mars. I'm calling to deal with the finalities of your contract."

Brad inclined his head. "I see. Unfortunately, I haven't completed all the paperwork. It'll take me another day or so to be completely satisfied with the report."

"Paperwork is not necessary for me to judge that the contract has been satisfied, Captain," Weaver said with a flash of white teeth. "I've spoken to young Mr. Johnson. He's obviously here, safe and sound.

"I'm releasing your base payment now. The bonuses and combat costs will need to wait for Governor Johnson's authorization, but I've already messaged her. If you'd provide me a list of what you expended and the cost of your repairs, I'll make certain to get that taken care of as soon as she gets back to me."

"Thank you," Brad replied sincerely. Prompt payment by one's employers was always nice. The man not haggling over the four torpedoes and replacing the reactive armor strips was even better.

"Lastly," Weaver said, "Mr. Johnson has authorized me to disburse a ten percent bonus out of his personal funds."

Brad's eyebrows rose. Colin Johnson had hardly impressed him as someone that generous. Then he caught the hint of an expression on Weaver's face. It probably hadn't been the kid's idea.

"I see. Pass my thanks on to Mr. Johnson."

"Oh, I most definitely will."

The man leaned forward. "Governor Johnson doesn't forget her debts, Captain. Your service has been exemplary, and her assessment of you to the Guild will be glowing. Speaking for Governor Johnson's extended family and close companions, if there is any aid that we can render you in the future, we shall be pleased to do so.

"Now, if you'll excuse me, I fear I have other business to deal with. I wish you a good day, Captain Madrid. May the Everlit guide your path."

"And may they keep the Dark from yours," Brad replied in the other half of the parting formula for the worshippers of the Church of Light.

The man's image flicked off his screen and Brad leaned back. Not too shabby for a first run. Not too shabby at all.

————

That great feeling evaporated as soon as MOSO security called him to come to their lockup in the middle of the night.

With a sense of resignation, Brad dressed and made his way off the ship. It was the middle of the local night, but the crowds were only a bit more subdued than when he'd last boarded the station.

The main security station was bigger than he'd expected. It was crowded inside, too. He wondered why they needed so many security officers. It seemed as if Mars would be a little more peaceful than the Outer System.

The desk sergeant, a harried man with a fringe of dirty brown hair, looked up when Brad stopped in front of the counter. "What can I do for you?" His tone indicated he really didn't care.

"I'm Brad Madrid, Captain of *Heart of Vengeance*," he replied with a firm grip on his annoyance. "I got a call that one of my people was here."

The man grunted and tapped on his console. "Yeah. Drunk and disorderly and assaulting a Fleet officer. Detective Huddleston wants to talk with you about him."

Brad sighed. He'd known this was coming for a while, but he'd hoped Marshal would pick a less sensitive place than Mars. And why the hell had he assaulted a Fleet officer? Probably over a woman.

"Then I'd best speak with the detective," he said with a headshake.

"You'll need to secure your weapons. The lockup is off to the right. Have a seat and she'll be out to get you shortly."

He went into the indicated room and found a series of lockers. They looked secure and he knew he'd never be able to argue them into letting him retain his weapons.

Once he'd locked them up, he pocketed the key and found a seat.

The waiting room had a selection of interesting people waiting for their turns with someone. He made a game out of trying to guess what their friends or family had done to get arrested. It helped distract him a little from the lump of anger sitting in his gut like a stone.

He hadn't used to be that way. Ever since the attack on Mandrake's Heart, he'd had a sense of rage that he could only barely control at times. While he had every right to feel that way, he needed to make his rage serve him, not the other way around.

The trick was keeping the demon on a tight leash. If it got loose at the wrong time, things could go very badly for him and his friends.

Ten minutes later, while he was still trying to figure out a way to balance his anger with his duty to get vengeance, a trim woman with dark hair who was dressed in a conservative dark gray suit stepped up the door. "Captain Madrid?"

He rose to his feet and stepped over to her. "Brad Madrid."

She held out her hand. "Margaret Huddleston. I'm a detective with MOSO General Crimes. That basically means I do initial investigations and hand them off if need be. Come up to my office and we'll talk about your guy."

If anything, the areas behind the counter were even more crowded. They must get a lot more trouble here than anyone in their right minds would expect.

She led him to an elevator, up to the third floor, and down the hall to a cramped office with a great view of the bathrooms. It was compulsively neat and the pictures on the wall seemed regimented.

"Have a seat," she said as she slipped behind the desk. "Your man was at a bar and he'd consumed a lot of alcohol at the time of the incident. According to eyewitness accounts, he got into an argument with a Fleet officer that escalated to shoving. A punch was thrown but didn't connect. Bystanders pulled them apart before anything really bad happened."

Brad sighed. "I wish I could say I'm surprised. I'm glad no one was injured. How serious are the charges?"

The detective shrugged. "The drunk and disorderly can be dismissed with a fine. The assault on a Fleet officer is more serious. I realize that a shove seems minor in the grand scheme of things, but physical contact is physical contact. That's technically assault."

"If Fleet decides to press the charge, we'll remand your guy for a hearing. With the backlog in the judicial system, the initial hearing won't be for a week or more. The actual process could take months to play out."

"Does he have to be here for that or can we post bail?"

She shook her head. "The Commonwealth is a big place and people disappear all the time. If Fleet decides to make an example of him, your guy is here for the duration."

Perfect. If Brad couldn't pour oil on troubled waters, he'd have to find a new pilot.

"Who do I have to talk with to try and fix this?" he asked.

"The wronged party in this is Captain Weldon Shelby with *Eternal*. He's supposed to come back tomorrow and file an official report of the incident. If you can convince him there's no need, I'll cut your guy loose with a stiff fine."

"Do you have his contact information?"

"Sure. I'll send it to your wrist-comp. It's the general number to *Eternal*. They'll get him your message and he can call you back."

"Thanks. Can I talk to Marshal?"

Detective Huddleston frowned. "Who?"

"My guy, John Marshal."

A corner of her mouth jerked up. "There's been some kind of misunderstanding. We're holding Mike Randall. He claims he's your chief engineer."

# CHAPTER SIXTEEN

BRAD FIGURED CALLING Captain Shelby in the morning was a better option, so he got what sleep he could and rose early. He'd slept like crap. No surprise.

Jim Shoulter, the junior engineer, came into the galley while he was eating breakfast. "Do you have a minute, Captain?"

"Pull up a chair," he said with a nod. "It's about Mike, isn't it?"

The man gave him an odd look as he sat. "Yeah. I don't think he came back in last night. At least, he's not answering his door or com. I'm a bit worried."

"I'll pass the word around shortly, but he got into a scuffle last night. He's in the security lockup. He's fine, though."

The tall man blinked and sat back in his chair. "A fight? Wow. I figured he was all bark and no bite."

"Just goes to show how we never really know someone as well as we think. Is everything under control in engineering?"

"Sure. There's some minor maintenance that I need to do, but it's all normal."

"Then keep doing what you need to do. If this takes longer than I hope, we'll discuss our options."

The man frowned. "Is it that bad?"

"It might be. I'll know shortly."

John Marshal sauntered into the galley and grinned at Dwayne Holmes as he took his plate of food from the wiry cook.

He sat down next to Brad and started eating without seeming to note the conversation already in progress.

"Man, last night was amazing," the pilot said between bites. "I ran into an old friend and we stayed up late dancing. And, well, you know."

Brad smiled a little. "I'm glad things worked out for you. Mike had some trouble."

He explained the events of the evening to Marshal. So much for his intention of telling everyone at once.

Luckily, Jason, Shelly, and Saburo came in right after he got started, so he was able to back up just a little and tell the tale in one go.

Saburo leaned back in his chair with an amused expression. "I have to say, I'd have expected that of Marshal, not Randall."

"Me, too," Marshal said. "I'm the guy that causes trouble. Mike is the one that fixes it. He's all bluster. He really shoved some Fleet guy?"

"So they tell me," Brad said. "I'll see if I can extract him from this in a little bit. It might be someone he knows. He was a Fleet officer before. Chief engineer on a battleship. Maybe *Eternal*."

Jason shook his head. "How did he get to that rank with his temperament?"

"The universe is filled with wonders beyond human understanding," Saburo intoned.

Brad laughed in spite of himself. "I suspect raw talent had something to do with it. Now get about your duties while I see if I can extract our engineer from this mess."

He was on his way back to his cabin when one of the enlisted mercenaries called for him over the shipwide intercom. "Captain, there's someone wanting to speak with you at the airlock."

Rather than answer the call, he changed course and was there in less than twenty seconds. It was Private Paul Metcalf. The burly mercenary was staring at a Fleet officer on his screen.

Brad noted the transmission was muted, so he took a moment to study the man. Based on the rank insignia—identifying him as a Fleet captain without an independent command—this was probably Weldon Shelby, *Eternal*'s chief engineer. The man was short but wide. He'd be a serious brawler, if that was his inclination.

"What did he have to say?" Brad asked.

"Just that he had business with you, Captain. From his tone, I thought you might be expecting him."

He supposed that was true. "Thanks, Paul."

Rather than use the screen, Brad opened the airlock and stepped out to meet the Fleet officer with his hand extended. "Captain Shelby? Brad Madrid."

The large man took his hand. "Captain Madrid. I'm sorry to meet you under these circumstances, but I think we need to talk."

"Step inside and we can use my office."

The officer looked around as they made their way toward the bridge. "I served on a *Fidelis* when I was just starting out. Tough little ships. Have you seen much action in her?"

"A little. She was a pirate before I captured her. We just got her out of refit and had a bit of a scuffle on the way here. Yeah. she's tough."

Once they reached his office just off the bridge, he gestured for the man to sit and pulled his chair out from behind the desk to join him. This wasn't the kind of conversation where he wanted to seem standoffish.

"It's early for a drink, but I can offer you some coffee."

Shelby shook his head. "I'm fully caffeinated already. Thanks for the offer, though."

The man took a slow breath and grimaced. "I'm sure you already know I had a spot of trouble with Mike last night. I tried to calm him down, but things spun a little out of control."

Brad wasn't sure that was the right way to describe the incident, but he didn't argue. "So, you know him."

Shelby nodded. "Sure. He trained me on *Eternal*. I was his assistant chief when he and Commodore Bailey got into the kerfuffle that cost him his career. It was a damned shame. The man is the best engineer I've ever met."

"It sounds as if you count him as a friend. Does that mean you'll consider not pressing charges?"

"I'd rather not, but it isn't completely up to me," the other man said tiredly. "Commodore Bailey sent me to make him an offer last night. Let's just say Mike didn't take it well. The commodore is insisting on the deal now."

Brad felt his expression harden as the demon inside him silently growled. "If you poke a bear, it isn't the bear's fault he mauls you. I don't approve of blackmail."

"Neither do I, but I'm not the one calling the shots."

"It sounds as if you are. Mike shoved you, not Bailey. You're the one about to put a friend you sought out through the meat grinder. Don't."

"I wish it were that simple, but I'm a Fleet officer under orders. If Commodore Bailey tells me to press charges, then I have to do it."

"I doubt that's a lawful order, but I understand. What was the offer? He's under contract to me, so he can't just go off on his own."

"The offer actually required your cooperation. I swear it wasn't blackmail. It's a straightforward job that Fleet wants to hire you for."

He raised an eyebrow. "Then you should've come to me first."

"Probably," the officer admitted. "It had been a long time since I'd seen Mike, so I just wanted to reconnect. In retrospect, that was probably a mistake."

"What did you expect him to do? Intercede with me to take the job? The man is as stubborn as they get. Even I know he'd balk."

Brad leaned forward. "It sounds to me as if you set out to get some leverage on me. This is a setup."

"Maybe. The commodore is the one who told me Mike was back and ordered me to broach the subject with him specifically. As one might imagine, they don't see eye to eye on a number of things."

The officer shifted uncomfortably in his seat. "Look, I really don't want to be in the middle of this. Will you at least hear me out?"

Brad allowed some of the anger inside him to show. "You put one of my officers—someone you claim is a friend—in a position you knew would make him go off," he growled. "You don't get to be a captain in Fleet by being an idiot. Don't act like one."

He rose to his feet. "This meeting is over unless you drop the charges. I'd rather he didn't go down like this, double-crossed by a friend, but I have a company that I'm responsible for. The Vikings will not be blackmailed. Neither will I."

Shelby stayed in his seat. "That's harsh, but even if you don't believe me, I don't want to see Mike in this position. Or you. Please, hear me out."

"No," Brad said firmly. "If you insist on throwing Mike under the bus, that's all on you. You're either his friend or you aren't. You're either a man with principles or you aren't. I don't negotiate with people I can't trust, and this is not the way to get me to help you."

The other man sighed and rubbed his face. "You don't know Bailey like I do. There will be consequences."

"If taking a stand were easy, everyone would do it," Brad said coolly. "Press charges and I'll fight you and Fleet on this. Drop them and I *might* consider the job. Even if you won't fight for a friend, you'd best realize you won't get a better offer from me. Either agree or get off my ship."

Shelby slumped a little. "Fine. I'll drop the charges. I didn't want to press them in the first place, and I really do like Mike. You're a lot tougher than I expected a mercenary to be, Captain Madrid."

"That's kind of a requirement for being a mercenary. Let's go spring Mike and you can take me to *Eternal*."

The other man frowned. "What? Why do you need to go there?"

"Because if I'm going to fight over this job, I'll do it with the person that actually wants to hire me. No offense, but you can only follow the line your commanding officer lays out for you. It'll feel a lot better for me to tell Commodore Bailey to stuff it myself than passing that through you."

That got a snort of laughter from the Fleet officer. "Part of me wants to be a fly on the wall for that meeting, but the rest of me wants to be far, far away from the fusion plant when it destabilizes."

Shelby stood. "It's obvious I have to cooperate with you, and as you said, the order is probably unlawful. That won't stop Commodore Bailey from making my life miserable, but I'll be able to sleep at night. Let's do this before I come to my senses."

He went back to the MOSO security center with Shelby. Detective Huddleston was off shift, but one of her compatriots started the necessary paperwork to get Mike out. Brad had to pay a fairly impressive fine—that was going to come out of Mike's salary—but everything was in motion.

The detective told them it would be a few hours to get everything taken care of, so they didn't wait around. Mike would find his own way back to the ship. Let him spend the time worrying about how Brad was going to tear a strip off his hide when this was all over.

With that taken care of, he followed Shelby back to the area of the station reserved for small craft. There was a Fleet shuttle waiting.

"You'll need to let Petty Officer Ramirez lock up your weapons," Shelby said. "Sorry. Fleet policy."

As much as Brad disliked that, he knew he wouldn't be able to negotiate. Just like the security station.

It was probably a good idea in any case. He was about to get into a screaming match with a Fleet commodore. It was best he did that without handy weapons, particularly with his new hair-trigger temper.

Brad removed his weapons belt and handed it to the Fleet noncom. "Take good care of them."

"You bet, Captain. I'll make sure you get them back right quick once you're done, too."

"Raul is one of my best people," Shelby said. "Your gear is in good hands."

The trip out to *Eternal* was uneventful. Brad took advantage of the port beside his seat to get a good look at the massive warship. The pilot must've been taking that into account, because they were passing close with an eye toward his side of the shuttle.

The battleship dwarfed even the largest freighters he'd ever seen. It probably wouldn't be fast, but it had more weapons than he could possibly imagine. Marines, too. It was probably stuffed full of fighting men. Why couldn't a ship like this one find the Terror and his base?

The bay they landed in was larger than *Heart of Vengeance*. That was a somewhat-humbling experience, but he made sure to keep his expression schooled. He was there to make a point. Gawking like a tourist wouldn't help him.

Shelby escorted him off the shuttle and into the crowded corridors. "I'll take you to the commodore's office and then wait outside for you. Like I said, I'd rather not get any of this on me."

"Good luck with that."

The captain chuckled. "Too true."

Once they reached the right deck, he led Brad to a compartment that was the same size as *Heart's* bridge—so easily twice the size of *Brad's* office. That was where the commodore's assistant sat at her desk. The young woman—a lieutenant, by her rank tabs—looked up when they stepped inside.

"Captain Shelby. The commodore said to see you in once you arrived."

She gave Brad a curious glance but didn't ask any questions as she rose from behind her desk. The woman knocked twice on a hatch to the rear of the compartment and opened it without waiting for a response.

"Commodore, Captain Shelby is here to see you. He's brought a guest."

"Send them in."

That wasn't a man's voice.

Brad had only a moment to adjust his assumption before Shelby led him into his commanding officer's presence.

Commodore Bailey's office was absolutely palatial. It could have easily held three of her assistant's compartment. It was tastefully decorated in subdued colors. None of the furniture seemed expensive, but it all matched. Unlike Brad's.

The commodore stood from behind her desk. From the way Shelby had spoken about her, Brad had expected a disagreeable man. What he got was a very small woman with golden hair in a neat Fleet uniform.

"Captain Shelby," she said, her voice a high alto. "I didn't expect you back so soon. Or for you to bring me a surprise guest."

Her tone indicated the man had some explaining to do.

"Sorry, I had to improvise. Commodore Angel Bailey, meet Captain Brad Madrid of *Heart of Vengeance* and commanding officer of the Vikings."

She let her gaze rest on Shelby long enough to promise trouble and then focused her attention on Brad. "Wait outside, Captain Shelby. We'll talk in a little while. Come in, Captain Madrid. We have much to discuss."

# CHAPTER SEVENTEEN

"Park it, Captain," Commodore Bailey said as she resumed her seat. "I assume Captain Shelby conveyed my requirements to you. Do you have any questions?"

"Just one," Brad said as he took the indicated seat. "What in the world makes you think I'll let you push me or my people around like this?"

She smiled without humor. "I would think that was obvious."

Her attitude set him to seething inside. "Then you're in for a rude awakening. I told Captain Shelby I don't negotiate with blackmailers. Too much like obeying pirates. Things never turn out well."

The woman eyed him and then leaned back in her seat. "So, you'd rather let your man go to jail? That's not very loyal."

"I'm wondering what you'd know about loyalty. You could have contacted me directly and made this just a business transaction. You chose to make it personal.

"Captain Shelby has some basic human decency. He dropped the charges. That's why I'm letting you talk. You have nothing to hold over my people now."

Her expression clouded. "He had no authority to do that."

"You want to talk about authority? You had none to give that order.

We both know it. If I pushed the matter, I could get you in some hot water over it, too. Let's stop playing these games. Tell me what you want so that I can tell you to get stuffed. I have a busy day ahead of me."

Her eyes narrowed as she sat up straight. "You've got a lot of balls, sitting in my office, talking to me that way."

"So I hear. You apparently have none, since your first impulse is to use leverage to get me to do what you want. Tell me, how does it feel, commanding a powerful ship like this? One that never leaves orbit to actually fight? It might as well be a defense station.

"Is that how you ended up commanding it instead of a real warship? They didn't trust you with a mobile platform in a real fight? Are you the desk-bound paper-pusher you look like?"

Those were fighting words. Ones he'd carefully worked out ahead of time to provoke a furious reaction. He had to admit he was getting far more satisfaction provoking this fight than he'd expected. He really was having problems.

Oddly, the words seemed to have the opposite effect from what he'd intended. Bailey actually chuckled as she leaned back in her chair again.

"I like a man that isn't afraid to come out swinging. I don't have to defend myself to you, but I commanded a cruiser for years. I've fought and killed more pirates than you'll ever see."

"It doesn't seem to have done that good of a job. There's still plenty out there. Cut to the chase, Commodore. Why play these games?"

"Honestly? I've never had much respect for mercenaries," she said with a hint of distaste. "If you want to get the best effort out of them, you have to assert dominance.

"I also can't stand Randall and I'm a vindictive bitch. Trust me when I say that he caused me more than enough trouble to deserve this."

She crossed her legs. "You're one cool customer, Captain. I'm as impressed as I am annoyed. Perhaps I made a mistake in approaching the situation like this."

"I'd say." Brad stood. "I'm sure you have a lot of work ahead of you now that you need to muscle someone else into working for you.

If you'll excuse me, I need to get some fresh air. I figure fifteen light-seconds ought to do the trick."

"At least hear me out. You've come all this way. Why not let me finish? Aren't you the least bit curious?"

He had to admit that he was, now that the demon inside him had been denied the fight it craved. "I can't imagine any set of circumstances where I agree to work for you."

"What if it involved slavers? You have some history with them. Can you honestly tell me you wouldn't want to stick a finger in their eye, Captain Madrid? Or should I call you Brad the Dutchman?"

Maybe she'd done a little research on him, after all.

"You do know how to troll people, don't you?" he asked slowly. "You could've led with that and it would've made both our lives easier."

"True, but it wouldn't have been nearly as fun. Though I have to admit that you fighting back makes this more satisfying. I do love a good fight. Please, sit back down and at least hear what I have to say."

Brad warily sat. She knew his history back to *Freedom*. Did she know more? As in who he really was? There was only one way to know for sure.

"How is Captain Fields?"

"He's good. I contacted him to get a feel for you once I knew who Randall was working for. I assume you recovered your memories, since you pulled that disappearing act on Ceres. That really got them excited, but they still traced you to Ganymede.

"That let me see how you really feel about slavers. That's a positive point with me, by the way. I wish we could kill them all."

"Then why don't you?"

She pursed her lips. "I think someone in Fleet's chain of command is working with them. Them and the Cadre. They've managed to consistently avoid engagements with us, and anytime we get word about one of their hideouts, they're long gone when we get there."

"So, why aren't you cleaning out your moles?"

"Who says we aren't? Someone broke into your new ship and stole the computer core. We sent one of our investigators to have a chat with you, and I believe she left a folder full of information for you to study. That's because we believe it had to be the slavers."

Brad nodded. "I'd agree with that assessment, but I'm not sure why that would make me work with you on anything. After all, you could be in league with them."

"You wound me," Commodore Bailey said. "Would I order Lieutenant Greer to read you in if I was working with the slavers?"

"That implies you were the one who ordered her to do it," he shot back. "You might be lying or playing some deeper game. You seem to be that kind of person. Cut to the chase, Commodore."

She sighed. "You're no fun. We believe the slavers aren't done with you yet. There's been chatter about your ship. Did you know they've put a price on your head? Rather, on your ship. A cool million credits for its verified destruction."

That was a surprise. "I had no idea. I'm still not sure why that leads you to harass my crew."

Commodore Bailey leaned forward. "I need someone that can act in places Fleet cannot. Someone with a grudge and some skin in the game. You seem like the perfect candidate to me. I can smell the rage inside you. You want to kill them all."

"I won't lie," he admitted. "I hate the slavers almost as much as I hate the Cadre. I'd be willing to do a lot to take them down."

"What if I told you they're linked?"

He shrugged. "That's not too surprising. Piracy and slave trading seem to go hand in hand."

She turned to her computer and tapped on a few keys. A screen on the bulkhead came to life, showing a meeting of some kind in progress. The long conference room was filled with rough characters. Based on the odd angle, Brad suspected the camera had been concealed.

The figure at the head of the table was all too familiar to him. It was the Terror.

Just the image of him sent a pulse a hot rage through him. He felt his hands grip the arms on his chair hard enough to threaten their integrity.

"This was taken by an operative we managed to get into a meeting between the slavers and the Cadre. We haven't identified most of the people, and our man vanished shortly after sending us this image. I assume you know the Terror."

Brad forced his hands to relax. "You know I do."

"Two of the people in this image were killed on the ship you now call *Heart of Vengeance*. This is a high-level meeting. You can see why those two facts strike me as odd."

It was odd. In fact, it was damned odd. Why would slavers of this high rank be involved in attacking the *Louisiana Rain*?

"I'll admit you've caught my attention," he said after a long moment. "I still don't see what you want from me."

She smiled. "I want you to be the bait for a trap. One the slavers will come running to spring."

———

Brad wanted to say no. He really did. He just couldn't bring himself to do it.

Instead, he drove a hard bargain. Bailey wanted him to put his ship at risk, knowing that the slavers would almost certainly attack. As much as he wanted to kill slavers, he couldn't take that kind of risk without ensuring his crew were well compensated.

Commodore Bailey put up only a token fight before conceding to his demands. It wasn't as if she could get someone else to do the job. It was a seller's market.

Satisfied with the terms while still being annoyed he had to work with the disagreeable woman, he made his way back to MOSO. Captain Shelby tried to get details, but Brad put him off. As much as he liked the man, he couldn't be sure he didn't work for the bad guys.

If this was going to work, he had to play things exceptionally close to the vest. That meant letting the rest of the universe think *Heart's* circumstances were completely different from what they really were.

Shelby dropped him off at the boat bay and headed back for *Eternal*. Probably for an epic ass-chewing. He didn't envy the man.

Brad headed back to *Heart* and discovered Mike had just arrived. He went to engineering and found the man looking over the work Jim had done while he was locked up.

"Got a second?" he asked the engineer.

"Maybe in an hour. I have to look at—"

"Let me rephrase," Brad interrupted. "Take a break and come talk with me. Now."

The burly engineer straightened and stared at him for a long moment. "Of course, Captain."

He led the other man to his office and closed the hatch behind them. Marshal, Shelly, and Jason watched them enter without comment. The hatch was thick enough to stop them from hearing anything, even shouting. A distinct possibility, he thought.

"Sit," Brad said as he moved behind the desk. "Tell me what happened last night. All of it."

The other man sat in the chair set before the desk. Brad expected him to be defiant, but he looked abashed.

"I screwed up by the numbers. That's the only way to say it."

Brad made a rolling motion with his hand. "Details. I've spoken with Shelby. I want to hear your side before I tear a strip off you.

"And I expect you to take it. You made a point in telling me how you didn't hold back in telling a superior when they'd screwed up. It's your turn in the barrel."

The big man slumped a little. "I deserve that. Weldon called me yesterday and asked to have a few drinks. I had more than a few while hashing over everything that had happened on *Eternal* back in the day.

"Then he asked if I could introduce the two of you. I didn't let him blow hot air up my ass, and when he admitted Bailey was behind our meeting, I snapped. Words were exchanged and I shoved him."

"And he called security?"

Randall shook his head. "No. There was an off-duty security officer sitting nearby. When the people around us pulled me off, he took me into custody. Shelby tried to talk him out of it, but they're kind of strict on MOSO."

Brad leaned back a little and considered the other man for a long moment. "Before we get into the rest, why is that? They've got a lot of security for a station in the Inner System."

The engineer shrugged. "It probably has something to do with them being the interface to the Outer System. They get a lot of people thinking the same loose rules apply here as do out there. Needless to say, there's some friction."

Brad could see where that might be the case. It didn't really explain things, but it was probably the best he'd get, just asking opinions.

He clasped his hands on top of his desk. "I arrived at the lockup thinking it was Marshal in the drunk tank. Frankly, I expected better of you. For God's sake, you used to be a Fleet officer."

The corner of the other man's mouth twitched. "One cashiered for conduct unbecoming, so I'm not sure that counts. Look, I know I've screwed up. I should've just walked out of there as soon as I found out what the meeting was about. Shelby set me up, but I should've been smart enough to see it coming."

"Yes, you should've been."

He considered the engineer for a full thirty seconds. "The fine for drunk and disorderly is impressive. It's coming out of your pay with an additional ten percent for my trouble. Considering what I'm doing for Bailey, I ought to charge you double."

Randall straightened. "Tell me you didn't let that bitch blackmail you. Tell her to go screw herself. Trust me, it feels good."

"To be fair, Shelby dropped the charges even though Bailey ordered him to keep the pressure on," Brad said. "I went to *Eternal* to tell her off in person, and I did. It *was* satisfying, but we're still doing the job."

The man's eyes narrowed. "It's something you want to do."

"Something I need to do," Brad admitted. "I'd have turned it down otherwise. I'll brief everyone in a few minutes, but I needed to settle this first. In addition to paying the fine, you're restricted to the ship during the next shore leave.

"And I expect you to do most of the menial chores in engineering over the next few weeks. Jim gets the easy stuff while you do your job and most of his. I'll let it sit at that, but this better not happen again."

"It won't. I'm sorry, Captain. I really am."

Brad rose to his feet. "I'll take you at your word. Let's go brief the crew on our next mission."

# CHAPTER EIGHTEEN

BRAD GATHERED his senior officers in the wardroom. Everyone was giving Mike surreptitious looks, except for Saburo. He was openly staring at the engineer with a grin on his face.

Before the noncom could say anything, Brad rapped his knuckles on the table. "Focus, people. We have a new job."

That got their attention.

"We're escorting a science ship out to Io."

"That doesn't sound very exciting," Marshal murmured.

"Neither did escorting a liner," Jason said with a smirk. "Wait for the other shoe to drop."

Brad raised an eyebrow. "What makes you think there's another shoe waiting in the wings?"

"If it was something that straightforward, you wouldn't be having a meeting like this. We'd just pull out of MOSO and get on about our business. You hate meetings."

"Now I'm going to have to start having random meetings to keep you guessing," he told the tactical officer.

Shelly elbowed her boyfriend. "Thanks, genius."

That got laughs from around the table.

"As it turns out, you're right," he told Jason. "The escort job is a cover. Fleet needs us to play siren."

The tactical officer frowned. "Like an ambulance?"

Saburo shook his head with a sad look at the confused man. "You really should read books with more words and fewer pictures. A siren was a mythical being that lured sailors to their deaths on the rocks with only their sweet voices."

"That doesn't make any more sense than running around going 'woooo-ooooo.' What does that even mean?"

"It means we're bait," Randall said in an irritated tone. "Fleet expects someone to come looking for us."

"Essentially true," Brad said. "It turns out the slavers are kind of miffed at us. They put out a bounty of a million credits on *Heart*."

That produced the expected silence around the table as they all digested the news.

"That seems a little extreme," Shelly said. "I don't recall ever hearing about pirates or slavers putting any prices on other ships. They take their risks and move on."

"Something about *Heart* worries them," he said. "The price is for the verified destruction of this ship. Not her capture."

Marshal frowned. "First they steal the computer, and then they want the ship taken out. Yeah, that does sound suspicious."

"Wait," Jason said. "Someone stole the computer? This is the first I've heard about this. I used the damned thing an hour ago."

Mike gave him a pitying look. "Before the refit, genius. Right after Brad captured the ship. Someone broke in, trashed the helm console, and stole the computer core. They wrecked all the peripheral equipment, too."

The engineer turned his gaze to Brad. "They missed something."

"Sounds like," he agreed. "Or at least they're worried they did. The commanding officer on *Eternal* thinks this ship is more heavily connected to the slavers than we thought. Two of the dead bodies from the raid where I captured this ship are connected to the upper echelons of the slaver organization.

"I can't go into the details, but she suspects they have Fleet penetrated. She wants to send us out to lure in a few more slavers to see if we can shake some information loose."

"Sounds risky," Shelly said slowly. "There's no guarantee that we'll get anything other than hired guns. Or that we'll survive the attack if they come in force. Maybe we should sit this out and tear *Heart* apart until we figure out what makes her so important to them."

"We're going to do that, too," he assured them, "but we're not going to sit on the sidelines. We'll take the fight to the slavers. And, through them, the Cadre."

The thought made him grin savagely, evoking a similar expression on Saburo.

"Finally, I and my people get to kick some ass," the mercenary noncom said.

"I sure hope so. You'll need to make sure you have everything you need to board an enemy ship. We want live prisoners."

"I'm already set," the noncom said nonchalantly. "Mike might need to get some gear for us to board wrecks after the fighting, though."

"Don't try to teach your grandmother how to suck eggs," the engineer sneered. "We're already set for that."

Now it was Saburo's turn to look confused. "Why would anyone want to suck eggs? Just scramble them and be done."

"Anyway," Brad said over Mike as he tried to respond. "Everyone needs to get ready to depart within the next twenty hours. The science ship is real and has a schedule. The part the slavers and pirates don't know about is that we'll have a silent escort of our own this time. A trio of Fleet's light corvettes are going to shadow us like we did *Louisiana Rain*.

"When the bad guys come calling, they'll wait until the enemy is committed and then strike. The hope is they can chase the other ships down and force them to surrender. Apparently, they're rigged with more engine than they need and will be able to generate more thrust than just about anyone. Us included."

Once he was sure they'd all caught the gist of what he was saying, he looked at Randall. "Mike, I want you to lead the effort scanning the ship for anything missed during the investigation and refit. If the slavers want the ship dead, then we need to know what they think we have."

He looked doubtful. "We pretty much tore *Heart* apart during the refit. I'm not sure how we could've missed anything significant."

"Consider this a professional challenge, then. Get help from anyone with spare time, including Jim. Now that I think about it, you'll just have to wait to serve out your sentence. Life is too short to wait on this."

The engineer nodded. "I'll start compiling a list of places. I think we need to start with your cabin. If there's a hidden compartment with secrets powerful enough to generate this kind of reaction, it's probably in there. Somewhere."

"If they found some slaver muckety-mucks, then it has to lead back to a slaver base or someone's identity," Marshal said. "The fact they wrecked the helm console leads me to think it's the first one."

"We'll only know for sure if we find it or capture someone on this mission," Brad said. "Someone we can convince to talk."

Saburo smiled coldly. "I can make them talk."

Brad was willing to bet he could.

The intercom came to life. "Captain, you're needed at the airlock." It was another one of the mercenaries.

"It sounds like we're done here," Brad said. "Our lives depend on getting everything ready. This time, we know they're coming for us. Either this trip, the next one, or one after that. Let's use that to our advantage."

He rose to his feet and headed for the airlock while they talked among themselves. Once again, he had a visitor. Two this time, with one he recognized.

Brad opened the airlock and smiled at the two women standing outside. "Lieutenant Greer. You're about the last person I expected to see on MOSO. Didn't I leave you at Io? And who is your friend?"

The Fleet investigator returned his smile. "I get around. May we come in? I'd rather not discuss business in a public area."

"That sounds suitably mysterious. Come right in."

Once he had them inside the ship, he led the pair to his office and once more closed the hatch for privacy. This time, he chose to pull out a spare seat and join them in front of the desk.

After they were all seated, he gave them his full attention. "What's going on?"

"I'm actually here to make an introduction," Greer said. "My associate needs to make sure you believe what she has to say, and I was the most convenient way to make sure that happened."

She turned to the tall woman sitting beside her. "This is Kate Falcone. She's an agent of the Commonwealth Investigative Agency." The last bit was said in a low voice.

He raised an eyebrow. "You're a spy?"

The woman smiled, an expression that accentuated her hawk-like features. "When I need to be. I'm more of a troubleshooter, though. I find fires and put them out.

"If you need a suitably spy-ish name, though, you can call me Agent Falcon. If you'll allow it, I need to ride with you on this mission. I'm hoping to meet a few old friends."

––––––––

Brad considered the woman for a long moment. "Why?"

"Because, like you, I don't trust that Fleet can do what needs doing."

He slid a sidelong glance at the Fleet investigator. She didn't seem all that perturbed at the statement.

"She's right," Greer said. "The Cadre and slavers have connections inside Fleet that give them word of any operation against them. Their success in evading major raids makes that a certainty.

"Worse, I think the rot goes higher. I'm sure the Commonwealth government itself is riddled with powerful people in the pay of, or even directly profiting from, the slave and piracy trades."

"That's a strong statement," he said slowly. "Why tell me?"

The smaller woman smiled. "Because I have confidence that you aren't working for the Cadre or the slavers. I can't think of anyone else I can be so certain of. Well, except for Agent Falcone."

The agent laughed. "Nice save. I'm touched, of course. The fact that

I came to her with instructions to introduce the two of us also plays some role, I'm sure."

"Of course it does," the Fleet investigator said as she rose to her feet. "That concludes my part of the program, I'm afraid. I'll have one of your bridge officers escort me out, Captain. Good hunting to you both."

Brad watched her leave and saw Shelly rising to meet her. Satisfied that the woman wasn't going to wander around his ship, he returned his attention to Falcone.

"We were just discussing what we could do with prisoners. My combat team leader is convinced he can make them talk, if we manage to get our hands on a few live bodies."

The woman nodded. "If we're talking about low-level people, sure. Bigger prizes will keep their lips firmly shut. Or, worse, convince you they're little fish. They have too much to lose.

"That's how I can help. We're very likely to get our hands on someone of significance, if we play our cards right. I'm trained in extracting information."

"I heard what Greer said," Brad said, "but I'm not convinced she told me the whole story. Why trust me?"

"Because you have so much to pay them back for, Captain Madrid. Or would you prefer *Mantruso*?"

That really set him back on his mental heels. Shock was quickly followed by the cold burn of rage in his gut. "I hadn't expected to hear that name again. How did you find out?"

"Hard work. Once the agency became aware of you, I started asking questions and having other agents do the same. No one had ever heard of Brad Madrid. The first place we could link you to was where *Freedom* found you."

The woman smiled a little. "If you're wondering how Commodore Bailey knew, it's because I told her. Don't worry. Only a handful of people have that information, and even less know about Brad Mantruso."

"I'd prefer to keep it that way," he said slowly, forcing his unexpected anger back down. "If the Terror knows I'm coming for him, he'll take steps to see that I'm stopped."

She raised an eyebrow. "Like having the slavers put a bounty on your head, just like they did your ship? Probably. Put your mind at rest. Only my director and I know you went Dutchman from *Mandrake's Heart*. Neither of us ever put it into any report."

"How do I know you or your director aren't working for the Cadre or slavers?"

Falcone shrugged. "It depends on how paranoid you're willing to be. You know what they say. The only way three people can keep a secret is when two of them are dead."

"I think we can safely say I'm not that paranoid," Brad said dryly. "How did you find me?"

"Several of our agents compiled lists of overdue ships in the general area you were found. Once I had that, I started going over the crew manifests. Records are never complete, but your uncle didn't have a reason to hide your presence. I matched your face."

He supposed this day was inevitable, but he'd hoped to put it off for a while. "And I can count on your discretion?"

The woman smiled widely. "Discretion is both of my middle names. I'll never mention your past again. There's no need. I'm much more interested in your current incarnation, Captain Madrid. We're going to become great friends, I think. We both want the same thing, you see."

Her voice turned cold. "I want to see every pirate and slaver floating dead in space. I will scour the system for them, and I feel confident you will help me."

Brad nodded slowly and gave her a small smile of his own. "I think we're going to get along just fine, Agent Falcone. Let's discuss our hunt, shall we?"

# CHAPTER NINETEEN

THEY LINKED up with the science ship the next day, right on schedule. From his seat on the bridge, Brad watched it undock. He knew that Falcone was doing the same from the small cabin they'd loaned her.

He'd offered her a spot on the bridge, but she'd declined, saying she'd take him up on that when they had some real work to do. Blamed a backlog of work she needed to catch up on.

That was probably for the best, he decided. It gave him an opportunity to discuss the new situation with his crew in privacy. Which, he admitted, might have been her intent all along.

"The science ship is clear of her dock," Shelly said. "They're boosting clear of MOSO on minimum thrust."

"Take us after them, John," he said.

"Don't we want to make it look like last time?" the pilot asked. "Like we're not even with them?"

"No. We want any observers to see us going about our business. The longer they think we're fat, dumb, and happy, the better. What about our hidden escorts?"

"No sign of them," Jason said. "Odds are that they left some time ago and are waiting out there for us to come to them. Hopefully not too far out."

"What are the chances we'll see them once we reach them?"

"Pretty good, with our sensors, and we have every reason to be looking hard."

The tactical officer turned in his seat. "What if they aren't out there, boss?"

Brad raised an eyebrow. "You've been spending too much time with Randall. They'll be there."

Privately, he had to admit he shared the same concern. If Fleet was as deeply compromised as he thought, this would be a stellar way to get rid of him. Send him on a throwaway mission where he expected secret backup and then let the enemy kill him.

Or have pirates meet him, pretending to be Fleet vessels. That would be an even better ambush.

He cleared his throat. "Still, it might be best to keep on our toes. I want weapons hot at all times, and we won't trust any stealthed ships too far. Keep an eye out for an ambush from them, too."

Jason's eyes widened as he caught Brad's meaning. "That's sneaky. We'd walk right into their arms. Not happening on my watch."

They followed the science ship out toward deep space and matched its speed when it went to full acceleration. The other vessel wasn't nearly as fast as *Heart*, so that wasn't a problem.

"Incoming signal from the science ship," Shelly said.

Brad straightened. "On screen."

The view of the other ship vanished and was replaced by an older man in a tunic that was somewhere between a uniform and casual wear. His beard was a deep white and he had laugh lines around his eyes.

"Hello?" the man asked. "I'm Dr. Garret Keller, lead scientist and mission commander on *Marie Curie*. Whom am I addressing?"

"Good morning, Dr. Keller. My name is Brad Madrid. I'm the commanding officer on *Heart of Vengeance*."

The doctor smiled. "What a suitably ominous name. Well, I just wanted to take a moment to touch base with you about our intended flight plan."

Brad raised an eyebrow. "We're just going to Io, Doctor. I know the way."

"I'm sure you do, but my people heard something about an attack on a liner between here and Io right before we left MOSO. It might be best to take a more circuitous route."

Brad allowed himself a smile. "We know all about that attack, Doctor. We're the ship that was guarding the liner. We have no reason to expect that group has any interest in your ship, though we of course would like you to maintain a higher-than-average state of readiness in case there *is* any trouble."

That was technically untrue, but he didn't want to panic the researchers. If Fleet hadn't informed them that they'd been selected as a stalking horse, it wasn't his place to inform them. As badly as that made him feel.

Besides, there might be someone in their crew passing information on to the enemy. Let them think he was presuming this to be a milk run.

"I have to say that doesn't completely assuage my concerns," the scientist said with a frown.

"You'll just have to trust us to keep an eye out for you, Doctor. It's the best we can do."

The man sighed. "I suppose so. Will you inform us if we're in danger?"

"Most assuredly."

"Then I'll take that back to my people. Thank you, Captain."

The transmission ended.

"I'm seeing something that might be one of our shadows," Jason said. "It's on the far side of the science ship. Not directly behind it, but close enough."

"Can you send a tight beam at them, Shelly?"

She shook her head. "They're too close to *Marie Curie*. They'd catch the edges of the transmission."

"If we have one shadow, we have three," he told the tactical officer. "Find them."

"It might take a bit. They have really good thermal shielding."

In fact, it took almost five minutes to locate a second ship. It was flanking them and significantly farther out.

"Target them with a tight beam, Shelly. John, make sure we're not in a position where a reply will clue *Marie Curie* in on our concealed escort."

"We're good," the pilot said.

"Ready when you are, Captain," Shelly said.

"Unidentified vessel, this is the mercenary ship *Heart of Vengeance*. Identify yourself and your companion vessels or I will have no choice but to assume you're hostile and take appropriate action."

A moment later, the main screen came to life and showed a scene that made Brad relax a bit. It was a bridge similar to his own—if a bit more cramped—occupied by men and women in Fleet uniforms.

The woman in the command chair smiled at him. "Captain Madrid, I'm Lieutenant Commander Brenda Andre of the Fleet light corvette *Sting*. You have good eyes. I didn't expect you to spot us so soon."

"I have good people. We tagged you and your companion on the other side of *Marie Curie*. We haven't spotted your third ship yet."

"I hope you don't. She's way out in front of us, scouting for enemy ships that happen to be lying in wait."

He nodded. That made perfect sense. "How do you want to play this?"

"We caught your exchange with *Marie Curie*. Let's play it just like that. If trouble comes calling, we'll have the other ship you spotted screen the scientists while we focus on the bad guys. With any luck, we can shoot them down before they even see us."

Brad smiled coldly. "I like the way you think, Commander. Let's go hunt some bad guys."

———

Time passed with the slowness of watching a pot boil. Jason started getting jumpy and seeing ghosts. That wasn't too surprising, since they were spending a lot of time on the bridge. No one was getting enough sleep.

It was John Marshal who spotted the enemy after Brad sent the tactical officer away to get some much-needed rest.

"I have a contact," he said late in the evening on day five. "They're coming up behind us and closing at a very slow rate."

"Signal *Sting* and then call the rest of the crew to battle stations."

Five minutes later, the rest of his people were at their consoles. The ship sneaking up on *Heart* was overtaking her at a relative snail's pace and was still hours away from being a direct threat, but Brad wasn't relaxing.

"*Sting* is moving a bit away from us so they can drop back and get a better look at the enemy vessel," Shelly said. "She says they'll be careful to stay out of easy detection range."

"Did they get any word from the lead corvette?" Brad asked. "If it was me, there would be a hammer to go with the anvil. Something pops up in front of us once the other ship gets close, and then they shoot us in the back."

"Caught between a rock and a hard place," Jason agreed. "We'd be at a huge disadvantage responding to either threat. It would be worse if there were a few more ships out there.

"Using the attack on the liner as an example, if they have three smaller ships ahead of us and one our size behind us, they could really plaster us."

Brad sighed. "As much as I hope that isn't the case, let's count on them detecting and neutralizing the Fleet ship up front before it even sees them. That's the worst-case scenario, so we'll plan on it. What could we do?"

"That depends on what our primary goal is," the tactical officer said as he turned in his seat. "If we're focused on defending the science ship, then we cover them as they make like a bird and fly the hell away. If we're intent on disabling and destroying the enemy, we let *Sting* handle the ship behind us and focus on the ships that pop up ahead."

"What if the ship behind us is a lot bigger than *Sting*?" he asked, playing Devil's advocate.

"They'll still bleed if someone punches their lights out from the dark. The worst case for us would be them spotting *Sting* and killing her. That would leave us handling a lot of ships by ourselves."

The other man considered what'd he'd just said. "Another possibility is that they'll slip into mass driver range and hose us down. If we didn't even know they were there, it would be a very last-minute surprise."

Brad rubbed his face tiredly. "We have to do the best we can with the cards we've been dealt. Fleet is watching over *Marie Curie*. We'll let them focus on her and trust them to do their job.

"Equally, we have to count on *Sting* at least delaying contact between us and the ship back there. They'll also let us know if the enemy starts shooting. They're professionals. So is the scout up front.

"Let's run with the initial plan to accelerate and engage any ships ahead of us. Then we'll come around and help *Sting* if we have to. If we can."

With the long delay before the trailing ship could even get into range to start shooting, he sent his people to eat and get some more rest. He'd crash in his office. He needed to be sharp when the moment came.

---

"Captain!" Jason shouted. "We're on!"

Brad jolted awake. Everdark, he'd been drooling on his desk. That was not how he wanted anyone to see the badass mercenary captain.

He wiped his chin as he staggered out onto the bridge and took his seat, trying to focus his attention. He hit the shipwide intercom. "All hands to battle stations."

Then he stared at the main screen. "What have we got?"

"The Fleet ship up front just tripped an ambush. She says she has engaged three hostile ships. There are torpedoes and mass driver slugs all over the place up there."

"What about the ship on our six?"

"Still in hiding, but they're closer to being in range. If they light off their drives, they'll be in mass diver range in less than twenty minutes."

Fleet had sprung the enemy trap early, Brad realized. The ship trailing them had hoped to get closer. The only question now was whether they'd attack or try to coast in on the fight after *Heart* engaged the ships ahead of her.

If he'd been in their place, that's what he'd have done.

"Full speed ahead. Light up the enemy ships as soon as you have any chance of getting hits with the mass drivers. Shelly, tell *Marie Curie* to head off at a right angle to our course."

His people got to their tasks while he focused his attention on the tactical plot. The fur ball up ahead was ugly. Apparently, the Fleet ship hadn't spotted the attackers until they opened fire. At least she'd been ready to fight.

In the space of five minutes, the battle ahead was settled. The enemy took out the Fleet corvette, but not before it blasted one of them down in return. Dammit.

"One of the remaining ships looks iffy," Jason said as he examined the carnage via his sensors. "I think Fleet got part of him. The drive output is lower now and he's limping along."

The two remaining ships ahead of them were on course for *Heart*. They were ignoring the science ship. If that kept up, the remaining escort would peel off and try to intervene in the coming fight.

"Shots exchanged behind us," Jason said. "*Sting* just punched out the trailer."

The Fleet vessel hadn't made it close enough to identify the enemy ship other than to get the impression it was big. They'd find out now how much trouble they were in.

The ship behind them lit off his drives and Brad realized they were in a *lot* of trouble. That was at least a destroyer back there. The light corvette *Sting* was heavily outgunned.

That didn't stop her from jumping in with both feet. The smaller ship turned on her bigger opponent like a wolf on a bear from closer than Brad had expected her to get.

Torpedoes exploded into the slaver's face from ludicrously short range. There was scant time for the outlaw gunners to react, and their attention must've been firmly on *Heart*, because they didn't respond for critical seconds.

When they did, it was with torpedoes and not defensive mass driver rounds.

At that range, the outcome was about the same as a knife fight in a com booth. *Sting*'s icon vanished in a flare of brilliance even as the destroyer's drives vanished from his repeater.

Brad's anger flared as he watched a brave crew die, but he had to stay focused on the fight ahead of him. Two smaller opponents were still coming for *Heart*.

"I have readings on the hostile ships ahead," Jason said. "I'm pretty sure they're both *Fidelis*-class heavy corvettes like us."

That was very bad news. Not as bad as fighting a destroyer and three heavy corvettes all on their lonesome, but still not a fair exchange of fire. Even if the remaining light corvette interceded on their behalf.

"Do we have a read on the enemy's course? Are they going to ignore *Marie Curie*?"

"It looks like they're more interested in us."

Brad considered that. "Shelly, send a message to the last Fleet corvette. If they can peel off the damaged heavy, we might have a fighting chance. The bastards have to be on the lookout now. Even a feint will do."

"Copy that. I'll see what I can coordinate."

Falcone appeared in the bridge hatchway. "This seems like a good time for me to join you, Captain. I've been keeping track from the cabin, but I'd rather be here if we're going to die."

He gestured for her to come in. "We set up one of the jump seats on the bulkhead over there. Strap in and keep the chatter down to important matters."

"Thank you, Captain."

The woman efficiently secured herself. "It looks like we underestimated the slaver response. We really need to find out why they want this ship in pieces."

"It must be pretty important," he agreed. "We've lost two of our three hidden weapons. I don't think the last Fleet ship is going to want to go head to head with a heavy corvette, even the damaged one."

"You underestimate them, I think. They're not going to back down. The enemy just killed a lot of their friends. They'll want blood."

Right about then, the remaining light corvette engaged her drives and powered in toward the oncoming enemy ships.

"It looks as if you're right," Brad admitted. "Now we get to see how this plays out."

Predictably, the damaged heavy peeled off and headed for the Fleet vessel. It was moving more slowly than Brad had expected, even in a damaged condition. The lead ship must've really mauled it.

"Can we get a read on that ship?" he asked Jason.

"It's down a drive unit, at a minimum," the tactical officer said after a minute. "One of the remaining units might be out of alignment, too. It's skating around as if the pilot can't measure the output consistently."

"Worse than *Heart* when we found her," Marshal agreed. "If the Fleet commander is smart, he might be able to use that to his advantage."

"Pull us to the far side of the enemy flight path," Brad said. "Let's make sure his buddy can't provide any covering fire. In fact, let's see if we can mess him up a little. Start unloading mass driver slugs at the damaged ship. We only have to get lucky once. He's already in bad shape."

The tactical officer shot him a dubious look. "If we dedicate all our Gatlings to him, we won't have them if we need them ourselves. Not without devoting some time to retargeting them."

"We can take the risk for a battle companion."

"You got it."

The odds of hitting the other ship, especially since it was on an unstable flight path, were exceedingly slim. Worth it, though.

"How long until torpedo range with the primary target?"

"Fifteen minutes until effective range."

"But not maximum range?"

Jason turned in his seat again, his frown back. "If we're willing to let the torpedoes go ballistic, no. They won't have any better chances of hitting than mass driver rounds, though. And they're a lot more expensive."

He was going to have to think about that if they made it out of this.

"How well can they see a torpedo after it burns out its drive?"

"They'll have a rough idea of where it is. Not a precise location, but something general."

"We're dodging, right?" he asked Marshal.

"I let a slaver tag us once and you never let me live it down. Yes, we're dodging."

"Good," he said. "Jason, launch some torpedoes to put the enemy off balance. Keep them guessing. Two salvoes."

The other man shrugged and turned back to his console. Moments later, the tactical repeater at Brad's side showed the torpedo launch.

The icons for it and the follow up-salvo made it most of the way to the enemy ship and began flashing as the drives failed.

All of the first set missed by a fairly wide margin. The second grouping was close enough to warrant targeted mass driver fire, though. Only, the other ship didn't fire. It used its drives to swerve farther away from the torpedoes, so none hit it, but that was a damned risky move.

"They didn't fire mass drivers," he mused aloud. "What if Fleet knocked them out in the ambush?"

A plan formed in his mind. It was reckless and his ship would pay the price if he guessed wrong. The demon inside him was pleased. Eager, even. Time to make them bleed.

"John, go to maximum thrust. Minimal dodging. Take us right at the bastard. Jason, Gatlings to defense. We'll let our torpedoes speak for us."

He expected argument, but his crew just implemented his orders. If the enemy did still have mass drivers, this would hurt a lot.

The two ships reached torpedo range right as the tactical plot updated to indicate the damaged enemy ship had taken hits from their mass driver rounds. Pure, blind luck.

Not enough to cripple it, but more than enough to put their defenses into disarray right as the Fleet corvette opened fire with torpedoes. They might make it after all.

But he didn't have time to watch. He had his own life-and-death struggle ahead of him.

"They're firing torpedoes," Jason said. "We have four incoming. This is going to get hairy."

"Keep pressing him."

They both spent torpedoes like they had an unlimited number. This exchange was going to prove costly for Fleet, assuming *Heart* came out the other side intact.

Even with all their Gatlings tasked to defense, some of the enemy torpedoes came far closer than Brad liked. One made it through everything they could throw at it and slammed into *Heart of Vengeance* at full speed.

The impact was like slamming into a wall while running full speed. Damage alarms blared and his repeaters lit up with lurid warnings about failed systems.

"We lost a third of our Gatlings," Jason shouted. "Evasive maneuvers!"

The other ship quietly blew up right at that moment. A full quartet of *Heart*'s torpedoes had slammed into the other ship, ending its existence in an expanding cloud of gas and debris.

His heart soared as he watched them die. This was what he lived for now.

"Torpedoes to defense," Brad snapped.

That was also a costly use for the weapons, but it beat dying.

*Heart* took one more torpedo impact, a glancing shot that slammed them all sideways in their acceleration couches. Then they were clear.

"What's the status of the last enemy vessel?" he asked. It was still on the repeater, engaged in a close torpedo duel with the Fleet warship.

"Leaking air and debris," Jason said. "They're badly damaged. So is the Fleet vessel."

"Take us around. Fire torpedoes as soon as we get into range."

Brad opened a line to engineering. "Talk to me, Mike."

"We're mostly in one piece. That hit up front knocked out a lot of secondary systems, and life support is offline. I'm pretty sure I can get it back up once you stop letting people shoot us."

"That part is about over. We're heading in to help the Fleet ship, but they're coming out on top."

"Then let me do my job."

The connection terminated without another word.

"They got him!" Jason shouted, his fist pumping in the air. "The Fleet ship took him out!"

A single look at the repeater showed the story. The other heavy corvette was gone. His side had survived the ambush. Some of them, at least.

"Take us to *Sting*'s last reported location," Brad ordered tiredly, his energy guttering out with his rage. "We'll make sure the destroyer is out of action and start search-and-rescue operations. Let the other Fleet ship go check on the forward scout. Once we're sure it's safe, *Marie Curie* can assist."

His most decisive battle with the Cadre and slavers to date was over. The demon inside him was pleased at how they'd made the enemy pay, but it was time to see how much it had cost them.

# CHAPTER TWENTY

To Brad's utter astonishment, there were survivors on what was left of *Sting*. The light corvette was blown open but had only split into two large pieces. Once they got close enough, Shelly started picking up short-range distress beacons and calls for help.

Saburo and his men led the way in after the survivors. The small ship had a crew of eight, and they managed to pull five living people from the wreck, including Lieutenant Commander Brenda Andre.

It was a good thing that Dwayne Holmes, one of the mercenaries, and Falcone both had significant medical training, or they might have lost two of the injured before *Marie Curie* arrived on scene with a real doctor.

The news from the scout in front was grim. There were no survivors from the other ship.

The operational corvette had taken damage and lost some of their people too, so half of the Fleet personnel with them had died in the fight. It made his blood boil. Even in victory, there would be no cheering today.

They transferred all of the wounded to *Marie Curie* and turned their attention to the tumbling destroyer. Its power was offline and it hadn't shown any hint it was ready to fire torpedoes. It might be completely dead.

Or it might be playing possum and waiting for someone to poke it.

Brad joined Saburo and his men in the shuttle. They'd find out soon enough.

Falcone numbered shuttle piloting among her skills, so Brad left Marshal on *Heart*. If this derelict came to life, he wanted his ship to get clear as quickly as possible.

They approached the hulk from the rear. None of the ship's weapons covered that angle. With the way the wreck tumbled, Falcone had to bring them in fast once the ship was swinging away from *Heart*.

*Sting* had really done a number on the enemy ship. One of her torpedoes had taken the pirate right in engineering and blown out the fusion plant before it could explode. Hell, it had cleared the entire compartment and actually dismounted one of the drives.

The other torpedoes had punched holes deep into the ship's armor all along her spine. While there might be survivors, there wouldn't be a lot of them.

"Damn," Falcone muttered. "Andre really kicked him in the balls."

"And how," Brad agreed with deep satisfaction. "I think we should use the cargo lock. It's intact and will have backup power. That section of the ship is more intact than a lot of the rest, too."

He turned in his seat. "Saburo, the hull is compromised everywhere. It's in one piece, but he could come apart without much warning. Keep the grenades to a minimum."

"You're taking all the fun out of this," the man grumbled. "We'll be careful, Captain. Let me say once more that I think you should leave this to us. I don't care how much you enjoy killing pirates; it's our job."

The words were innocuous, but the mercenary's expression was not. He was watching Brad closely and with more than a hint of concern.

That splashed a little water on Brad's rage but didn't extinguish it. He'd see the bastards pay.

"We'll let you go in first, but I'm coming along and so is Agent Falcone," he said firmly. "We need intelligence. Don't forget we want *a few* people we can question."

He made sure to emphasize *a few*. He'd rather not let any of them survive.

"That's all up to them," the mercenary said nonchalantly. "If they fight, we'll stop them. All I can do is offer them the chance to surrender. Which, by the way, is far better than they deserve."

That answer satisfied Brad.

Falcone snorted. "Since the penalty for piracy is death, I suspect we won't get many takers. The best chance we have to get live prisoners is to pull any wounded off the ship as we go. If they're like *Sting*, we might get lucky."

She deftly brought the shuttle to the enemy's hull right beside the cargo lock and latched on with monofilament grapnels.

"I'm locking the controls so no one walks off with our ride. The code is 123-0-789-0. Not too complicated in an emergency, but not so easy that an intruder will figure it out before we get back."

The security officer buried inside Brad wasn't exactly pleased with her cavalier notions, but he wasn't going to argue. They had pirates or slavers to capture. He'd figure out which group they were once this was all over.

They made their way out the airlock and crouched beside the cargo entrance to the dead ship. There in deep space, it was pitch black when the hull rotated away from the sun. Even when they were in the light, it was dimmer than he'd like.

The constant movement meant there could be pirates in the shadows that he might not see until the last moment. Or at all. He'd find out when the shooting started.

Falcone used a small torch to cut away the controls. "This is probably locked and will certainly announce our arrival to someone if I don't bypass the security."

It took her five minutes to satisfy herself and activate the airlock. The cargo bay was in vacuum, so she opened both locks at once.

They weren't carrying cargo. The compartment was filled with dead men and women.

"Holy shit," one of the mercenaries muttered as they entered the tomb.

"Cut the chatter and make sure everyone is really dead," Saburo snapped.

"It looks like they were preparing boarding parties," Falcone said. "They hadn't suited up yet. *Sting* took them down with no warning and killed their biggest offensive force."

Brad played his light around the compartment and tried to suppress a surge of unholy joy. This was just what they all deserved.

The large area had a few emergency lights, but nothing close to what was needed to see everything clearly. There were dozens of enemy troops there. Lots of weapons, too, including heavy weapons.

"Looks like slavers," he said. "Pirates wouldn't have so many guns."

"I've never understood that," Falcone said as she scanned the compartment. "Why limit yourself to a blade, pistol, and the occasional shotgun when you have frangible rounds?"

"Tradition and risk minimization, I suppose. If we ever capture a live pirate, I'll ask him." Fat chance.

They closed the airlock behind them. He didn't want any potential evidence floating off. Then they headed deeper into the ship. The crew hadn't fared much better than the boarding party. It seemed they weren't going to find many live slavers.

"The next section has air," Saburo said from up front. "We can get through the personnel lock in the pressure door. There might be paying customers after all."

Saburo sent four of his men through the emergency bulkhead. One of them reported back almost immediately.

"We're taking fire and advancing. It isn't too heavy, but mind your heads."

Brad let the rest of his men go through before he and Falcone advanced. The fighting had pushed farther up the corridor by then. It was weird how he couldn't hear the shooting until the lock filled with air to carry the noise.

The resistance wasn't all that bad, but a pistol wielded by a terrified slaver crewman could still kill the toughest mercenary. Saburo took no chances, having his men lay down withering fire until the shooting stopped.

The mercenaries advanced slowly, checking each of the bodies as they passed. The bleeding corpses were mostly men, but a few females filled the slaver ranks. Brad would never understand what could drive people into this kind of sick madness.

That's when he discovered they'd missed someone in one of the cabins. A woman triggered a mono-blade and came barreling out with a shriek.

He drew his own blade and barely got it up in time, deflecting her slash away from Falcone and into the bulkhead. As much as he hated the idea, he was going to try and take her alive.

The woman wasn't that skilled, which actually made his defense more dangerous. One never knew what an inexperienced fighter would do next.

Before he could attempt a risky disarm, Falcone shot the woman several times. The slaver collapsed.

"I was going to take her," he said as he checked the woman. She was dead. Part of him was pleased, but the professional side of him was mildly annoyed.

"Maybe," Falcone said, holstering her pistol. "Maybe not. Sorry to cut in on your dance, but I'd rather have you alive and uninjured than get a prisoner."

"No live ones," Saburo reported a few minutes. "Sorry about missing that one, boss."

"Don't stress over it. This looks like crew quarters. A lot of the slavers were probably at duty stations. Maybe we'll find some up front."

In fact, they did. Ones with more guns.

The scene reminded him of the slaver attack on *Louisiana Rain*. The bridge blast doors were partly open, and an unknown number of slavers were crouched behind them. The fight was eerily silent since the attackers had transitioned back into vacuum.

Brad cycled through frequencies on his suit radio until he found the channel the slavers were using. It wasn't encrypted like the mercenary signals.

He cut over someone shouting for the slavers to keep firing. "This is Captain Brad Madrid of the mercenary frigate *Heart of Vengeance*.

You came looking for us. Here we are. As much as I'd like to shoot every single one of you, I'm calling on you to surrender."

"Screw you," the first man shouted. "We're already dead men. We'll go down hard, taking you with us."

With the fusion plants gone, they'd have to do it the old-fashioned way: with guns or blades.

"Perhaps not," Falcone said. "I am Agent Falcone of the Commonwealth Investigative Agency. If any of you surrenders now and cooperates fully, I'll see that the death penalty is taken off the table. That offer has a very short shelf life, so you'd best take it before I change my mind."

Needless to say, that started quite the argument among the slavers.

While they bickered, Brad switched over to the encrypted frequency. "You're not really going to let them off, are you?"

He tasted bitter disappointment at the idea. A few prisoners were one thing. There might be a dozen slavers in there. They had to pay.

"There are worse things than death," she retorted. "I was thinking the lead mines on Mercury."

He shivered and then smiled. That was where the Commonwealth sent their worst offenders. The living conditions were as good as modern technology could make them, but on those sun-blasted plains, the mining facility was exceedingly dangerous.

Prisoners arrived with a life sentence, and they served it as quickly as one might imagine.

"I'll wager you don't mention that up front," he said dryly, satisfied with the proposed punishment.

"Damn straight. Otherwise, they'd fight to the death for sure."

It sounded as if the shouting man was losing the argument. His men—for he sounded like their commander—weren't interested in dying today.

A loud grunt and a curse sounded, and a new voice came on. "We surrender. We're tossing our guns out."

Brad watched the weapons come flying over the blast shield. Mostly pistols, a few rifles, one shotgun, a pile of mono-blades, and knives by the score.

Once the flood stopped, Falcone spoke again. "You'd best make sure there aren't any more weapons. If we find anyone holding out, they get escorted to the nearest airlock."

Half a dozen additional knives and a pair of pistols came out.

"That's it. We're done."

"Come out one at a time with your hands up," Brad said. "Move slowly and obey my men."

A dozen men and one woman walked out of the bridge with their hands up. Saburo and his people quickly searched them for weapons and strapped their hands behind their backs with disposable cuffs.

Brad led the way onto the bridge. It was as much a wreck as the rest of the ship. A single figure in a vacuum suit lay sprawled on the floor. Probably the pirate leader.

To his astonishment, the man was still alive. He had blood on the inside of his helmet, so he wasn't doing that great. It looked as if someone had shot him in the back and then slapped a patch on his suit. Considerate, that. Or cruel. He couldn't decide which.

The man was crawling toward the captain's chair, so it was a good bet he had a weapon concealed there.

Brad planted a boot in the man's back, eliciting a scream of agony. "Where you going, sport? The party is the other way."

"Screw you," the slaver moaned.

"No, screw you. I have some bad news. You didn't take Agent Falcone's generous offer, so as ship's captain I can declare you guilty of piracy. The penalty is death and I can make sure the sentence is carried out right now. It's up to you to convince me otherwise."

Falcone held up a pistol. "Look what I found stashed in the armrest. Naughty man."

She squatted near the slaver. "I'd love to help you out here, but Captain Madrid is absolutely right. You're going to have to do some damned fast talking to avoid the airlock. If, of course, you don't just bleed out first."

"I'll never tell you squat."

"Saburo, escort Captain Fancy Pants to the forward airlock," Brad said. "I could just pull his helmet off, but I'm feeling traditional today."

"Yes, sir."

The wiry mercenary and two of his men hoisted the wounded slaver to his feet, secured him with disposable cuffs, and dragged him forward. It wasn't far. They could still see the other prisoners from beside the airlock.

Part of this charade made him a little sick to his stomach in spite of the burning hatred trying to eat its way out of him. Sending him Dutchman might be satisfying, but if he did, he'd be the one that had to live with doing so for the rest of his life. A sobering thought.

As a slaver officer, he would know useful things. Even if he didn't talk, the others would be able to hear everything the three of them said over their radios. This would be a good time to be instructive.

Brad shoved the prisoner into the airlock and Falcone trailed them.

Once the three of them were inside, he closed the inner hatch and brought the pressure up. Then he removed the slaver's helmet and his own. If he was going to do this, he wanted the other man to see the face of his executioner.

The brawny man was heavily bearded and he had a scar running across his nose. Blood dripped from his lips. The shot to his back must've clipped a lung. The wet sound of his breathing confirmed that.

"The only question now is whether I jettison you with your helmet on or off," Brad said coldly. "Convince me to leave it off and this is over quick. Be an ass and I put it on and leave your hands cuffed while I send you out to die slowly. Be particularly troublesome and I'll add some extra air to your suit first."

The man looked as if he wanted to spit in his face, so Brad turned him around to face the outer door.

"Look out the port," he said softly. "That's the last thing you're going to see. Do you want to do that for hours or seconds?"

The man hyperventilated a bit before he shook his head. "I can pay for my life."

"Your money is no good here."

"Data! I have information on the slaver leadership that those traitors don't."

"The fact you call them traitors means we can't trust a thing you tell us," Falcone said coolly. "You'll say anything at all to save your skin but lie about the important parts."

"Tell me why you're chasing me," Brad said. "How did you know I'd be here?"

"The leadership put a price on your head," the man said tiredly. "A million credits for the verified destruction of your ship. We have ears in Fleet. We knew you'd be heading for Io today. Hell, we came running once we heard you was on Mars."

"What's so important about my ship?"

The man shrugged. "Nobody said. It used to be one of ours, so I was thinking it was just revenge."

No way. Not for a million credits.

"I'm not hearing any information worth your life," he said after a moment. "You better reach deeper."

"I came from a meeting where our leadership talked with the Cadre. The Terror was there. It was a big deal."

"Where was the meeting held?" Falcone asked.

"Deep space. We brought the bigger ships together to talk strategy. The Terror wants us to up our activity around Mars. That's why we were so close."

One question answered, though the information raised new ones. "What exactly did they discuss?" he asked.

"Can't say. I wasn't at the table."

"This is a lot of nonsense," Falcone said. "You're holding out on us."

"I'm still the only slaver commander you've captured. You're not going to kill me." He sounded smug.

"Put your helmet on," she told Brad. "I'm bleeding off the atmosphere."

Sure she was bluffing, he resealed his helmet.

Falcone reached over to the airlock controls and started dropping the pressure slowly. "Before it gets so you can't hear us, you should know that I'm only stopping if you give me a base location."

The man laughed wetly. "The leadership don't trust the likes of us with base locations. They have pilots that meet up with us and take us where we need to go. Same for the Cadre."

That complicated matters. Brad wondered how they'd ever locate the major bases without getting their hands on a pilot with the coordinates.

The man coughed again and spat up a little more blood. "Wait," he gasped. "I have some hardcopy in my safe."

"Once again, we could have guessed that," Falcone said. "One last try. Tell me something worth my time or we say goodbye."

"There's a boss on Ganymede."

She reached out and reversed the pressure. Air flooded back into the lock.

"Finally, you begin to interest me. Tell me about him."

The slaver coughed and spat up more blood as he gasped. "I saw him at the meeting. More of an ass than most. Sneered at everyone. The leadership acted like he was somebody important."

"That's pretty generic," Brad said. "Details."

"He runs a spaceship company. I think his name was Dean. Only saw him for a minute before they whisked him into the meeting. I wasn't even supposed to see that much."

Brad felt his lungs freeze. "Astro Transport?"

The man straightened. "Yeah. Dean with Astro. That's the guy."

"Tall guy, big muscles? Long brown hair?" That was completely the opposite of the short, balding, red-faced Breen whom Brad had met on Ganymede.

The slaver shook his head. "Not even close. Kinda short with very little hair. Big voice, though."

"Just checking."

That was far more confirmation of Breen's identity than Brad had ever expected to get. The fact the weasel was a slaver boss stunned him. The man was right there in plain sight. And he'd gone after one of his own liners. Why?

He and Falcone kept pushing the slaver, but it became clear that he didn't have any other world-shaking information.

"I think we're done here," she told Brad. "Let's wrap this up."

She then reached over to the control panel and blew the outer lock. It flew open and sent the helmetless slaver tumbling into the void with a rapidly expanding puff of air.

Brad might have followed the suddenly dead man if she hadn't grabbed him tight. He started to say something, but she made a slashing gesture across her throat.

"Use the encrypted channel," she said on that frequency. "I don't want the prisoners hearing this."

It took him a few fumbling moments to change over. "Why did you do that?"

Part of him—the dark demon in his gut—gloried in the man's death. The tattered remains of the young man he'd been quailed at what had just happened.

"Because he richly deserved it. That was too easy, by my way of thinking. Only the fact he gave us something useful made me show mercy, just like you said."

"I was bluffing!"

"I wasn't."

He couldn't say she was wrong, but he'd yet to kill anyone who hadn't tried to kill him first. As much as he'd wanted to do exactly that, actually doing it brought him face to face with the monster inside him. He didn't like what he'd seen.

Her expression softened a little. "I knew you wouldn't do it, Brad. Not in the end. It's not your way, so I did what had to be done. He's not the first pirate or slaver I've executed after we captured them. He won't be the last. Justice is served.

"Also, it'll make the other prisoners cooperate more completely. They won't lie or hold things back if they know I'll space them. Which I will."

Brad took a deep breath. "We should get back inside. We need to tear this ship apart and get what data we can."

"You recognized the man from Ganymede." That hadn't been a question.

"Fabian Breen," Brad said. "He wanted to seize my ship. I guess he was behind the break-in and theft of my computer after all. I'm not sure what we can do about it, though. The man is an ass, but he's a member of the community there. No way they'll believe he's a slaver without proof."

She smiled coldly. "Then we'll get proof. I'm a really good investigator."

# CHAPTER TWENTY-ONE

IT TOOK them three days to scour the wrecked destroyer—a missing Fleet vessel, it turned out. The slavers had changed her name from *Vigilant* to *Chained Woman*. Sickening but hardly unexpected.

Worse, the papers in the safe had been of little practical value and the computers had been blasted into ruin. The only useful data they'd get off the wrecked ship was from the prisoners.

Lieutenant Commander Andre and the other Fleet survivors had moved to the light corvette *Striker*. Brad headed over to the crowded little ship as soon as they finished going over the derelict.

She met him at the airlock, her right arm still in a cast and sling. Primitive but effective until they got somewhere with more advanced medical care.

The right side of the woman's face had a spectacular scar and her nose was bandaged. He hadn't heard, but he expected it was broken just because of the bruises that made her look like a raccoon. The woman was in good condition compared to some of her compatriots.

"Captain Madrid," she said in a formal tone. "Welcome aboard *Striker*."

He smiled and dipped his head. "Thanks. How is everything

holding up here? I don't recall if anyone told me what damage she suffered. If they did, I've forgotten."

"You've been busy. Come on in and I'll show you to our wardroom, such as it is. We can talk freely there."

Brad fell in behind her and threaded his way past the crewmen still doing repairs. They all gave him warm smiles.

Andre and he squeezed into the cramped wardroom and she closed the hatch. "The damage is relatively minor, all things considered, but more than enough to keep Lieutenant Commander Meriden busy.

"He sends his apologies for not being there to meet you. He and the engineer are trying to salvage one of the drives. It's bad enough but better than what happened to *Sting* and *Troubadour*." The last came out in a sad sigh.

"I'm sorry you lost so many people," he said softly. "You got a raw deal."

"We're Fleet. We don't hold back when people need us."

"In case you hadn't heard, the destroyer was a Fleet ship once. *Vigilant*. The bastards renamed her *Chained Woman*."

Her expression soured. "I heard. I sent that information back to Mars when I reported. Oh, and I have news of my own. We have reinforcements on the way. They'll relieve me and escort you the rest of the way to Io. Congratulations, you're getting a cruiser. *Freedom*."

Well, that might be a bit awkward. Particularly if they didn't know who they were coming to escort. He'd find out soon enough if Commodore Bailey had told them anything. Based on her personality, she probably hadn't.

"When can we expect them? I'm feeling a little naked out here; no offense."

"None taken. They're coming at flank speed, so they'll be here in another twenty hours."

"Are you going to get into trouble for going toe to toe with the destroyer?" He couldn't bring himself to call the ship by the slaver name, but it felt wrong to use her old Fleet identification.

"We'll see. I lost my ship, so they'll seat a board of inquiry. Against the forces we faced, I'm surprised any of us made it. They had three heavy corvettes and a destroyer arrayed against your heavy corvette and our three lights. We're here and they're not. I suspect my career will survive."

Her eyes narrowed a little. "I hear you're holding the surviving slavers. Mind telling me what you have in mind for them?"

How the hell had she heard? He had the slavers locked into *Heart*'s hold, chained to the very hooks that other slavers had used to move their prisoners.

His people wouldn't have talked. The commander didn't know Falcone was on his ship, so she couldn't have told anyone. Who had leaked the information?

"That's right," he finally admitted. "How did you know?"

"I didn't. Not until right this moment. Your expression gave you away when I put you on the spot. Feel free to tell me why you haven't turned them over to me yet. This had better be good."

She was damned smart. It served him right for not planning ahead for something like that.

"I can't go into specifics, but I have the authority to hold them." That was true, since Falcone had ordered him to do so. "You don't have room for them here, anyway."

"That's beside the point," the Fleet officer said harshly. "Those bastards killed half my people and destroyed two Fleet vessels. You *will* turn them over to me."

As much as he wanted to, he couldn't. Not quite. He'd stared into the abyss and it had stared back at him. He *knew* what the lieutenant commander wanted—and he wasn't prepared to let her pay the price that came with it.

"Regretfully, I will not. You want revenge for what they did to your people. I get that, but I can use them to get me closer to the slaver leadership. *Freedom* gets here soon. We'll let her captain make the final decision."

Since Falcone was the ace up his sleeve, he already knew how that would play out, but the chance of getting her way would be a salve to the commander's pain.

Andre sighed and slumped a little in her seat. "That's probably for the best. Revenge is exactly what I want. What needs to happen is justice. I'm praying the two are the same in this case, but that's a better call for someone like *Freedom*'s captain to make."

Her words were like an accusation, stripping away the pretense from his hungry rage. He had to be honest with himself. Vengeance was what he craved, but was he willing to pay with his soul to have it? One way or another, he needed to answer that question while it still made a difference.

"What will you do once *Freedom* arrives?" he asked, changing the subject.

"I'll take us back to Mars. As I said, *Striker* took some drive damage, so we'll need a few weeks to make the trip. There are other ships on the way to escort us home. Then comes telling everyone what happened a few million times.

"Thank the Everlit we managed to recover the data recorders from *Sting* and *Troubadour*. That's going to make things somewhat easier. I appreciate you passing on your sensor readings. All of that will make a good composite of what we saw."

"Considering what we faced, I think our ambush was a rousing success," he said. "The price was high, but I've already picked up a few leads that might hurt the slavers."

He probably shouldn't have said that, but he wanted to give her hope. To make sure she understood their sacrifice really meant something.

"Keep that to yourself," he added hastily. "The slavers and Cadre have ears in Fleet. I doubt there are any on this ship, but if they get wind of what we're up to, they'll get away again."

She shot him a penetrating look. "I hope you aren't just yanking my chain. Okay, I'll keep my mouth shut, but you have to promise that I'll hear what comes of this. The whole story."

"I swear it. Trust me on this, if we roll the slavers up, everyone will hear about it."

---

Brad was back on *Heart*'s bridge when *Freedom* arrived. This was the moment of truth. Time to find out if Captain Fields had been read into the whole story.

"Incoming signal from *Freedom*," Shelly said.

He took a deep breath. "On screen."

The stunning view of the Fleet cruiser vanished to be replaced by Captain Fields in his command seat. The one Brad had modeled his own after.

The officer opened his mouth to speak, but his eyes widened and nothing came out.

"Captain Fields," Brad hurriedly said to cover the awkward gap. "Brad Madrid. It's a pleasure to meet you. I can't say how good it makes me feel to have *Freedom* keeping an eye on us."

Fields closed his mouth and smiled, though Brad noted it was a tad wry. "Captain Madrid. Fleet lives to serve. I wasn't sure what I expected to find out here when Commodore Bailey commed me, but this isn't it. You and the Fleet personnel pulled off an amazing victory."

"We should talk about that in person."

"Oh, yes. I think that's a capital idea. I'll send a shuttle over to pick you up right away. If you don't mind, I'd like to meet with you privately before you bring any of your officers over."

Brad felt the corner of his mouth twitch. "That sounds like an excellent plan. I do have a passenger aboard that needs to be present, though."

The other man's eyebrow rose slightly. "Oh? If you think that best. We have a few things to speak about that require some…ah, discretion."

"My associate is very discreet."

"Then I look forward to meeting you both in person. Until then."

The communication ended.

Shelly frowned. "Is it just me or did he sound a little weird?"

"I'm sure it has something to do with what Commodore Bailey told him," Brad said as nonchalantly as he could. "Or perhaps with what she didn't tell him. I'll find out soon enough."

"Maybe it's a trap," Jason said, frowning. "He might be in the pay of the Cadre or slavers."

"I seriously doubt that. Not after everything I've heard about him from Commander Andre. Even if he was, his crew can't all be bad guys. I'll be perfectly safe."

The tactical officer didn't seem convinced, but he only shrugged. "You're the captain. A shuttle just came out of the cruiser and is on the way over."

Brad rose. "Then I'd best go meet it. I'll be back shortly."

Falcone was waiting at the lock when he got there. She'd dressed in the same uniform his crew used. He wondered who she'd borrowed it from. The woman was far too tall to have used one of Shelly's, and any from his male crewmembers would need a bit of tailoring to fit so well.

"Nice uniform," he ventured.

"I hope so. I stole it from your closet."

He raised an eyebrow. "I don't recall giving you the code to get into my quarters."

"You didn't."

"You do get around, Agent Falcone. It looks good on you. Are you going to be able to put it back the way you found it?"

"The alterations I made were fairly minor. You'll never know."

*Heart* shuddered a bit as the shuttle docked. Brad opened the lock and the two of them made their way through and onto the Fleet boat. It didn't surprise him one bit to find Lieutenant Mackenzie piloting the small craft.

The woman smiled at him politely, as if she'd never met him before. "You must be Captain Madrid. Lieutenant Helen Mackenzie."

He took her hand. "It's good to see you again, Lieutenant. My associate already knows I was aboard *Freedom* at one time."

"Kate Falcone, Commonwealth Investigative Agency," the other woman said as she extended her hand. "We'd like to keep the connection as close to the vest as we can."

"I'll bet," the pilot said wryly. "You gave the captain a real shock. Allow me to say that you've gone a lot farther in the last few months than I'd have expected, Brad. Well done."

"I had some help."

She gave him a penetrating look. "I assume you recovered your memories. Is this who you were all along?"

He shook his head. "No, but it's who I am now. I wish I could say more, but I'm sure Captain Fields will pass along the details to you and everyone else that knows me."

"Not so you'd know," the pilot said as she sat back into her couch. "He's cleared the boat bay and corridors between it and the wardroom. Only he, the bridge crew, and I know who you are. He plans on keeping it that way for the time being."

That sounded like an excellent idea to Brad. He really doubted there were spies aboard the cruiser, but it paid to be cautious.

The pilot flew them over to the cruiser in just a few minutes. The boat bay looked exactly as he remembered it, though eerily empty of people. Mackenzie shut the shuttle down and escorted them off.

As she'd indicated, the corridors they passed through were empty. It was like walking through a ghost ship.

The pilot rapped on the hatch to the wardroom and it slid open. "Captain Madrid and his companion are here to see you, Captain."

Fields stood there, eyeing Brad with a mixture of curiosity and something else for a long moment before he turned to his pilot.

"If you'd keep watch outside the hatch, I'd appreciate it. No one in or out."

"Aye, sir."

Brad gestured for Falcone to precede him in, then closed the hatch behind him. "Captain Fields, it's good to see you again. This is Agent Kate Falcone of the Commonwealth Investigative Agency."

The older man shook her hand and then turned to him. "And to think I was offering you a midshipman's tabs two months ago. Let's just say you've wildly exceeded my expectations, Captain."

Brad grinned. "Well, things *have* taken a few unexpected turns, I'll grant you. Agent Falcone and I have quite the story to tell you."

The officer gestured toward the conference table. "Sit while I get us something to drink. I have to confess that I expect this will be fascinating."

# CHAPTER TWENTY-TWO

"So, let me see if I have everything straight in my mind," Captain Fields said once Brad and Falcone had laid everything out, minus Brad's original identity, of course.

"You've got a lead on a slaver on Ganymede, but you don't want me to report that to my superiors. I can't begin to tell you how upset that would make them. I have a duty to report this so officials on Ganymede can take action."

Falcone smiled politely. "We have no proof. Not even decent circumstantial evidence. It's my job to find out for sure. Then I'll be the one taking the action.

"And if we tell anyone, word will certainly get out. The Cadre and slavers have every governmental organization in the Outer system penetrated. Almost certainly the Inner System, too. Tell me I'm wrong."

The Fleet captain shot her a disgruntled look. "You damned well know I can't say that. They have more than enough money to buy people off. That doesn't change my duty, though. I'll get into a lot of trouble if I keep this quiet."

"Not if I issue an investigative injunction requiring you to coop-erate with me," she said smugly. "Which I'm doing."

He raised an eyebrow. "Can you do that? I mean, am I bound to assist you to that degree?"

"You are if I have enough backing." She pulled a data chip from her pocket and slid it over to him. "This should cover that nicely."

Fields picked it up and slid it into a handy reader. After a few moments, he laughed. "I suppose it does, though this sounds like something out of *The Three Musketeers.*"

Brad felt himself frowning. "Excuse me?"

The officer focused his attention on Brad. "This is an order from Admiral Weber—the man who runs Mars Defense Command—to any and all Fleet personnel to assist the bearer to any degree that is otherwise lawful. I suppose keeping my mouth shut falls inside those parameters."

"I remember the story now," Brad said. Bailey, it seemed, wasn't operating entirely on her own—and Commonwealth Fleet didn't go any higher than Weber until you reached Earth orbit. "We might need more than that, though. If Fabian Breen really is senior in the slavers' organization, we might get a lead on where they have major bases. The pirate commander said they kept that information tight, so only trusted pilots knew the specifics, but that could've been a lie."

Captain Fields's expression became more serious. "If we get a slaver base location, I'm not going to have enough firepower to be certain we take it cleanly. Those bastards kill their prisoners. One thing you can count on slavers having plenty of is slaves. We'll need more ships and people to do it right."

"I have a few ideas along those lines," Brad said with a smile. "And speaking of prisoners, Agent Falcone has the survivors from the slaver destroyer on my ship.

"Commander Andre wants them spaced—and so do I, when it comes right down to it—but Falcone made a deal with them. I told Andre that you would make the final decision, but only because I couldn't reveal my ally."

"So, you're making me the heavy?" Fields asked wryly. "That's not very nice."

"If we make a major break in the slavers' organization, I'll let you take the official credit, too," Falcone said. "Look, this is critical. These bastards will wish I'd let the two of you space them by the time this is all done. Trust me on that."

"I don't give a rat's ass who claims credit," Fields said bluntly. "I just want to kill every last one of them. If I can make that happen, you'll have my complete cooperation. Admiral Weber gave me a fig leaf that I can use to run naked through the town square with, if I need to.

"I'll tell the good commander I'm keeping them close for the moment. I'll take them aboard, too. I suspect I have a more appropriate place to keep them secure than you do."

"Better, perhaps, but hardly more appropriate," Brad said. "I have them in *Heart*'s old slave hold."

That earned him an appreciative nod. "Very nice. I heartily approve of the irony. Still, do you want to chance them getting loose in the middle of a fight?"

"No. You can have them. What you do with them is between you and Agent Falcone."

"I'll send boats for them as soon as we're done, then. Commander Andre and the survivors have already indicated they're ready to start back to Mars, so we can work out any other details on the way."

"I worry about what Fleet will do to her," Brad said with a sigh. "She really kicked the slavers' asses, but she lost her ship."

"Don't worry about official repercussions," Fields said. "I've already reviewed the preliminary reports she filed. Her conduct was impeccable. She did *everything* right. The fact she survived is a testament to her skills and those of her people. No, she's going to be fine, career-wise."

The officer sighed heavily. "It'll be the ghosts of dead friends that haunt her dreams. The people she's always going to believe she could've saved if only she'd been just a little better, just a little more prepared."

"We all have those ghosts," Brad admitted. "The only thing we can do is be worthy of the sacrifice they made for us."

The officer's eyes narrowed. "That's something from your past," Fields observed. "You did get your memories back. I'd wondered."

Brad nodded. "The details aren't important to this discussion, but I did. There are people I wished I'd been able to save. Like I told you the first time we met, the Terror and his ilk are going to pay.

"I consider the slavers a down payment on that account. Not only are they worth eliminating in their own right, but their loss will hurt the pirates, too."

"I think we've about covered everything for the moment," Falcone said. "We'll have plenty of time to work out the details as we head to Io. The most critical thing is that we keep the slavers from suspecting we know anything more about them now than we did before the attack."

"We barely do," Fields grumbled. "I'll keep the number of people that know about the prisoners limited to people I trust implicitly. I'll also have my officers ride herd over all the communications gear.

"We're on radio silence from here on out, so far as the crew is concerned. We can talk back and forth with your ship, but I'll lock the coms down to the bridge and my office. In fact, I'll secure them with a code only I and my XO know."

"And once we get to Io?" Brad asked.

The officer smiled coldly. "Then I wave goodbye and head off on our next mission. Only, that means waiting at a prearranged location nearby, still under radio silence. If you find something, we'll be along real quick."

Falcone shot the Fleet officer a matching grin. "I'll get what we need. Their leadership has no reason to suspect we know about Breen. The dead commander wasn't supposed to know he existed. Oh, the prisoners know about him, too. They were listening in when I questioned the man."

"Then I'll make doubly sure they don't speak to anyone at all. We can do this."

Brad gave them a cold smile all his own. "Yes, we can. Thank you both for everything you're doing. Now, if you'll excuse us, we need to get back to my ship and refine the plan. We'll talk again tomorrow."

"Before you go, I think a toast is in order."

The Fleet captain rose to his feet and went over to a locked cabinet. It yielded to his thumbprint.

Once he opened it to their view, Brad saw various alcoholic beverages. That made him laugh. "I thought Fleet frowned on things like booze."

"This is for special occasions," the man said with an airy sniff. "Only the executive officer and I can get in. Name your poison."

It took only a minute for him to pour the requested drinks and return. He raised his glass. "To the death of the slavers."

Brad raised his glass in return. "And the Cadre, too. We'll get them all eventually."

"I can drink to that," Falcone said.

———

They discussed every aspect of the situation they could imagine as the three ships made their way to Io. Some parts were going to depend on the situation they found when they got to Ganymede, but there was a fair amount they could game out in advance.

The first thing that became clear was that they were going to need to do this the old-fashioned way. They couldn't trust anyone to help them. They'd need to do everything regarding Breen in-house.

In fact, the planning sessions definitely had the feel of a criminal enterprise.

"We're not going to get arrested for this, are we?" Brad asked during their final session.

They'd deliver the science ship to Io safe and sound in just a few hours. Then they could get to the important business ahead of them.

Falcone raised both eyebrows. "Are you worried you wouldn't make it in prison? You seem pretty tough to me. I was watching while you and Saburo went at it. Almost Agency-level stuff. Very impressive. I think you can stop anyone from shanking you, and you can probably sweet-talk your cellmate."

"You sure know how to reassure a guy," he said dryly.

Her expression became serious. "We'll be fine. I wrote a get-out-of-jail free card for you in the form of a contract between the Agency and the Vikings. You're operating under my supervision for this. My protective shield is yours, and you're getting a pretty decent bonus for working outside the normal parameters of your regular job, I might add."

That made him smile. "I'll have to review it. Did you include combat bonuses and sweeteners for going above and beyond?"

"Of course. If we get enough to arrest Breen, you'll be pleased. If we get a lead on a major slaver base, you'll be thrilled. If we take them down, well, let's just say no one involved will have cause to complain."

"That sounds good to me. If we manage to locate a base, I'll speak with Factor Kernsky and get some help that won't tip anyone off. She lost a lot of friends taking down the Terror's old ship, *Black Skull*. She's not in their pay."

Falcone nodded. "I've already checked her out and we're on the same course. A few mercenary companies working in conjunction with *Freedom* will give us the force we need to crush them, if we act with a little surprise on our side."

A rap at the wardroom hatch preceded its opening. Shelly was in the corridor. "Sorry to disturb you, but we're coming up on the protective zone around Io."

He raised an eyebrow. "You could've just called."

His com officer's eyes twitched toward Falcone. "Actually, I wanted to talk to you for a few minutes. Alone. It's a personal matter."

The agent rose smoothly to her feet. "We're done anyway, so I'll go print out that contract. We can hash out any details before we dock."

Once Falcone was gone, Shelly came in and closed the hatch behind her. "I really hate having to say this, but I think I've detected a tight beam communications signal from our ship."

Brad sat up abruptly as what she said registered. "What?"

"I found it purely by accident. I was getting some interference and I started searching around for the source. I think it's coming from the front of the ship near one of our regular com arrays."

"And you didn't want to tell me in front of Falcone because you think it belongs to her?"

"I don't know who it belongs to, but she's the newest element. I can't imagine any of the rest of the crew being involved. I wanted to give you the information without her knowing so you could decide what to do, Captain."

He nodded slowly. She was right, of course. "Is there anything else you can tell me about the beam? Like where it's going to?"

"The Io shipyards, I think."

He stood slowly. "Does anyone else know about this?"

"No. I just found it."

"Keep it that way. Did it just start transmitting?"

"I have no way of knowing. We're at exceptionally long range for it to get to the shipyards cleanly, though. Jupiter is at a really disadvantageous position, and the radiation is likely killing the low-powered transmission.

"My money says no, but that won't last long. The closer we get, the clearer the signal will be. We're also moving clear of Jupiter's interference. My best guess is that we have half an hour at the very most."

His mind raced as he considered his options. He didn't believe Falcone was involved. They'd had a lot of traffic around the ship after the ambush, though. Sadly, it was possible someone had gone out and planted it while a boat was docked.

Or it could've been installed while they were at MOSO on Mars. This wasn't the time to point fingers of blame. He needed to make sure it didn't give away anything important.

"Tell Jason to slow down while I look into it. Hell, have him change course a little so it has a worse angle. I'll get Mike to go look at it right now. He'll disable it."

His com officer nodded sharply. "Are you going to tell Falcone?"

That was the big question, wasn't it?

# CHAPTER TWENTY-THREE

BRAD FOUND Mike Randall testing something on a bench in engineering. "Drop what you're doing and suit up. We have some kind of transmitter on the hull."

The engineer cursed and dropped the part he was working on as he ran toward the engineering lock. "Where is it?"

"Somewhere near the com array up front. It's a tight-beam transmitter of some kind."

"On it. Jim! Get a suit on and come help me find something! Move!"

Brad raced toward the bridge. If someone detected that signal, the end result was likely to be an ambush.

Partway there, he slowed. He really needed to tell Falcone. She'd find out what he was doing in short order anyway. Better to show her the trust he felt up front.

This was taking longer than he liked, though. He hit the intercom to the bridge. "John, bring us to a stop. Shelly, ask *Freedom* if they can move between us and the shipyards. Hell, see if they can jam the signal."

Once the two of them indicated they were working on it, Brad stopped outside Falcone's cabin and rapped sharply on the hatch.

It slid open to reveal the agent. "I just finished printing the contract."

"Forget that. We have a tight-beam transmitter on the hull."

Her eyes widened in surprise but quickly narrowed. "*Personal business*, my ass. Your com officer was coming to tell you about it. She thinks I did it."

"She doesn't know you as well as she knows everyone else. I'm telling you because I know you didn't do it."

The agent nodded. "I guess that's what matters. We need to prep for an ambush."

"Already in progress. I had Marshal stop us short of the shipyards. Shelly doesn't think the signal is strong enough to get past Jupiter until we move closer. *Freedom* is going to see if she can block or jam it while my engineers locate the transmitter."

The two of them headed for the bridge at a run. Falcone and Shelly exchanged looks, but there was no drama from either woman. That suited him fine.

Once Brad was securely in his chair, he focused his attention on the com officer. "What's our status?"

"*Freedom* is between *Heart* and Io. They've got the beam blocked with their hull. Based on the strength readings they've given me, I strongly doubt anyone has picked it up yet."

"Is it just a notification that we've arrived, or is there some specific message?" Falcone asked.

"It has position information. Precise heading and thrust. It's acting like a normal transponder, except for the fact it's looking for a specific receiver. Well, not exactly. There is an extra message attached. My guess is that it's meant to be forwarded by the receiver into the regular com network around Io."

"What kind of message?" Brad asked. "Something encrypted? Data pulled off our ship?"

The woman shook her head. "A plain text message that reads, 'I expect that bonus you promised me.' It's not some kind of hidden code, either. Just a one-liner."

"Sounds like someone went to a lot of trouble to put the thing in place and they want to be sure the man or woman with the cash pays up," Falcone said. "I wish we could know who it's going to. Is there any routing information?"

"None at all," Shelly said. "The receiver must already have that built in."

"Dammit. Maybe we can find the receiver and pull the code out of it."

Brad shot the agent a doubtful look. "Have you seen how large the shipyards are? Fat chance. Still, maybe you're right. We should explore the possibility. Perhaps the scientists on *Marie Curie* can help us narrow the search area."

"Bridge, this is Randall. We've found the transmitter. Do you want me to disable it?"

"No," Brad said. "Not until we decide the best way to handle it. What can you tell me about it?"

"It's a custom job. Pricy, by all appearances. It hasn't been here that long."

"Engineer Randall," Falcone said, leaning forward. "Can you put a minimum timeframe on how long it has been there?"

"Yep. It was here during the most recent ambush. Some of the torpedo debris scored its casing. I can also see some minor pitting. It was never designed for long-term use. My bet is that someone slipped it on our hull at MOSO. Definitely not before."

"You sound pretty sure of that," Brad said. "Why?"

"Because the idiot put it near one of the reactive strips we used in the fight protecting the liner. No way this could have survived that. Hell, I'd have seen it when I was replacing the strip. This was done at MOSO."

"Can you remove it without triggering a self-destruct?" Falcone asked.

"It's a damn toy. No protective features at all. I can turn it off, pick it up, move it, reprogram it. Whatever you like."

A slow smile spread over the woman's face. "Can you turn it back on in the same configuration?"

"Sure. Just like it had never been messed with."

Falcone turned to Brad. "I think we should take it off the hull while we decide how to best use it. I have an idea you'll like."

"Turn it off and bring it inside, Mike," Brad said.

"Copy that."

Once the com channel was closed, Brad turned to Falcone. "What do you have in mind?"

"Let me hold off on that until we get together with Captain Fields and Dr. Keller, preferably over on *Freedom*. A girl has to have some secrets."

He shook his head with a smile and a snort. "Shelly, signal *Freedom* that we'd like to meet her captain and the good doctor in about an hour. If the scientists have anyone that might be able to help locate and hack the com receiver, please have them bring them along."

"You got it."

Brad rose to his feet. "I'm going back to engineering to wait for Randall. As soon as he gets in, we'll head over to the cruiser. Good work, everyone."

———

An hour later, Brad sat in the cruiser's wardroom with Falcone, Captain Fields, Dr. Keller, and a reedy-looking woman that the scientist had forgotten to introduce. The illicit transmitter sat on the table, where they could all see it.

Randall had been right. It was almost literally a toy. The kind of hobby gear someone could buy in specialty shops. It still had the label on it.

"So," Fields said slowly. "Someone planted this on your ship so people here would know if you made it through the ambush. That probably means you have company around here somewhere. Good thing you found this beforehand."

He looked over at Brad. "What's your plan? Disable it and waltz in as if it were never there?"

"Actually, Agent Falcone has a better plan," Brad said with a wolfish smile. "I have no idea what it is, but she tells me I'll like it."

Falcone picked up right where he left off. "First, we need to know if our handy scientific team can help us locate the receiver it's targeting."

Keller shook his head. "*Narrow* is somewhat of a misnomer in this case. At the range it can get a message across, the receiver could very well be anywhere in the Io shipyards."

"That's disappointing," Brad sighed. "We'd hoped to track down who was receiving this message."

"Oh, I didn't say *that* was impossible. You just have to expand your thinking a bit."

The scientist gestured to the woman beside him. "This is Evelyn Wandry, our resident communications wizard. She's come up with a solution that is quite innovative, though highly illegal."

"The law can be flexible in some cases," Falcone said. "Talk to me."

The woman nervously cleared her throat. "The message you mentioned is attached to the data so that it can be forwarded to the standard com network. If I attach a Trojan to it, I can have the recipient call us with his identity."

Brad raised an eyebrow. "Is that even possible? I thought communication companies had safeguards in place to prevent that kind of thing."

The woman smiled a bit shyly. "They do, but the battle between security and accessibility is always ongoing. Everything is a tradeoff. In this case, if one is sufficiently knowledgeable and willing to accept that the network might catch on after a while, almost anything is possible.

"I don't believe I could do this very many times before the provider noticed what I was doing and took preventive measures, but it will almost certainly work once. The greater risk is that the recipient might notice the outgoing transmission. It's brief and I can have the program mask many of its tracks, but without knowing everything about the end user's system, I can't account for all the variables."

"How likely is someone to notice?" Fields asked.

The woman shrugged. "Normal people would see nothing. A paranoid individual might have a dedicated monitor to track every action his system takes. Perhaps even one that makes sure the Trojan doesn't even get a message back out."

Brad frowned. "Could you have the Trojan leave a trail we could track to the target? Perhaps that's the smarter play. Just log the path as it goes without triggering a response."

"Sure. That's not nearly as challenging." The woman sounded disappointed.

"How long will it take you to prepare?"

That got her smile back. "Five minutes. I brought everything I need with me."

"Excellent. I'll leave you and Dr. Keller to it, then."

"Use the table over against the bulkhead," Fields said.

Once the scientists were huddled over the transmitter, Fields fixed Falcone with a stare. "What do you have in mind?"

The agent grinned. "They're expecting to jump a heavy corvette. They'll have enough force to make it happen fairly quickly. What if they accidently found themselves slugging it out with a Commonwealth cruiser?"

"That would probably leave a mark," the Fleet officer admitted. "So, you want us to plant the transmitter on our hull and walk into the ambush?"

"It would be best if you masked your nature as much as you could. Then they'd commit and bad things would happen."

"Won't they be suspicious when you come in alone?" Brad asked.

The officer shook his head. "We won't be. If we can mimic an unobservant heavy corvette, you can pretend to be a science ship. We'll have our charges follow us at a sedate pace. They aren't what the enemy is looking for, anyway. They'll be safe enough."

"Do you think that will fool the slavers?" Brad asked uncertainly. "A cruiser is pretty big."

"We can mask some of our thermal signature. If a ship is transmitting the locator beacon for your ship, they'll explain away any variances. By the time they realize they've made a colossal blunder, we'll be all over them."

———

Brad wasn't so sure this plan was going to work, but he was more than willing to give it a try. *Freedom* was in front of *Heart*, curving around Jupiter until the Io shipyards were in direct line of sight. Shortly after that, Io itself came into view.

The science ship was dawdling way back. No one would see them until the lead ships were almost to the yards. If they got that far, there wouldn't be an ambush.

Falcone was with Fields on *Freedom*. That made her orders a bit more official, he supposed.

"Four ships just detached from one of the outer facilities around the shipyard," Jason said. "They're boosting for us at high speed. I think there are two heavy corvettes and two light ones."

"Open a channel," he said.

By prearrangement, his signal was going tight-beam to *Freedom*, who would then retransmit it more widely. No one else would realize the bigger ship wasn't the source. It would serve to reinforce the illusion that the slavers were dealing with *Heart* and a science ship.

"Unknown vessels, this is the mercenary warship *Heart of Vengeance*. Identify yourselves, cut your acceleration, and change course."

They didn't respond, so he repeated his warnings and threatened them with destruction. Then he cut the channel and let *Freedom* move ahead.

The enemy ships actually launched torpedoes before Captain Fields went to full power and returned fire. He then declared his identity and demanded their surrender.

By that time, the hostile ships were far too committed to escape. The cruiser's broadside was more than the enemy could launch as a group, even before *Heart* joined the fray.

The bloodlust was roiling inside him, but Brad forced it back down. He needed to be in control. There was a time and place for vengeance. This wasn't it. One mistake could kill a lot of innocent people.

"Jason, pick one of the enemy heavies and open fire. Keep the shipyard in mind. I don't want any mass driver slugs coming near it or any innocent vessels in our area."

"Roger," the man said, hunched over his console. "Firing."

Compared with the cruiser's output, *Heart* was a lightweight, but that didn't mean his ship was helpless. The heavy corvette he targeted was already sorely pressed, so the extra torpedoes came sailing through his defenses with devastating results.

"Target destroyed. Moving to the other heavy. It looks like the lights are trying to break contact. No way they can get clear. We're getting some return fire, but *Freedom* is still their primary target."

"Is *Freedom* in danger?"

"Negative. Their defenses are handling everything the slavers are throwing."

"We're being hailed by Io Security," Shelly said. "They're demanding everyone stop shooting. Shall I respond?"

Brad shook his head. "No. Let *Freedom* take the lead on that."

"The heavy is maneuvering to bring *Heart* between them and *Freedom*," Marshal said. "That's going to allow us to close with them faster if I accept the challenge. Shall I make a run at them?"

Maybe he could indulge the demon a little. "Do it. Flank speed."

At these ranges, the Gatlings were proving to be far more effective than usual and the torpedo travel times were measured in seconds rather than minutes.

"One of the lights just cooked off," Jason said. "*Freedom* is maneuvering to close with the other light but is still firing at the remaining heavy. He's taking hits, but we're going to be at point-blank range real fast. It looks like he's lost most of his torpedo tubes."

"Gut him," Brad said with a snarl.

This was the kind of short-range fight *Sting* and the slaver destroyer had engaged in. With about the same balance of fire—in *Heart*'s favor this time—considering the other ship's damage.

"Hits on the enemy," Jason said. "Multiple hits. He's breaking up. There goes his fusion plant."

"Taking evasive action to avoid debris," Marshal said. "We're past him. Shall I come back around?"

"Don't bother," Jason said. "He's cooked. The last light corvette just blew up too. That's everyone."

"Don't fall for that," Brad said. "We treat the area as hostile until we're sure. Take us back around to *Freedom*, John."

Shelly turned in her seat. "*Freedom* is transmitting stand-down orders to the Io forces. All the civilian shipping is scattering."

"You know what I'm going to enjoy about this?" Brad asked as he felt the rage drain out of him. "Letting someone else explain why we got into a torpedo duel in their front yard. How long do you think it will take us to get to Io now, John?"

"The distance is deceptive," Marshal said. "If we were free and clear, we could dock in half an hour. With all the hubbub, I'd imagine it will take us the rest of the day, even with Captain Fields providing the cover."

If anything, Brad suspected his pilot was being overly optimistic.

"Shelly, call *Marie Curie* and tell her to join us. We'll be here a while."

# CHAPTER TWENTY-FOUR

IT TURNED out Brad's worst-case guess about how long they'd be waiting was far too hopeful. The Io security forces kept them tied up until late the next day. To his annoyance, *Marie Curie* was ushered in to dock with no fanfare at all.

Oh, Falcone might have been able to speed things up for them, but she was playing things quiet. She'd slipped back over to *Heart* before the security forces stopped all small craft in the area. She'd pretend to be one of his crewmen, if need be.

Once Io Security grudgingly allowed them to dock, *Heart* headed in. To say that they were under heavy guard once they arrived was something of an understatement. Security was out in force. Disapproving force, based on their expressions.

"I think I'd curtail your planned night life for a while," Brad told Marshal. "These boys and girls seem more inclined than most to frown on infractions."

"Don't they just?" his pilot asked. "I think I'll stay in tonight. You know, rest up for later."

"That's good advice for all of us," Brad said. "Too bad I have to go meet Dr. Keller and his hacker."

"That sounds like my cue," Falcone said. "If security noted the intrusion or finds out now, I'd rather not have anyone arrested."

Once Brad called Keller, the two of them rose and made their way to the airlock. A squad of heavily armed security people stood just outside. They didn't actually say no one was allowed off the ship, but they tried to exude that message by hulking over Falcone and him.

A third of their number peeled off to follow the two of them closely. This was going to be awkward. How could they hope to do any penetration of the com network with all this company?

He'd figure that out once he met with the scientists, he decided. Why borrow trouble?

The scientists were waiting at the agreed-upon café. He sourly noted that they didn't have any guards at all. At Keller's gesture, he and Falcone sat at the table and ordered coffee.

"Goodness, what big friends you have," the scientist said brightly. "It's almost as if they think you need protecting. How considerate."

"You can be both perceptive and ironic," Brad conceded. "The question now is how we get to searching for the trail of breadcrumbs you left with suspicious eyes looking over our shoulders."

"Simple enough. We checked the com network when *Marie Curie* docked yesterday. We already have the data."

Brad took the data chip the man slid across to him. "Weren't you worried about being detected?"

Wandry looked faintly scandalized, causing Brad to shake his head in amusement. "Did you track the transmission?"

"Sure did," the woman said. "It went to a disposable com. That wasn't very helpful, but planting the step-by-step log of hops turned the tide. The call was received somewhere in the governor's office."

That was a surprise. He'd have expected the slavers to keep something of a lower profile. Brad knew that the governor wasn't in league with them, but no one could vet their staffs well enough to keep the bastards out.

"Can we narrow that down any at all?" Falcone asked. "I'd rather not wander around the center of Io's government, asking if anyone happens to be a slaver."

"It's possible the com unit is still active," Keller said. "At close range, we should be able to locate it with a fair degree of accuracy."

"How close are we talking about and what constitutes a 'fair degree of accuracy'?"

"Perhaps fifty meters," the scientist said. "And we'll be able to pinpoint the location within half a meter."

"That's pretty good," Brad admitted.

"It is," Falcone agreed. "That means we have to be able to ditch our escort and get into the building. I'm not quite sure how we do that without pissing them off.

"Then, once we're inside, we need to be able to get to the area where the slaver is located. The governor's office is probably large, so it might take us dozens of scans. Security *will* spot us. I can pull rank, but that's going to tip our hand."

Brad grinned. "Not if someone with access lets us in. I happen to know someone like that who owes me a favor."

————

It took him a surprisingly short amount of time to get Ilene Johnson on the com. Admittedly, having her private number helped. He expected the call to go through Jack Mader, but the woman answered it herself.

"Yes?"

"Governor Johnson, it's Brad Madrid. I hope I haven't caused you too much chaos."

She gave a short bark of laughter. "You *do* know how to make an entrance, Captain. Yes, I'd say you could call this a bit chaotic. Slavers operating right here around Io. That infuriates me. Thank goodness that Fleet cruiser was there.

"Though I must admit I'm still trying to figure out how the slavers mistook a cruiser for your formidable little ship. Might I take it you had something to do with that?"

"I did. It was part of a scheme to flush out some higher-ranking bad guys, for which I need your help. Might I call in that favor?"

"Absolutely not. Finding slavers is my business and pleasure. Save the favor for when it's not something I'm already determined to help you with. What do you need?"

He eyed their watchers. "We've picked up some friends from Io Security that are cramping our style. Also, we'd like to come explain things in person, if we can find a spot in your schedule."

"Easily done. Come straight to my office and I'll send them off to watch people that truly need watching."

"Thank you, Governor. We appreciate your help."

"Thank *you*, Captain Madrid. Keep doing what you're doing. I like it a lot."

Brad ended the call and opened his mouth to say something, but the expressions of disbelief on everyone else's faces stopped him for a moment. "What?"

"You are a wellspring of surprises, Captain," Falcone said dryly. "I had no idea you were close friends with the governor of Io. You don't happen to know the Commonwealth Director of Intelligence, do you? I'd love the chance to discuss our budget with him."

"You know how it is," he said with a grin. "We mercenaries get around. It really *is* who you know."

Once the group finished their drinks, he consulted his wrist-comp and headed off toward the government center. Their watchdogs trailed not so discreetly in their wake.

The building they came to was low, its bulk below-ground, but that didn't stop it from being ornate. The exposed surfaces were either made of worked stone, sheathed in white marble, or both. The security screening area up front was also suitably imposing.

Half a dozen men and women staffed a protective barrier where visitors had to submit to scanning and the temporary confiscation of their weapons. Not what he wanted to do while hunting for a slaver, but he needed in.

Brad got into line, but one of the women motioned for him to come forward. "Captain Madrid? Step though here for a special screening, please."

"I have associates," he said as he complied.

"They can come too."

The Io Security forces made to follow, but the other guards blocked them.

"We'll take it from here," a man behind the counter said. "You can either wait or return to your regular station."

The security forces looked even more annoyed at that than Brad had felt about the extra screening, but they backed off.

The woman led the four of them past the screening rooms and right to an elevator. That wasn't what he'd expected, but he wasn't going to complain.

They rode down in silence to the lowest level. The offices there were large and luxurious, much more so than any Brad had seen so far in the Outer System. There wasn't nearly as much art, but it was well displayed, elegant, and no doubt exceptionally valuable.

The security officer brought them to a spacious office with the emblem of Io on the frosted glass wall. A well-dressed young man rose from behind the desk and smiled.

"I have them now. Thank you."

The aide—not Jack Mader, to Brad's surprise and concealed pleasure—waited for the security officer to leave and then escorted them all to the door at the rear of the room. "The Governor will see you immediately."

Without knocking, he opened the door and gestured for them to pass.

Governor Johnson's office was large and tastefully decorated but didn't have any expensive art on display. Here, the furniture seemed to be the point. Everything was made of wood. The workmanship was astonishing. They were in fact works of art, to Brad's mind.

The governor rose from behind her desk and gestured toward a seating area off to the side. "Please sit. I realize it's early, but would anyone like something to drink? I can have tea or coffee brought if that's more to your taste."

"I'm good," Brad said. Once the rest had declined, he introduced everyone.

Governor Johnson shook hands all around. "Dr. Keller, I suppose I'm your boss, indirectly. The Government of Io contracted your services to deep-scan Jupiter for potential gas mining. I confess I didn't suspect you'd fall in with Captain Madrid."

She shifted her eyes to Falcone. "Nor did I expect he'd show up with an agent from the Commonwealth Investigative Agency. This is all suitably mysterious, particularly when I take the slaver attack and *Freedom* into account. Am I going to find out what's going on?"

Brad grinned. "You're in charge. I suppose I should fill you in on everything that's happened since we last met."

He told the people with him how he'd worked for the governor and then segued into what he'd done since then. Governor Johnson hung on every word, scowling when he described the ambush and loss of life.

"Dammit, these bastards are everywhere," she said with a scowl. "How can they be so well plugged-in?"

"That's actually why we're here," Falcone said. "We believe the attack was instigated by someone in your employ. Or at least in this building."

Johnson stared at the woman for a long moment. "I sincerely hope you're mistaken, but I wouldn't doubt anything at this point. What leads you to that conclusion?"

"Ahem," Keller said. "I'm afraid that's where the crew of *Marie Curie* come in. Captains Madrid and Fields asked us if we could trace the signal from the transmitter. With Agent Falcone's blessing, we attached a Trojan to it.

"One that merely mapped the nodes the message traveled through. I recognize that's technically illegal, but she indicated that we were doing the work under her warrant. I do hope that won't get us in trouble."

Johnson shook her head. "I'm not going to fuss, Doctor. I can pardon crimes on Io and wouldn't hesitate to do so, but you're fine if you had an Agency warrant. So, you traced it here? Can you be more specific? I have a lot of people working in my government."

The scientist shrugged. "I can't tell you who received it. The com was a disposable. We were hoping it was still here and that we could get your blessing to scan the building."

"Done," Johnson said at once. "I'll call security to send a few people down to escort us around. What kind of process will this need?"

Wandry spoke up. "I can get a return within about fifty meters. That will allow me to pinpoint the com to about half a meter."

The scientist pulled a device from her pocket. "This is it. All I have to do is press the button and it sends out a signal. If the com is within range, it will let me know with a chime."

She pressed a button and the device chimed.

All of them stared silently at the woman for a long moment.

Governor Johnson spoke first. "You're telling me that the com the slavers signaled is within fifty meters of my office *right now*?"

"Apparently so," Wandry said, her tone bemused. "Off in that direction about forty meters." She pointed.

"That's my special assistant's office," Johnson said quietly. "Jack Mader. You've met him, Captain. He's been with me for almost two decades in one position or another. Are we seriously saying he works for the slavers?"

Considering his dislike of the man, Brad certainly hoped so. Taking him into custody would be a real pleasure.

"There's one way to find out," Brad said as he stood. "Let's go ask him."

"No. Let me get security down here first. If he *is* a slaver, this might turn violent. Then we can be sure he doesn't have a chance to try anything."

The governor called for security, indicating it wasn't an emergency. "No need to get everyone excited. That might tip him off."

They all waited impatiently for the requested security team, and then the governor led the way to Mader's office. The young woman at the desk out front smiled at them. "Oh, Governor! You just missed him. He stepped out to see someone about a project."

Johnson smiled. "That's fine, Sarah. Could you call him for me? I really need to have him come back right now."

"Certainly." The woman pressed a button on her com and waited. Mader didn't answer.

Brad looked at Wandry. "Is the com still in there?"

The woman checked. "Yes."

Johnson pushed past the desk and into Mader's office.

Brad put his hand on his pistol, but it didn't matter. There was no one there. Based on the open cabinets and hastily searched contents, he wasn't coming back, either. Two coms sat on the desk. One was probably the disposable and the other had to be his official unit.

The governor turned to the security team. "Seal the building. I'm issuing a detention warrant for Jack Mader. Find him."

Twenty minutes later they had the official word. Mader was gone.

# CHAPTER TWENTY-FIVE

BRAD WATCHED the security monitor as it showed a recording of Jack Mader departing the government center. The man didn't seem to be in a hurry as he made his way past security, even seeming to joke with the guards as he hefted a bag over his shoulder.

He could only imagine what the man had inside the bag.

Falcone wanted the man and his goodies very badly. She and the governor were working feverishly behind the scenes to lock Io down and locate the traitor. Governor Johnson took lead because Falcone still didn't want her participation known.

Brad didn't think they were going to catch the man, even though they'd only missed him by a few minutes. The bastard had clearly prepared an escape plan, and he'd executed it coolly under pressure. No, he was probably already off Io.

He really hoped he was wrong. He hadn't liked the man from the first moment and would love to have a heart-to-heart chat with him about the slaver attacks. His escape left a bitter taste in Brad's mouth.

Still, he had to play this as if the man was already gone and assume he'd warned any co-conspirators about his cover being blown.

Brad stepped over to where Falcone and Governor Johnson were listening to a woman from Io Security drone on about all the measures they were putting into place that would certainly stop Mader from escaping.

"He's gone," Brad whispered in Falcone's ear.

She nodded minutely. "I know," she said softly.

"We need to get into his place and see if we can find anything. Then we need to move on Breen. Maybe we need to do that first."

"Already ahead of you. This isn't our week. Breen is off Ganymede on a business trip. Been gone two weeks already. They don't expect him back for as long as a month more."

They just couldn't catch a break. "What do we do in the meantime?"

"We carry on with the plan." She turned her back toward the presenter to give them privacy. "We'll search Mader's place. Maybe we'll get lucky.

"Then we head for Ganymede and break into Breen's place. We keep that low-key. He has no reason to avoid coming back home. We can pick him up then."

Brad considered her for a long moment. "Do you think we'll get lucky?"

The woman snorted. "Bad luck, maybe. When I joined up, my partner told me the best attitude to have was to believe that everything was going to go wrong and none of the promising leads would pan out. Then I'd be thrilled when something broke my way. He was amazingly prescient."

"What's the plan on getting into Mader's house?"

"The governor already swore a warrant out against him, so all we need to do is let Io Security move in. We'll go with them and turn the place upside down."

That took a lot longer than Brad expected or wanted. It seemed the bureaucrats in security had plenty of paperwork to fill out. More than two hours passed before they made entry into Mader's home.

*Palatial* didn't begin to cover it. The exterior looked well-to-do but concealed a surprisingly opulent interior. Lush furnishings sat on deep carpets made of only the best materials. Works of art that rivaled the collection in the governor's offices adorned every wall and more niches than one could easily count.

"Being a special assistant pays better than I'd expected," Brad said as he looked around.

The security detectives were already fanning out to take images of everything, leaving him standing near the entrance with Falcone and Governor Johnson.

"Not this well," Johnson ground out between clenched teeth. "Not even close. If I'd had any doubts the man was in someone's pay, I don't anymore."

"We need to get to his home office," Falcone said. "Forgive me if I don't exactly trust your security people not to trip something and wipe his system."

She led them on a quick search through the house, revealing even more lavishness. So much so that Brad wondered if the man ever expected to be found out. No way he'd have been able to cart any of this away with him. He had to have known he'd be forced to abandon a lot of money at some point.

Or had he expected to get away with everything? That seemed overly optimistic, but the Cadre and slavers had had their way for years.

They found his office in a sublevel. The smell of burned equipment told him it was a smoldering ruin before they entered it, however. It had been ultramodern and extremely well equipped.

"He came back here and made sure we wouldn't get anything," Falcone said in a low voice as she looked around at the destruction. "Dammit."

"Impossible," Johnson said. "I dispatched security to watch this place first thing. He couldn't have moved in and out so fast."

Brad leaned over and looked at one of the ruined comps. "This wasn't smashed. Someone set off a small charge inside it. It was rigged to self-destruct."

"He might've done this remotely," Falcone suggested. "One call and he could wipe everything and then blow it. That's what I'd have done."

"I'll have my people go over everything, but that's going to take time," Johnson said with a bitter sigh. "At least I know how the damned Cadre always knew what I was doing. Mader was involved in everything. I trusted him completely."

Falcone turned to him. "We don't have time to waste. If Mader was in league with Breen, he might be on his way to Ganymede even as we speak. If he wrecks any evidence there, we're back to where we started."

"Is there anything I can do to help?" Johnson asked.

Brad considered that and nodded. "Yes. If I take *Heart* to Ganymede, it might raise some eyebrows. Could we borrow *Marie Curie* and her crew for a little while? They might prove invaluable in getting data out of Breen's systems without leaving too many tracks."

Johnson nodded decisively. "Use them as long as you need. I'll do anything I can do to stop these bastards or catch Mader. I can intercede with the government on Ganymede, too, if you need it."

"Let's hope they never realize we were there," Falcone said. "That's the only way we're going to get to the slavers or the Cadre. We have to work in the shadows. If they see us coming, they'll scatter and we'll never catch them all."

———

Their arrival at Ganymede was low-key. *Marie Curie* docked without incident and let her crew off for leave. Brad and Falcone dressed in the same bland jumpsuits as the ship's crew and came out with a number of people dressed just like them.

The scientists had preceded them out, their clothes seemingly designed to draw the eye but not in a good way.

Brad wasn't sure why brilliance and good taste in clothing seemed to never travel in the same company, but the civilians were adorned in a wild array of colors and styles that didn't even come close to matching, even on the same individual.

Perhaps they'd done it intentionally. It certainly served to draw every eye on the docks. No one noticed Falcone or him slipping away from the rest.

She led him on a circuitous path to be certain no one was tailing them. Half an hour later, she declared them clear.

They rented a small room suitable for visiting crewmen who were tired of the ship life but too poor to afford good accommodations. The room held a single bed, large enough to suggest a second class of patron. Everything had a worn appearance. The place hadn't received new furniture in a long while, it seemed.

Looking at the bed, Brad was glad he wouldn't really be sleeping on it. At least he hoped not.

"What now?" he asked, taking a cautious seat on a rickety chair.

"We change and go scout Breen's neighborhood. You first. I still need to see about getting some equipment."

He stepped into the dingy bathroom and winced. "I wouldn't count on coming out of this place cleaner than you came into it," he said as he started stripping.

"That was kind of the point," she said. "No one will give us a second glance here. Or ask any awkward questions."

Brad wasn't certain that would be the case when they left. His change of clothes was of significantly better quality than the crew uniform. It had to be so they could blend into the high-class neighborhood Breen lived in.

Once he was dressed, he packed the shipsuit into a small bag that wouldn't stand out and stepped back into the bedroom.

Falcone was just finishing up something on her wrist-comp and stood. "Perfect timing. We'll get out of here and meet up with my contact as soon as I change. He'll have everything we need."

She ducked into the bathroom and made a disgusted noise. "You weren't kidding. What a dump."

Fifteen minutes later, they were walking out of the hotel, hopefully never to return. Their clothing drew curious glances, but no one messed with them as they made their escape. From the knowing leer the hotel clerk gave them, they'd been classed under "discreet affair"— and the only thing better than going completely unnoticed was being put into a box and forgotten.

The agent led him to a shop dealing in secondhand comps in a working-class section of the city. She paused as she started to go inside.

"Wait out here and keep lookout. I should only be ten minutes or so. If I'm not back in fifteen, go back to the ship."

He raised an eyebrow. "Are you expecting trouble?"

She shook her head. "Not really, but you never know. This guy fences stolen goods, so he might do something unexpected. He's not on our payroll. Just someone we've used as a supplier in the past. Without his knowledge, of course."

"Ah. I'll hit the café across the street and get us some coffee. That'll let me linger a bit. If you don't come out in fifteen minutes, I'll come in after you."

Falcone patted his cheek. "That's so sweet. Don't worry about me. I can take care of myself."

He wagered she could.

Brad sauntered across the street and bought two coffees to go. Then he took up a table with a view of the shop.

As she'd predicted, it took Falcone about ten minutes. She walked out, her oversized handbag virtually bulging with stuff.

"What's in the bag?" he asked as he handed her the second coffee. "And this is surprisingly good coffee."

"Tools of the trade, so to speak. Everything I need to bypass Breen's security and get past his locks."

Brad raised an eyebrow. "And it all fits in there? Impressive. I'm shocked it all comes as a kit."

She shot him an amused glance. "It's not like that at all. I told the guy what I needed, and he put it together for me."

"Out of materials on hand."

"That is his job in this part of the underworld. Buying and selling stolen goods, as well as getting gear for those who need and can afford his services."

"For anyone who walks in off the street?"

She shook her head. "Absolutely not. I have impeccable references. Otherwise, he'd have sent me packing while pretending he had no idea what I was talking about."

It was getting into the local evening, so they didn't cause too many raised eyebrows as they transitioned to Breen's neighborhood. The homes here were mostly behind protective—though decorative —barriers.

Breen's home was aboveground, a luxury in a place that normally used below-ground accommodations. The exterior boasted imported wood and quarried stone from Mars. A true statement about the man's wealth.

It struck Brad as not being coincidental that neither Breen and Mader seemed to care if they displayed signs of their wealth. Though, to be fair, Mader had kept his behind closed doors.

"Any word on how wealthy Breen is?" he asked. "This is pretty blatant."

"He's actually the majority shareholder in Astro Transport. He doesn't spread that around, but anyone that cares can dig it out."

"I just don't get that. Why was he selling out his own employees? *Louisiana Rain* was his liner."

She shrugged. "Who knows? Insurance? Someone on the ship knew too much? We'll ask him when we put him in an interrogation room. Right now, we need to get into his place and find something that will let me space him and everyone else he works with."

Brad didn't notice anyone watching, but he still felt as if everyone could clearly see what they were up to. Frankly, he wished he could watch Falcone work. As a former security officer, he'd love to know how she bypassed locks and security systems with such ease.

A minute later, she opened the front entrance and he gratefully followed her inside. The foyer was dark but she pulled a tiny light from her bag and scanned around for anything of concern. They looked clear so far.

"I'll lock the door and rearm the security system," she said quietly. "That way, if anyone checks, everything will look good."

He stepped over to the stairs while she accomplished that. They led up, but he was relatively sure the door under them led to another set of stairs going down, just based on how it was positioned. And the fact that it had a second security system.

"Up or down?" he inquired when she stepped over to him.

"Down."

This time, he kept one eye on her and was impressed by both the equipment she used and her skill at manipulating it. This system took several minutes for her to bypass. He wondered if that meant it was of higher quality than the one on the house itself.

Once the light turned green, she unlocked the door under the stairs and opened it. There was indeed a wide set of stairs going down.

He started to say something pithy but froze when the security system on the front door beeped and then shut down.

Someone was coming in behind them!

# CHAPTER TWENTY-SIX

BRAD FOLLOWED Falcone into the stairway heading down, closed it behind them, and locked it. There was a simple security control beside the door that allowed him to arm the system with the touch of a button, so he did.

Once that was done, he checked the display. It offered him two exterior views: right outside the door and into the foyer. He chose the latter and watched the front door open. Two men in private security uniforms came in.

They didn't seem overly concerned, so he doubted they had triggered any kind of alarm.

"Mark us down as having checked the place," the older man said to his young companion.

The kid frowned. "Shouldn't we do a walkthrough?"

"The owner is off Ganymede. He'll never know. Besides, the security system was armed. No one came in."

That seemed to offend the young man. "At least check the interior system. There's a note that we have to look at it every time. It says it's right over here."

He walked over and looked at the door Brad and Falcone hid behind. "It's on."

"See? All secure," the older man said. "Just like I said. We can lock the place up and be back to the office early."

"After we check the other houses on our list," the kid said repressively. "I need this job. I'm not going to screw off because you want to get back to the video screen."

"I was like you once, kid. You'll get over it."

Brad let out a slow breath once the two had armed the exterior security system and departed. "That was close."

"We could've been away from the door and fine even without this hole to hide in," she assured him. "You're talking like the kid. Why worry when everyone else screws off?"

"Does that make you the old guy?" he asked with a smile.

"Only on the inside. Let's go down and see what Breen didn't want anyone else to see."

The answer was "everything."

Brad eyed the office and workshop in the basement. He couldn't speak for what might be in the computers, but the shop held something he recognized.

"These were the computers that the burglars took off *Heart of Vengeance*," he told Falcone as he gestured to the cores on the table. "I guess Breen was behind it after all."

"Check them out while I look in the office," she said. "Be sure there aren't any remote means to turn them into slag."

He walked into the workshop and examined the cores' exterior casings. They looked intact, but Breen might have installed something. Or it could've been there before Brad captured the ship.

Brad used some handy tools to carefully open the access panels. Once he could see inside, he examined everything for remote-kill devices.

"Nothing," he said. "These look fine. We'd have to plug them into an appropriate control system to get at their data, but they seem intact. How are you doing?"

"I'm pulling some remote-controlled explosives," she called back, as if she'd told him she was considering noodles for dinner. "Someone really wanted to make sure no one got at his home computer. It's wired into both security systems. Good thing I'm an amazing burglar."

He didn't think he'd ever understand her.

"I'll search the rest of the workshop while you clean that out."

The workshop was a pretty big room and it was far from empty. Various bins and shelves contained a lot of equipment and parts. It looked as if Breen enjoyed working on computers.

His examination of the contents was relatively straightforward until he found one of the lockers filled with explosives. A lot. All seemingly wired into a remote panel and com unit.

That wasn't good. There seemed to be enough here to blow up the entire house.

"This place is wired for remote destruction," he called out.

Moments later, she stood next to him, examining the setup. "Yeah, this is pretty extreme," she admitted. "It looks as if he wanted to make sure he could eliminate all the evidence. I'd best disarm this first."

"That pretty much matches my feelings," he agreed dryly. "Is the office safe?"

She nodded. "I still need to complete disarming the remote-wipe functions, but the equipment won't burn."

He headed into the office to take a look around and stopped dead in his tracks. He'd already been able to tell that the office was as well decorated at the rest of the house, but that wasn't what captivated his attention.

The near wall had a piece of art that he hadn't been able to see from outside. It was worth far less than most of what he'd seen elsewhere in the building, but one that was infinitely more valuable to him.

It held the intricate curtain of metal strands that he'd last seen aboard *Mandrake's Heart* before the Terror had sent him Dutchman. The artwork he'd made his uncle that had sat on the bridge of the lost freighter.

---

"Are you sure that's yours?" Falcone asked before waving the question away. "Never mind. Of course you are. Well, that's a pretty direct link between the slavers and the Cadre, I think."

Brad stood there grappling with his spontaneously aroused anger and captivated by the unexpected ghost from his past. "A recent one, too. That means someone close to Breen had been aboard *Mandrake's Heart*. That really makes me wonder if my uncle or any of the other crew are still alive."

He forced himself to turn away from the sculpture and faced the computers. "The answer is on those."

"Maybe," she said. "Maybe not. You might very well have another avenue to find your uncle, though."

He shifted his gaze to her. "Like what?"

She held out a tablet. It showed the image of a small device. "This is a portable course plot. The kind a harbor pilot might use to mark all the local landmarks when piloting a foreign ship through familiar space.

"It's the same kind of thing that the slavers said their pilots used to keep the location of their base from anyone on the crew of a ship they brought there."

Brad examined the image. "Where did you find this?"

"Here in the office. I took the tablet with me when I ran back in to deal with the bomb. I think the accompanying text might interest you."

It took him a few moments to bring that up. The image turned out to be an attachment to a message from a nondescript account. All it said was *make sure to get the computer cores, helm memory, and this.*

"That's why they wanted to destroy *Heart of Vengeance*," Brad said as understanding flooded him. "This is somewhere on my ship. It's probably in a bin with all the other detritus that Randall hasn't finished processing yet."

"Or he's already broken it down," she said softly. "Our luck hasn't been that great so far."

"We're still here, aren't we? Do we have enough proof to bring in some of your people now?"

Falcone looked around. "With your computer cores linking him to the slavers and the sculpture tying him directly to an act of piracy, I'd say we do. Still, we don't want to tip our hand. I'll bring in some people I can trust to start digging into the computers quietly.

"Meanwhile, you need to get a message back to your ship. Have your people find this device and get their asses here. I want the scientists on *Marie Curie* to examine it. As with everything else these bastards have done, it's probably booby-trapped."

Brad nodded and stepped away from her, bringing up his wrist-comp. Using the number Dr. Keller had provided, he called the scientist.

The man appeared on the display. "Keller."

"Doctor. I was wondering if you could send a message to *Heart* for me. Something inconspicuous."

"Of course."

He took an image of the tablet screen and sent it along. "Let them know I want them to search the salvaged gear for this device. It's incredibly important that they find and preserve it."

"What is it?" the man asked as he leaned forward to examine the image.

"It's potentially the key to locating the slavers. It's a device used by pilots to hold course data. Once they find it, they need to get to Ganymede so your people can unlock it. I'd count on it being encrypted and on it having self-destruct programming if someone attempts to get into it without the right codes."

The other man smiled. "You do know how to provide some interesting projects, Captain. I'll get the word to them at once. Was the rest of your mission successful?"

Brad looked over at where Falcone was summoning assistance. "Very much so. Remember, keep everything calm and low-key. We don't want to tip anyone off."

"Trust my discretion, Captain."

"I do. Thank you, Doctor."

———

Over the next hour, a dozen men and women infiltrated Breen's residence. None of them looked like security, but Falcone literally welcomed them with open arms. That was good enough for him.

The newcomers quickly made a plan to get all the gear out of the house and began executing it. While they worked, others started searching the house from top to bottom. No stone would remain unturned and they'd scan every wall, ceiling, and floor for hidden doors or compartments.

"I want this removed, too," Falcone told them, gesturing at Brad's sculpture. "It's important evidence. Treat it with kid gloves."

He was ridiculously grateful for her concern for his feelings. Then it occurred to him that she might be telling the man the literal truth. His artwork was the link tying Breen to the Cadre.

She stepped over to him. "They'll take care of this place. No one will ever know you or I were here. We don't have enough data to wake anyone up yet. We might as well get out of here and get some sleep."

"Do we have a place to go?"

Falcone nodded. "I had them get us a pair of rooms at one of the local hotels. A decent one but nothing that would stand out."

Part of him hated leaving the search for evidence to others, but he knew this wasn't his strength. Let the professionals do their part. He'd be at the forefront of the fighting once they located the slaver base.

———

The two of them quietly extracted themselves from Breen's neighborhood and made it to the hotel without comment.

Brad showered and fell into a dreamless sleep. One that felt it had barely begun when his wrist-comp signaled for his attention.

He grabbed it off the nightstand and sat blearily up. "Go."

"Captain Madrid?" It was Dr. Keller.

"Yes. Sorry. I was asleep. Is something wrong, Doctor?"

The other man smiled. "No. Something is right. Your pilot just called. They've located the device. They're on the way."

Relief flooded through Brad. He'd been afraid the lead wouldn't pan out. "That's good. What's their ETA?"

"They won't arrive here until early afternoon local. Rather, they wouldn't if they were actually coming to Ganymede."

He felt himself frowning. "I don't follow."

"Your man said that the reasoning behind you taking our ship was still in force. I'm having my people move *Marie Curie* to meet *Heart* away from Ganymede. We'll shave a number of hours off the time until my specialists get the device and draw less attention. I hope you don't mind my altering your instructions."

Brad rubbed his face. "No, that's actually sound thinking. You need to be ultra-careful with that device, though. It's the only directions to get to the slaver base we have."

"You may count on my people's skill and discretion. We'll do everything within our power to get the information safely and quickly."

"Call me the moment you have access, Doctor. And thank you. I won't forget this."

"Neither will I. Sleep well, Captain."

Brad disconnected and looked at the time. He wasn't going to be able to go back to sleep now. He'd be getting up to start the day in an hour anyway, so he might as well make an early start of it.

Today was going to be critical. He had to corral the support he needed to take the slavers without tipping his hand.

He had to assume the Cadre and slavers had the Mercenary Guild as penetrated as everything else. They'd get a report if he just showed up. So, he'd need to make contact in a way that wouldn't draw undue attention, yet get him in without any fuss.

Brad smiled. He knew just how to make that happen.

# CHAPTER TWENTY-SEVEN

Unlike the Mercenary Guild, the odds of anyone watching the Arbiter Guild offices were slim. After all, he'd already won that fight. They wouldn't waste personnel at unlikely areas.

Arbiter Kenna Blaze's building was almost tranquil so early in the morning. The only person who'd shown up so far was the young man Brad assumed was manning the desk.

"Is that her?" Falcone asked, sipping her coffee as she leaned against the wall along the street.

Brad looked at the image she was transmitting to his wrist-comp. He'd elected to stay out of sight in a sheltered alley behind the agent.

"That's her."

Falcone pushed away from the wall and casually headed to meet the other woman. "Excuse me. Are you Arbiter Blaze?"

The angle was bad for Brad to see anything, and the image from the agent's wrist-comp was even worse. All he could detect was the surprise in the arbiter's voice.

"Yes. Do I know you? If so, I apologize, but—"

"You don't know me, but you know this man."

The image on the wrist-comp moved until Brad saw the arbiter.

"Arbiter Blaze, if I might have a few minutes of your time, I think you'll want to hear what I have to say."

The woman's eyes widened. "Captain Madrid. I must confess I didn't anticipate meeting you again so soon. If you need to speak with me, might I suggest my office?"

"I'm a little concerned that the people who damaged my ship are trying to kill me, so I'd rather not be seen. Do you have a back way in?"

"You do know how to make a mysterious entrance. Yes, the building has a place around back for deliveries. No one will be there now. Should I let you in now?"

"That would be wonderful."

She smiled a little. "I confess that I can't wait to hear what is going on now. I'll see you in a few minutes."

Brad made his way around the building on one side while Falcone took the other. Neither of them saw any indication the building was being watched. The wide dock used for deliveries led up to a double-wide door that opened at their approach.

"Captain Madrid and mysterious friend," the arbiter said from just inside. "Please come in. We can go directly to my office without Achmed seeing us. No one will know you're here."

Falcone nodded approvingly as she looked around the arbiter's office a minute later. The pale wood paneling and plush white carpet seemed to meet with her approval.

Blaze sat behind her desk and gestured for them to take seats across from her. "What brings you to see me in such an unusual manner, Captain?"

Brad settled into his seat. "I assume you heard about the battle at Io."

"The ships that attacked a Commonwealth cruiser? It's all over the news. Were you involved?"

He nodded. "I was traveling with the cruiser. The attackers thought they were getting me because we fooled them. They were slavers."

Arbiter Blaze made an expression of distaste. "I'm glad you blew them up. Those people are a scourge on the universe. How can the Arbiter Guild assist in that task?"

"Perhaps it's time for me to introduce myself," Falcone said. "My name is Kate Falcone and I'm an agent of the Commonwealth Investigative Agency. Captain Madrid is assisting me in taking on the slavers. We need your help to move the investigation to the next level."

"Then you shall have whatever assistance I can provide," Blaze declared, "though I'm uncertain how settling a dispute will impact this situation."

Brad smiled. "We're certain they have the Mercenary Guild under observation. We need to get access to forces that we know won't get word to either the slavers or the Cadre.

"I'm hoping to convince you to call Factor Sara Kernsky and invite her here. Then I could speak candidly with her and no one would associate the meeting with me."

The woman reached out and touched her com panel without taking her eyes from his. Moments later, a male voice inquired what he could do for her.

"Paul, please call Factor Kernsky at the Mercenary Guild. I need to speak with her about a case. I'm afraid it's urgent, so if you could get her right away, that would be wonderful."

Once the call ended, Blaze considered them. "You've been very busy since you took possession of your ship, Captain."

"You could say that," he said with a wry smile. "It's only been a short while and we've had three battles with the slavers. Four, if you count when I seized her."

"I'll wager you won't be on their Christmas list."

"Only as a gift, perhaps. I'm definitely on the naughty side of the equation. On another note, I found the computer cores that were stolen from my ship."

The woman perked up. "You've secured my complete attention. That theft was a black mark on my guild and I'd love to see it erased. Where were they?"

"In Fabian Breen's basement," Falcone said. "We believe he's in the local leadership of the slavers."

The other woman frowned. "Breen? The man was an ass, but I've known him as a businessman in the area for decades. Are you sure?"

Falcone nodded. "The proof we found is beyond circumstantial. It's a definite and solid link."

"Okay. Assuming he's part of the slavers' organization, why break into a slaver ship and steal the computers?" Her eyes widened. "They had something important on them."

Brad smiled widely. "We think we're going to get coordinates to a major slaver base. Once we do, the Mercenary Guild is going to be the hammer that smashes them flat. We can't let them know we're coming."

The com chimed and Blaze answered it. "Blaze."

"Arbiter Blaze, this is Sara Kernsky. My schedule is fairly packed today. Could we meet tomorrow afternoon?"

Blaze shook her head as she looked at the screen on her desk. "This is far too urgent to delay. I can't go into details over the com, but I need you to come to my office right away. Alone."

There was a long moment of silence. "I'll be there in twenty minutes. I do hope this is worth all the cloak-and-dagger."

Blaze smiled coldly. "I think you'll love it. See you in twenty."

———

Sara Kernsky stopped in her tracks once Arbiter Blaze opened the door for her. The factor raised an eyebrow and stepped inside.

"Captain Madrid, this is an unexpected surprise. Is there a dispute between the Mercenary Guild and you that I'm unaware of? I assure you, we can probably come to terms without involving the Arbiter Guild."

He smiled. "We have no problems between us, Factor Kernsky. Arbiter Blaze is merely assisting me in making certain this meeting is private and unremarkable. I don't want people to know I'm even on Ganymede.

"This is my associate, Kate Falcone of the Commonwealth Investigative Agency. If you'd come in and have a seat, we've got quite the story for you."

They all sat down in a set of comfortable chairs and Brad told them the whole story: what they'd accomplished, what they hoped to do, and how they needed help doing it.

Once it became clear he was talking about the slavers, the factor's expression became quite serious. She listened intently and asked no questions.

After Brad finished, she remained silent for a few moments. "This is the most extraordinary tale I've heard since the Guild went after *Black Skull*. I can see now why you're worried they'll find out what you intend."

She shifted her gaze to Falcone. "I need to verify this story is true. One doesn't commit mercenary companies without being absolutely sure. No offense to you or Captain Madrid, but I have to make some calls.

"I know someone in the Commonwealth Investigative Agency that should be able to confirm you're with them. And I'll contact Captain Fields on *Freedom*. If they both confirm your story, then I'll start setting things up to help."

"You can have your friend verify 'Agent Falcon is in flight.' That code phrase will get him the confirmation that I'm active on Ganymede and that this is a valid request for help from the agency."

"Be discreet," Brad said softly. "These bastards have people everywhere. Make your lines of communication as secure as possible, and be completely sure you trust the people you tell this to."

Kernsky smiled and shook her head. "I've been at this a long time, Captain. You don't have to tell me how to do my job. Besides, my contact in the agency is beyond reproach. Arbiter Blaze, do you have a secure com screen I could use?"

"You can use mine. We'll step out and give you some privacy."

"No need."

The two women switched places and Kernsky entered a number. Someone they couldn't see picked up and Kernsky smiled. "Angie, I need you to check on something for me."

"Sure," the unseen woman said. "Hit me."

"I need you to verify someone is working on Ganymede and that a request for help is valid. I was told to tell you that 'Agent Falcon is in flight.'"

The silence from the other end was profound. "I don't need to check. That's valid. Sara, what's going on?"

"I can't say right now. We'll talk later. Thanks."

Kernsky disconnected and stared at Falcone. "When my sister vouches for someone, that carries a lot of weight. She's been in your local office for ten years. Time to confirm the rest."

The factor called *Freedom*. That wasn't as simple as it sounded, but it wasn't overly complex. The time delay due to the distance was enough to be noticeable, but not too bad.

"Captain Fields," she said after a few minutes. "Sara Kernsky with the Mercenary Guild."

"Ah, Factor Kernsky," Fields said. "I was just talking about you with a mutual friend a few days ago. He should be on Ganymede."

"He is. I'm just confirming he has your confidence."

"To the hilt. Fleet is backing his play."

She smiled. "That couldn't be clearer. Thank you."

The factor ended the call and stared at Brad. "You really think you can get the location of the slavers' base?"

"Let me make a call and see what the progress is."

Brad brought up his wrist-comp and made the connection to *Marie Curie*. It was closer than *Freedom*, so the transmission lag was noticeably shorter.

"Keller," the scientist said a few minutes later.

"Doctor, let's not mention names, just in case. How goes the project?"

The older man smiled. "Much more simply than we'd anticipated, actually. That old saw about possession being nine tenths of the law applies in the case of bypassing security, too. We cracked the encryption ten minutes ago. Without going into specifics, we have the data you wanted. How do we get it to you?"

Brad grinned. "I want you and my ship to head out into deep space. Call Captain Fields and arrange an out-of-the-way location where we can all meet. Have him send it to me as a secure message. He can use the last name of the man he assigned as my tour guide when we first met as the key."

The older man smiled widely. "All this skulking about makes me feel like a spy. I'll do that right away. Just in case, I'll have him send the coordinates we found along with it. One can never be too careful."

Brad ended the call and looked at everyone else. "That's the final link in the chain. If we can gather enough force before Mader can warn them, we should be able to smash the slavers where they live. If we can crush their leadership, we can get the handle we need to end them as an organization."

Kernsky nodded. "Their base will have formidable defenses. We'll want to strike before they have a chance to use them. I'll begin contacting companies I trust and issuing overriding contracts.

"I can get enough trustworthy mercenary companies without giving them any details. So long as we head into space to join up and they lock down communications, we should be secure from leaks."

The factor smiled harshly. "Make this work and you'll have earned a reputation no one can ever take away from you, Captain. Well done."

He nodded. "Now all we have to do is strike them hard and fast. Time is of the essence, with Mader in the wind and Breen off Ganymede. It wouldn't surprise me if they both ended up at this base. I want to make sure they don't slip away again or we'll have to do this all over again someday."

# CHAPTER TWENTY-EIGHT

AN ASTONISHINGLY SHORT for interplanetary travel but nerve-wrackingly painful four days later, Brad sat in *Freedom*'s wardroom with Captain Fields, Sara Kernsky, Dr. Keller, and a dozen mercenary leaders commanding almost three dozen ships. He'd just finished running through the full story again.

Commander William Branson of Heimdall's Raiders spoke up first. "Well, I'll be damned. And this is all confirmed?"

Fields made a noncommittal gesture. "We know the information is potentially good, but we can't verify it without poking our heads into the hornet's nest. I have no reason to suspect it's some kind of elaborate trap, if that's what you're asking."

The big mercenary nodded, his expression dark. "They'd pull back a stump if they came after us. Worse than when they sent those little ships after your cruiser. That doesn't worry me. My concern is that we avoid jumping an innocent mining station."

That was valid, Brad thought. The coordinates in the recovered device had pointed them at an isolated mining base serving the asteroids Jupiter dragged behind itself in orbit. Pretty far off the beaten path, but a place that would have a fair number of miners.

If the place was legitimate, those would be innocent civilians. If it was a slaver installation where the work was done by prisoners, they'd have to be even more cautious. As everyone knew, slavers had no qualms about executing their slaves to prevent wagging tongues.

Since Brad knew the slavers or the Cadre had *Mandrake's Heart*, the stakes were even higher. His uncle and old crewmates might be in the firing line too.

"Perhaps that's where I and my fellow scientists might be of assistance," Dr. Keller said. "*Marie Curie* is outfitted with probes designed to tease secrets from deep inside Jupiter. To say its sensors are…well, sensitive is something of an understatement.

"I propose we modify them to disable the active sensor bands and use them to passively gather data around the mining facility. If it's a normal civilian outpost, no one will even see them. If it's more, there is a risk, but much less than sending in a ship to do the same."

That set off a lively debate among the mercenary captains. Some of them wanted to go right in and bring the hammer down if there was any sign this facility belonged to the slavers. The woman running the Pythons was the strongest advocate of that approach.

Captain Fields took the opposite side of the coin. He wanted to get a complete layout of potential forces and facilities before they committed any ships at all.

Brad knew he had the least experience of any of these people, so he let them argue for a bit before he ventured an opinion.

"Both plans have their plusses and minuses," he said. "I propose we split the difference. Most of the ships wait and come in hot. They don't have to attack until we're certain what we're dealing with.

"Still, the slavers will kill their prisoners if they think an attack is likely. We need to get strike teams in to quietly infiltrate the base. Then we can stand between the slavers and their victims while the cavalry comes screaming in."

Kernsky cleared her throat. "I think that's a good idea, but forgive me if I suggest someone with a bit more experience lead that mission. No offense, Captain Madrid, but you're new to the game. A rising star, perhaps, but we need a steady hand at the controls for this."

Commander Branson grinned. "I know the perfect man for the job:

me! In fact, Captain Madrid owes Heimdall's Raiders a favor. I'm calling it due."

Brad didn't mind. "Please. I suggest we take a very large team to infiltrate the base. We can leave just about everyone on their small craft and have them grapple with *Heart* on the way in. The acceleration will be low unless we're spotted and someone starts shooting.

"We can communicate via low-powered coms and settle on a final boarding plan once we get into position and see what we're dealing with."

"We're talking basically putting this intrusion team up front and using the ships to take out the fixed defenses in a second wave," Fields said. "We land enough men to swamp the defenders while your lead elements keep the innocent people safe. I like it.

"The first thing we need to do is verify we're in the right place. I say we send probes in without any transmitters at all. Let them collect data, and one of us picks them up on the far side. We'll need to have ships coming in on multiple vectors to be sure we stop anyone from running."

Kernsky nodded slowly. "If we're sure that this isn't the place, a tight beam to warn us off won't hurt. No signal means we're good to go and we kick off phase two on a preset schedule. *Heart of Vengeance* will slip in, carrying the strike teams. Once *Heart* detects all hell breaking loose on the mining station, they call us all in for phase three."

"I'll take a few of the smaller ships around to the other side," Fields said. "With *Freedom* at hand, that should help balance things out. I figure we should all be in position in about twelve hours, if we stay clear of detection range."

"We have to assume they have listening posts out to detect incoming ships so that they have time to run," Falcone objected. "Take twice that long and go way out. Then we come in slowly and be careful to avoid any sentries. Better safe than sorry."

The Fleet officer considered that. "Agreed."

They spent the next three hours wrangling the details, but the big picture was settled. Brad let the older professionals make sure they didn't miss anything while he started planning the raid itself in his head.

The demon deep inside him was raring to go, and that made him even more determined to keep it on a tight leash. His uncle's life might ride on his maintaining control. And there would be more victims down there. He just knew it.

He had to locate the prisoners first. If they screwed that up, he'd never be able to live with himself. Revenge was fine and good, but much sweeter if he took everything away from the bastards first—and didn't get any innocents killed along the way!

———

So Brad and his people would have the best data, they'd gone around the mining station with *Freedom*. Waiting for the probes was nerve-wracking, but the tiny devices came up on them exactly on schedule.

Boats from the Fleet cruiser retrieved them while the strike team leaders waited in the wardroom to see if this was going to pay off. It only took a few moments for Brad to relax a little.

"No way this is a mining facility," Fields said as he examined the first images. "Look at all these ships parked out here. Sure, a few freighters would be appropriate, but there's more than two dozen vessels. I see a few freighters, but at least half are fighting craft."

Brad tapped one section of the large display. "Can you enhance this any?"

The image was surprisingly high-resolution, and it enlarged with plenty of detail for him to make a positive identification. "This is the freighter *Mandrake's Heart*. I know for a fact the Cadre took her a few months back."

Everyone looked at him closely, but no one asked how he knew.

Fields nodded slowly, understanding in his eyes. "Then we're in the right place. I'm hereby greenlighting phase two. Let's look at the facility itself."

Brad didn't know who'd built the original mining facility, but it looked as if the core was a real operation. Someone had stabilized a large asteroid at some point and placed a smelting unit on the surface. Heat exchange was probably a bitch.

That explained a lot of the domes and external facilities he saw, but not all of them. Not even most of them. It seemed as if the slavers had honeycombed the asteroid with tunnels and placed domes all over it.

What could they use them all for? And one towered over the rest. What did they do there?

Branson provided the answer. "Look at this ship floating nearby. It looks as if they're stripping it. The valuable parts will probably be sold on the black market, and the hull will end up getting melted down. No evidence left.

"They could also use some of the parts to modify the other ships, and sell some of them to people who aren't concerned with a legal history for their purchase. Sort of like a chop shop on a grand scale."

"What about the big dome?" Brad asked. "What do they use it for?"

Fields smiled without the least bit of humor. "Prisoners, I suspect. See the big hatches on the outside at surface level? Ones like that are normally used on ships as bay doors for small craft. Those are too close to surface passages for that. I'll wager they plan on using them to vent the atmosphere if there's trouble."

"How do we stop that?"

Branson smiled coldly. "We land people on the surface and weld the hatches closed from the outside. If they can't open them, they'll have to go to plan B. See the personnel hatches next to the big ones? Once we send the main strike teams in, we have the welders go in and watch over the prisoners."

"And where do we send in the main teams?"

The mercenary tapped several locations on the asteroid. "These locks don't look as well used as the others. See how the surface dust is so heavy on them? Odds are good these lead to less-traveled areas of the base. We pick some that are fairly close to the prison dome, just in case, and send in teams to start interdicting the slavers."

"I have a few more suggestions," Fields said. "Have *Heart of Vengeance* use her Gatlings to put mass driver slugs into the tunnels around the smaller domes. That'll keep the slavers from getting rein- forcements to the big dome for a bit.

"Also, I think you need to get into the larger dome faster. What if they have explosive charges? You'll want to make sure there aren't any other self-destruct mechanisms. Get it wrong and hundreds—potentially thousands—of people will die."

That made Branson nod. "I like the way you think, Captain. The teams can verify where the majority of the prisoners are, too. That makes using mass driver slugs on the other domes a little less risky."

"But not completely so," Brad said. "We'll never be sure where the slaves are when we go in. We can't possibly do that without having better intelligence."

"What if someone could tap into all their communications?" Wandry asked. The scientist had come along in case there was a problem with the probes, and had been sitting quietly in the back of the wardroom.

Fields gave her his full attention. "What are you thinking?"

"It should be possible to get taps into the com system. Then we could potentially see everything in the rest of the base. At the very least, we could do something up front to be sure no one knew we had people in the big dome before we're ready."

Brad frowned. "How do you do that?"

"See where the dome connects to the rest of the base? Those are power and com junctions right there. If I can get into them on the outside, I can record the data. Once I have enough for a loop, I can overwrite the information going to the security systems. They wouldn't even know we'd gone in until the main attack gets under way."

Branson grinned. "Now, *that's* what I'm talking about! How long would you need?"

The woman shrugged. "It depends on the level of protective security in the system. Anywhere between five and thirty minutes to get access. Say fifteen minutes of recorded data."

"So, if we allow for an hour, you think that's enough time?"

"It should be, unless these people are far more paranoid than I expect."

"They're slavers," Brad said. "*Paranoid* doesn't even begin to describe them."

"That's not what I mean," the scientist said with a shake of her head. "How likely do they think it is someone will hack them from right out on the surface? If I jack into their system right under their noses, they'd have to have prepared for insiders doing that all along."

"I wouldn't count against that," he warned. "They might very well worry about someone in their own ranks betraying them."

"That's why I gave us half an hour to get in," the scientist said smugly. "I'm a pro at this kind of thing. Look how fast I got into their encrypted navigation device. Something that they had to worry would fall into the wrong hands."

Fields inclined his head. "Point taken. Still, that means you'd be in a very hostile environment. People might end up shooting at you."

"Don't be ridiculous," the woman said. "I'd stay out on the surface. If someone comes looking for a fight, I'll run back to the shuttle like a good little noncombatant."

That evoked general laughter.

"I think that plan has the greatest possibility of success," Fields said. "We'll divide up the landing areas and start making contingency plans. We have another twelve hours to get into position, so I want to get *Heart* moving in eight."

"I'm taking the dome," Brad said, leaving no room for argument. "I'll have some of the others with me, but I'm in charge of that aspect of the strike."

No one argued, which was good. If his uncle was alive, it was his responsibility to keep him that way. The final act of this little play was about to get underway.

# CHAPTER TWENTY-NINE

GETTING close to the base wasn't going to be easy. The slavers had numerous small sensor platforms scattered around the area to keep an eye out for exactly what *Heart* was planning to do.

Thankfully, Fleet had some tech that would at least make it possible. The cruiser's engineers had been hard at work installing thermal bafflers to his ship.

Amusingly, they managed to fully outfit the corvette with the spares they kept aboard to replace battle damage, and still had their own gear in place.

Brad waited until he had the word that all the small craft were bound to his hull by monofilament grapnels, and then had Marshal give the ship enough thrust to take them to the base once they'd shut the drives down and started coasting.

The plan was to detach the small craft and make their insertion while *Heart* used just enough thrust to park among the ships waiting for the slavers to disassemble them. From there, the corvette could power up and move very quickly, if need be.

The base wouldn't have as heavy a sensor net so close in. Brad was counting on that to mask the corvette slowing.

Once *Heart* was in position, she could fire her Gatlings without fear of discovery. The defenders wouldn't know precisely where the assault was coming from until they managed to backtrack the damage and guess the area of space the ship had to be in.

*Heart* could use the parked ships as cover, too. That wouldn't save them for long once the enemy started shooting at them, but the slavers would have other problems to deal with in very short order.

Brad's gut was tight as they killed their drives and started the ballistic element of their insertion.

"Have we locked down everything?" he asked Randall over the intercom. "We can't let them spot us."

"*Freedom* says we're as black as space. No thermal detections. Relax, Captain. These bafflers are amazing. I wonder if we could keep them when this is all over."

"Take that up with Captain Fields. Thanks, Mike."

The probes had mapped out several armed sensor platforms, so Brad knew where to look as they came closer to the base. They passed within ten thousand kilometers of two and neither made a peep. They'd gone undetected.

"Coming up on detach point, Captain," Marshal said. "Five minutes."

Brad rose to his feet. "You know the plan. Keep safe and come running if we need you."

He made it back to *Heart*'s shuttle and strapped into place beside Saburo. "Are we ready?"

"No. Can we have a do-over?"

Brad gave him a hard stare and then smiled. "You really need to keep the day job."

"That's my plan. I'm adding something significant to my resume today. Yes, we're all set. Every boat has reported green. We can depart on schedule."

A few minutes later, right on schedule, they detached from *Heart*. The ship pulled slowly away as they changed vector, leaving the smaller craft to proceed in unpowered flight. They wouldn't brake until they were right on top of the asteroid.

He'd been warned the deceleration would be savage, but it

exceeded his expectations, causing spots in his vision before the shuttle came to rest on the asteroid's surface.

Monofilament grapnels locked it into place before Saburo led the men out. No one spoke, so as not to warn any of the slavers that they had guests. Everyone already knew their part in the plan.

Low-powered suit thrusters made for quick movement on the dark surface of the asteroid. They happened to be facing away from the sun and Jupiter at the moment, so there wasn't much to see.

Brad took personal responsibility for Wandry, shepherding her to the power and com junction boxes for the large dome.

The scientist went right to work, opening the panels and examining the contents for a long moment before pulling tools out of her bag. Five minutes later, she turned to him and gave him a thumbs-up.

Brad leaned close so that his helmet touched hers. "You're in?"

"You bet. This wasn't secured at all. Well, not against anyone that knows the first thing about communications security." Her voice sounded muffled when transmitted by vibration through the helmets. "Give me fifteen minutes to record a loop and I'll give you the high sign when we're live."

It felt more like hours, but he focused his attention on the team nearest his location. They were using cold weld on one of the large airlocks. It worked chemically and required no bright lights for anyone to wonder about.

He leaned back over and touched helmets with Wandry again. "Did you see any prisoners in there?"

"Oh, yeah. It looks like one of the old refugee camps you see in historical vids. Check it out."

She held up a handheld monitor.

The image was small, but he could see numerous camera feeds in rotation. The inside of the dome looked like a cross between an illegal trash dump and a prison. Saying it was filthy was being far too kind.

Also, their estimate on the number of prisoners was badly off. There were easily a thousand people in there. Minimum. More pessimistically, he'd have to bet on at least fifteen hundred. He'd pass that information on when he kicked the attack off.

The camera angles weren't the best at seeing the guards, but there were some. A major concentration of them sat at a position near the main airlock leading to the rest of the base. Several dozen men and women manned heavy weapons to keep the prisoners docile. Just the sight of them made his blood boil.

He motioned for Saburo to come over and touched helmets. "That's your target. I want them dead before they warn anyone we're here."

"Copy that," the mercenary said. "Two dozen dead slavers coming up. I'll go set up outside the personnel airlock with the best angle."

Brad once more touched helmets with Wandry. "Can you see the rest of the base?"

"No. The feeds are outgoing only. Once we get inside, I might be able to tap into any interior systems on the other side of this short passage."

"That might not be the safest place to be."

"Have you seen those people?" the scientist demanded. "How can I cower in a corner with them depending on me? Hell, no. I'm going."

Brad smiled. Courage came in all sizes and forms. "How are you doing on recording the loop?"

"Three minutes left. It'll take me another fifteen seconds to get the feed switched. When I do, I'll cut all coms into the dome. No one will be warning anyone we're here. I'll also cut the power to the interior lock. They won't be able to run."

"Excellent," Brad said, pleased. "Give me the high sign when we can go. If there is a problem, wave both arms."

"You got it."

He made his way over to Saburo and his men. All of them were arrayed outside a small airlock and looked ready to go. One of the men had some kind of portable rocket launcher for the guard post. It had a rotary magazine and at least six munitions.

Brad readied his rifle and watched Wandry. The moment she gave him a thumbs-up, he hit his suit transmitter. It was set to go right to the shuttle, and that would retransmit his message at full power.

"Viking Actual to all units. Prisoner count is estimated at fifteen hundred, repeated, one five zero zero. Initiate ingress. Go! Go! Go!"

Saburo and his men piled into the airlock as soon as they got the outer door open. Someone hit the cycle button and the pressure started increasing. This was it.

————

The inner door opened and the man with the heavy weapon stepped inside. He handled the switch from virtually no gravity at all to maybe half a $g$ without issue.

The rest of them waited as he opened fire. The backblast from the rocket launcher scorched the bulkhead beside the airlock, and an intense explosion rocked them.

The sound was more furious than the damage, he knew. The explosives were designed not to breach hulls. That said, they obviously maimed and killed people, based on the screams coming from the target zone.

His men rushed into the dome after the heavy-weapons gunner fired three times, setting up behind the nearest cover and opening fire with their rifles.

Brad dropped into place beside Saburo and picked a staggering slaver as his target. The man was beating on the airlock door behind the security post. The one Wandry had cut power to. The sight of the emaciated prisoners cowering all around them left him with no mercy to spare, so he shot the man in the back with no guilt at all.

In ten seconds, they'd killed every slaver in sight. That was their cue to advance and make sure it really was clear of enemy combatants.

Strike teams that had used the other exterior airlocks to get inside began sweeping the crowd, making sure there were no slavers in the mix. That seemed unlikely, but one never knew.

Brad pulled off his helmet and started shouting toward the prisoners. "Everyone! Listen up! We're here to rescue you, but you need to keep back. If we think you're a threat, we might accidentally shoot you. Let us secure the base and then we can tell you what's going on."

That really set off a lot of chatter and excitement, but Brad didn't have time to spare them, even though he wanted to search the milling people for his uncle. He had more important fish to fry.

He put his helmet back on, signaled for someone to bring Wandry inside, and focused his attention on the reports streaming back in over the radio. It seemed that they'd caught the slavers flat-footed. The strike teams were making good progress rolling up the bad guys.

That momentum would change as soon as the enemy got their feet underneath them and started fighting back. The good guys really needed to punch out the heaviest concentrations of slavers now, while they had a fighting chance.

One of the mercenaries got the scientist inside and she walked through the bodies around the slaver guard post with her eyes closed. That didn't stop her from getting right to work as soon as she was in place beside the controls.

"I've reactivated the com, subject to my password," she said. "No one can use the lines into this dome but me." She sounded as if she were talking just so she could hear her own voice.

"There," she said after a minute. "I'm seeing data from the rest of the base. I can start scanning the channels and locating heavy concentrations of people. I've got our people dialed in, there won't be any mistakes."

"Are you seeing any threats?" he asked.

"Give me a minute. I have to get my bearings. I see several places where the enemy is gathering, but I don't know where they are yet."

A few more seconds went by and she jerked. "I found one. They're not too far away from us and look like they're headed in our direction. I recognize the guy you were looking for, too."

Brad leaned over and looked at the screen she was working on. There were dozens of armed men streaming down a corridor. The man in front was Fabian Breen. He was in a vac-suit and was directing his men forward while hefting a bulging pack.

"Saburo!" Brad called out. "We have company on the way. We need to move into the base and keep them back while Wandry calls in strikes on the rest."

Once his noncom had gathered the strike forces together—about forty men in the dome—he nodded. "We're ready to open the hatch. Everyone else stand back."

At his signal, Wandry opened the lock doors and his men rushed through. The enemy hadn't quite reached the area, so they were able to get to the smaller dome next to them and set up defensive positions in peace.

That's when Brad heard the distant shriek of alarms. Loss of pressure. The mass driver slugs were starting to arrive. He hoped Wandry could keep them on target, though it wouldn't matter for the strike teams. They were all suited up.

That's when the slavers rushed through the hatch ahead of them and ran into a hail of bullets. The front rank died, but Brad didn't see Breen among them. He must've held back at the last moment.

The exchange of fire became intense, and he was glad they had cover. The slavers were being forced to run through their fields of fire to get at them and paying for the privilege in blood.

"Wandry," Brad called out over the radio. "How many of them are still in front of us?"

The woman didn't respond for a moment. "Not a lot. Two or three dozen. I'm more concerned about the ones cutting around you."

He ducked low so he could focus on what she was saying. "Repeat that. Cutting around us how?"

"There are half a dozen of them exiting a lock from the corridor ahead of you. It looks like they're coming to the outside of the dome."

Brad remembered the pack Breen was carrying. If it was filled with explosives, the man could breach the dome.

"Saburo," he snapped. "I need a dozen men right now. Send them after me and back out the lock in the dome. Wandry will tell you where."

He didn't wait for a response before heading back to the prisoner dome at a run. If he didn't stop Breen, hundreds of innocent people could die.

# CHAPTER THIRTY

BRAD CYCLED through the lock in a rush, weapon up and searching as he transitioned to microgravity. The asteroid had rotated to face Jupiter, so he spotted the slavers as soon as he came out.

Four of them were looking around with pistols in their hands while a fifth was propping the pack against the dome's exterior wall. They saw him at about then and opened fire.

Unlike Brad, they clearly had no training in firing a gun in zero *g*. Or, apparently, for dealing with the recoil of a firearm when operating in grav-boots. This was clearly *not* Breen's A-team.

Brad had no idea how close the initial shots came, but they didn't get off a second volley before they went sprawling backwards with only their boots allowing them to keep a semblance of balance. One of them even lost his footing. With no gravity to speak of, the slaver wouldn't be seeing the ground again anytime soon, most likely.

Ignoring them all, Brad shot the man with the pack five times, using his suit thrusters to counteract the recoil. One shot was probably enough, but he wanted to be sure.

The dead slaver—Breen, he hoped—kicked spasmodically and floated away, blood leaking from his suit.

That's when Saburo came out with reinforcements. The men spread out and expertly shot the flailing slavers in short order.

"How many did you say there were, Wandry?" Brad asked over the radio.

"Six."

"Crap," he said to Saburo. "We're missing one. Probably Breen, with our luck. We need to spread out and find him before he does something else. Get that bomb dealt with, too."

"That's easy."

The noncom used his thrusters to fly out to the pack, grabbed it, and tossed it straight up. It quickly vanished into the darkness.

"That was a little dangerous, don't you think?" Brad asked dryly. "What if it had gone off?"

"Then I wouldn't be getting my ass chewed out later?"

"Got it in one."

Saburo quickly sent men off in every direction, choosing to remain with Brad. "Which way shall we go?"

"Which direction was the nearest shuttle docking area? Maybe he was looking to get away while his men planted the charges."

The mercenary checked his comp. "This way, I think."

Both of them headed away from the large dome and quickly made it to a substantially smaller one with a roof-mounted shuttle hatch. It was open.

"Do you think he's gone already?" Saburo asked.

"Only one way to find out."

Brad expertly flew up and literally ran into a shuttle exiting the dome. It wasn't going that fast, so the impact only jarred him. He managed to grab on before the pilot kicked the thrusters to full and sped away from the asteroid. He only had time to hear Saburo's surprised shout before he was out of suit radio range.

He managed to hold on but lost his rifle in the unexpected encounter. He'd need to rely on his pistol and blade. If, of course, he could get inside the shuttle. If not, he'd have to wait until it docked and find a way into the ship Breen was using to escape.

That's who it had to be, he thought.

The shuttle was of a standard design, so there were handholds on the outside to facilitate extravehicular activities. Brad held on tightly at all times and quickly deployed a safety line to one of the provided attachment points. No way he was going Dutchman again.

He worked his way to the airlock in short stages. He'd attach a new line and then disengage the previous one with the manual disconnect. It took perhaps fifteen minutes to make the short journey.

Unsurprisingly, the airlock wasn't secured. There wasn't much point. After all, how often did a shuttle pilot have to worry about hitchhikers?

If the layout of the shuttle was standard, Brad could guess where Breen was with a high degree of certainty. Unless, of course, the man suspected the person he'd run into was somehow still outside. Or if he'd even seen Brad at all.

Hmmm. There weren't any obvious cameras, but the controls would let the pilot know the airlock was cycling. That left the man plenty of time to get into position to ambush him.

If he saw the indicator. That was the conundrum. If Brad guessed wrong, he'd come in facing the opposite direction from the man trying to kill him.

Well, if Breen didn't know he was out there, it would take him time to react. Best to play it safe. Get in as fast as possible and be ready for an attack from the rear of the shuttle.

It would take the airlock fifteen seconds to cycle to vacuum. Then he'd face the same time pressurizing. He'd be trapped once he committed himself, too.

The bloodlust briefly threatened to overwhelm him, but he savagely repressed it. He couldn't—he wouldn't—allow his trauma to make him fail. He had to go into this with all his faculties.

Taking a deep breath, he pressed the control outside the airlock and watched it begin to cycle. Fifteen seconds later, he was inside and the pressure was starting to build.

This was the moment of truth. He pulled both his blade and pistol. He'd use the blade for a close attacker and the pistol for the more distant pilot's controls.

The gravity was on inside the shuttle and he shot out like a sprinter off the line. A shout of surprise immediately preceded several pistol shots from up front. The other man hadn't been quite ready.

Brad put several rounds into him and then grunted as someone shot him in the back, a heavy slug that punched through his suit's armor. There were two of them!

Already feeling weaker, he rolled and slashed with his blade. The first swing was lucky and took half the man's pistol and a number of his fingers.

That sent the ambusher staggering back, clawing at a blade on his belt with his off hand. He should've practiced the maneuver. And he should've paid more attention to Brad.

He was so focused on getting his weapon out that he stood there and let Brad cut his legs off at the knees. The strike was an automatic response he'd drilled far too many times to count. One he instantly regretted as it probably meant Breen would die before they questioned him.

Groaning with pain, Brad levered himself to his feet and kicked the blade clear of the man's twitching hand. He saw it was Breen.

A look at the front of the shuttle told him the second man was dead in the control couch, his eyes staring sightlessly at the two living combatants.

Not that Breen was going to be alive more than a few seconds without medical assistance.

"Aren't you going to save me for the critical information I could give you?" Breen gasped out.

"You mean you'd cooperate?" Brad asked as he sat heavily on the floor. He had to make the attempt, he supposed, as much as he wanted to just watch the man bleed out.

He grabbed the man's safety line and wrapped it tightly around his bleeding stumps. The pulsing blood slowed to a trickle but didn't stop.

"I figured you as the kind to hold out and taunt us with everything we'll never get from you," Brad said. "Or to lie. That was my second guess."

The other man laughed weakly. "I suppose you know me better than I'd guessed. You think you've won, don't you? I'll tell you this for free. We're only the leading edge. The Cadre will come for you soon enough."

"We found Mader on Io, by the way," Brad ventured.

That seemed to surprise the slaver. Then the man laughed again. "Serves the Cadre bastard right for underestimating you. After the hell he gave me, I only wish he'd come out to rub my face in it in person.

"I don't know how you unraveled my organization like this, but the Cadre will just create another one. We're useful to them."

Breen was fading even with his severed limbs bound. Brad could see it in his color. The bleeding had been too intense and the man was going into shock. If he wanted answers to any questions, Brad had best ask them while the man was still alive.

"I've wondered since the start. Why *Mandrake's Heart*? What did she have that drew the Terror in person? Not the cargo of monofilament. He could've sent anyone to capture it. He came himself."

Breen was already sagging, but he smiled. "You'd be shocked if I told you. And don't expect any of the crew to tell you. They aren't here, though I hear the Terror kept his hands on some survivors. This base is *nothing* to what the Cadre has, by the way. You'll probably find them there, suffering."

The man used his good hand to rub his face. He'd taken the gloves off sometime after getting on the shuttle. "I imagined this moment. Thought I'd come out on top. Who the hell are you, Madrid?"

"The man who is going to end your organization and the Cadre once and for all."

The demon inside Brad wanted to drag the dying slaver to the airlock and send him into the Dark in style, but he was so tired. Tired in a physical sense, but spiritually, too. He wasn't going to let the demon have him. Not anymore.

Moments later, Breen's breathing slowed and then stopped. The man was dead.

Rather than waiting for someone to come for him, Brad climbed to his feet, reoriented the shuttle, and headed for where *Heart* was hiding. He called ahead to let them know he was coming and was injured. That was the last thing he remembered doing.

————

Brad woke up in *Freedom*'s infirmary. There was a weird kind of symmetry to seeing the familiar ceiling again. At least this time, he still had his memories.

Dr. Merrine looked down at him as soon as he caught her attention by moving. "Ah, I see our guest is awake, again. Welcome back."

"We need to stop meeting like this, Doctor."

She laughed. "I heartily agree. Your crew rendezvoused with your shuttle and got you here as quickly as possible. You were shot twice and lost some blood but won't have any permanent injuries."

Not physically, anyway.

He knew better than to try to sit up. Instead, he relaxed. "What about this mission? Did we save the prisoners?"

The doctor rested her hand on his shoulder. "You did. Captain Fields just landed the marines. The asteroid base is fully under our control now, and you kept the slavers from harming their prisoners."

Brad let out a shaky breath. "Did we catch any slavers?"

"Some, or so I hear. We won't know the final count for a few hours. Rest."

That proved easier than he'd have liked. Sleep took him in seconds.

He roused what felt like only seconds later but had a different woman staring down at him. No, two women.

"Agent Falcone. Factor Kernsky." His voice sounded a trifle stronger.

"We're glad to see you made it," Falcone said. "Saburo was seriously pissed that you left him behind like that. He said something about trading ass-chewings with you."

Brad laughed and then groaned as his back started hurting. "He should know better than to complain. You snooze, you lose."

He groped for the glass of water and took a sip to gather his thoughts. "You're up here. I figured you'd be down there, gathering intelligence."

"We'll get some, but not as much as I'd hoped. Breen wiped the computer. I'll deal with the prisoners we caught and see if any of the ships we captured has data that will prove useful. It's the best I can do.

"And in case no one told you, the mercenaries chased down every ship that ran. None got away. We made a clean sweep. Did Breen tell you anything useful?"

Brad shook his head. "Not really. That the Cadre would rebuild the slaver organization and that they'd be coming for us all soon enough. That this was their one main base and that the Cadre has at least one big one, too. That could have been a lie, though."

He considered telling them what Breen had said about the crew of *Mandrake's Heart*, but decided to keep that to himself. If his family and crewmates were still alive, he'd keep working hard to find them. No need to telegraph his plans.

No need to single them out, either, or the Terror would guess who he was. He still felt it necessary to keep that to himself. Maybe that was idiotic, but it was how he felt—and if the Terror learned who he was, that same family and crewmates would suffer for his actions.

Falcone clapped him on the shoulder. "I've got to head back down and start working with Captain Fields on how to get the former slaves off this place. They'll all need to be debriefed. They might be able to point us at other facilities, though several slavers have confirmed part of what Breen told you. This was their one big base.

"You do good work, Captain Madrid. Look for a really nice bonus in the near future. It was a pleasure working with you and I hope we can do it again real soon."

The agent squeezed his shoulder and walked out of the infirmary.

Kernsky watched the other woman walk out before turning back to him. "With how this turned out, I'm not sure I'd be happy with that expectation."

He laughed and then groaned again.

The factor took a step back. "I'll let you get some sleep, but rest assured you and your company have earned some serious credit with the Guild. Hell, with a lot of guilds. You brought down the slavers. That's an achievement you can be proud of. Well done, Captain. Well done."

She walked out the door and left him lying there with his own thoughts.

He might have stopped the slavers, but the Cadre was still out there. The Terror was still out there. He'd make the bastard pay one day very soon. He'd killed Breen and he'd do the same to the Cadre leader. Shari demanded it.

But he couldn't do it with this darkness inside him. He had to be in control, not a slave to the Dark. He had a problem that was too big for him to solve on his own, and it was time to admit it.

He pressed the call button beside his bed, and Dr. Merrine quickly appeared.

"Are you in pain?" she asked.

"Yes," he said hoarsely. "But not the physical kind. I need to talk to someone about the rage inside me. The anger I can only barely control. I'm tired of it dominating me."

She pulled up a seat and sat. "Then you've come to the right place. This is a Fleet cruiser, Captain Madrid. I'm almost as good a counselor as I am a surgeon and I'm told I'm a terrific listener."

# ABOUT THE AUTHORS

#1 Bestselling Military Science Fiction author **Terry Mixon** served as a non-commissioned officer in the United States Army 101st Airborne Division. He later worked alongside the flight controllers in the Mission Control Center at the NASA Johnson Space Center supporting the Space Shuttle, the International Space Station, and other human spaceflight projects.

He now writes full time while living in Texas with his lovely wife and a pounce of cats.

———

**Glynn Stewart** is the author of *Starship's Mage*, a bestselling science fiction and fantasy series where faster-than-light travel is possible–but only because of magic. His other works include science fiction series *Duchy of Terra*, *Castle Federation* and *Vigilante*, as well as the urban fantasy series *ONSET* and *Changeling Blood*.

Writing managed to liberate Glynn from a bleak future as an accountant. With his personality and hope for a high-tech future intact, he lives in Kitchener, Ontario with his partner, their cats, and an unstoppable writing habit.

# OTHER BOOKS BY TERRY MIXON

You can always find the most up to date listing of Terry's titles on Amazon at
author.to/terrymixon

*Scorched Earth*

The Vigilante Duology with Glynn Stewart

**Heart of Vengeance**

*Oath of Vengeance*

Bound By Stars: A Vigilante Series with Glynn Stewart

*Bound By Law*

*Bound by Honor*

*Bound by Blood*

Want Terry to email you when he publishes a new book in any format or when one goes on sale? Go to TerryMixon.com/Mailing-List and sign up. Those are the only times he'll contact you. No spam.

# OTHER BOOKS
# BY GLYNN STEWART

For release announcements join the
mailing list or visit **GlynnStewart.com**

## STARSHIP'S MAGE
Starship's Mage
Hand of Mars
Voice of Mars
Alien Arcana
Judgment of Mars
UnArcana Stars
Sword of Mars
Mountain of Mars
The Service of Mars
A Darker Magic
Mage-Commander (upcoming)

**Starship's Mage: Red Falcon**
Interstellar Mage
Mage-Provocateur
Agents of Mars

Pulsar Race: A Starship's Mage Universe Novella

## DUCHY OF TERRA
The Terran Privateer
Duchess of Terra
Terra and Imperium
Darkness Beyond
Shield of Terra
Imperium Defiant
Relics of Eternity
Shadows of the Fall
Eyes of Tomorrow

# SCATTERED STARS

**Scattered Stars: Conviction**
Conviction
Deception
Equilibrium
Fortitude (upcoming)

# PEACEKEEPERS OF SOL

Raven's Peace
The Peacekeeper Initiative
Raven's Course
Drifter's Folly (upcoming)

# EXILE

Exile
Refuge
Crusade
Ashen Stars: An Exile Novella

# CASTLE FEDERATION

Space Carrier Avalon
Stellar Fox
Battle Group Avalon
Q-Ship Chameleon
Rimward Stars
Operation Medusa
A Question of Faith: A Castle Federation Novella

# SCIENCE FICTION STAND ALONE NOVELLA

Excalibur Lost

# VIGILANTE
## (WITH TERRY MIXON)
Heart of Vengeance
Oath of Vengeance

### Bound By Stars: A Vigilante Series
### (With Terry Mixon)
Bound By Law
Bound by Honor
Bound by Blood

# TEER AND KARD
Wardtown
Blood Ward

# CHANGELING BLOOD
Changeling's Fealty
Hunter's Oath
Noble's Honor
Fae, Flames & Fedoras: A Changeling Blood Novella

# ONSET
ONSET: To Serve and Protect
ONSET: My Enemy's Enemy
ONSET: Blood of the Innocent
ONSET: Stay of Execution
Murder by Magic: An ONSET Novella

# FANTASY STAND ALONE NOVELS
Children of Prophecy
City in the Sky